Karma for Beginners

Karma for Beginners

By Jessica Blank

Hyperion • DBG New York

First Edition
1 3 5 7 9 10 8 6 4 2
This book is set in 14-point Perpetua.
Printed in the United States of America
Library of Congress Cataloging-in-Publication Data on file.
ISBN 978-1-4231-1751-3
Reinforced binding
Visit www.hyperionteens.com

SUSTAINABLE FORESTRY INITIATIVE
Certified Fiber Sourcing
www.sfiprogram.org

THIS LABEL APPLIES TO TEXT STOCK

For Mom, Dad, and Natasha

Karma for Beginners

ONE

. . .

*To open up your consciousness, you must detach yourself
completely from the life you thought you knew.*

I had to fight for this hamburger. Twenty minutes: in the
rest stop parking lot and the bathroom, by the pay phone
while my mom called work to make sure they had the
forwarding address for her last paycheck, and then
the entire time in line, past the fried chicken and
the biscuits and the french fries and the milk. My mom
didn't give in till we were at the register, when she
finally said, "Fine," held her hands up to heaven and
closed her eyes, apologizing to the endless wheel of
karma, while I ran back and grabbed the hot crinkly
foil-wrapped cheeseburger and brought it to the cashier,
in front of whose astonished face my mom was still
praying.

I was born a vegetarian. Really: my mother, Sarah,
spent her pregnancy, which straddled 1971 and 1972,
on a diet composed exclusively of brown rice, adzuki

beans, and overcooked broccoli. When I was born I got the same stuff, just pureed. I was eight years old before I tasted meat: one day when my mom left me at my friend Hillary's, I was taken on a forbidden trip to McDonald's and bought a forbidden Happy Meal with a forbidden hamburger inside. My favorite part was the little rectangles of onion, sweet and soft, the bite flash-frozen out of them. My least favorite part was the hour I spent throwing up afterward because my digestive system had never encountered meat. And my *least* least favorite part was explaining to my mom, when she finally showed up, why I got sick. My mom said the throw up was karma, and when I got to the dry heaves I should imagine how the cow felt.

This time, though, when I unwrap the burger my mom doesn't say anything. She just sits there steaming while I go to the Fixin's Bar for ketchup and mustard and perfect bright green pickles made much more deli-cious by the artificial color, and when I get back to the orange plastic table and eat the whole thing, she shoots me a look made out of daggers. She can't stand losing.

She gets an A for effort, though; she used all her tricks in line. First the warning: "Remember what hap-pened last time you ate meat?" Next the guilt trip: "You're already fourteen years old. Don't you think it's time to develop some compassion?" Then the lesson: "You're eating all that poor cow's pain, you know. It stores up as toxins in your blood. Plus you'll have to do a lot to balance out that karma."

But I didn't fold. Instead, I used my trump card. I waited till we were in earshot of the register, and then I said: "You're taking me out of my school and away from my friends and off to live in the cold woods with a bunch of people who worship some weird guy in orange robes. The least you can do is let me *eat*."

I got the burger.

It was sort of a lie, I know. I don't have any friends to be taken away from. And it's not *so* weird, the place we're going; it's an ashram, not unlike the New Age centers she's been going to on weekend trips for work-shops since I was five. But this time we're going to *live* there: no house, no school, no backyard or apartment or car. No drive home at the end of the weekend intensive; no slipping back into the crowd of my classroom where nobody asks my deep inner dreams and I can just sit at my desk and listen to other kids talk about TV shows and laugh like I know what they're talking about. None of that; just a room, stacked up on all the other rooms, and a name tag, and a four a.m. wake-up for chanting. Forever. I wanted a hamburger.

I climb back into the passenger seat, the revenge burger rumbling in my stomach, and strap the seat belt tight across my chest. She leaves hers undone.

"I've decided to forgive you for that little act back there, Tessa," she tells me. "I understand transitions can be stressful."

"Great. Thanks," I say.

"I know it must be tough to leave right when you're starting high school. Did you feel special about your new school?"

I look at her like: *special?* "No, Mom, I didn't feel 'special' about it. I don't care."

She squints like she doesn't quite believe me, which just makes me madder, and then she turns her key in the ignition. We pull onto the highway, dart between trucks and slide into the fast lane. I grip the sides of my seat, brace my feet against the dusty dashboard, but no matter how tight I wedge myself in we still keep moving.

That's sort of how it always goes. As soon as I get to know the trees and the kids and the walk to school, it's time to follow some guy or get away from one: skip out on last month's rent, pack our stuff in boxes, and strap the futon on the car. So I don't really think of any of my schools as "special." Mostly I don't think of them as any-thing, except another place I'm gonna leave. The buses are always the same—ripped upholstered seats and the popular kids in the back, too-loud laughter circling them like an electric fence, and when the bus stops you just spill out into another set of Lysoled halls and sparkly clean linoleum and fake wooden-plastic desks. I've been wearing weird secondhand clothes since kindergarten. I just read my books and the teachers think I'm smart and the kids think that I'm stupid and everyone lets me alone until it's time to leave again.

My life so far we've lived in Akron, Dayton, Youngstown, Venice Beach, then Akron again, plus one summer in Big Sur where my mom cleaned guest rooms at a Retreat Center in exchange for a tent in the redwoods and use of the outdoor hot tubs between three and five a.m. So we're portable. My mom says it's important to be portable, and then she'll talk about the sixties when everyone was On the Road except her because she was still fifteen and locked up in my grandparents' yellow split-level.

This trip she'd gotten up to 1969 when she ran out of banana chip–sunflower seed mix and I whined that I was hungry and we had to stop at Roy Rogers for lunch. I was hoping she'd forget about the beginning of the seventies by the time we got back in the car.

No such luck. "Tess, I wish you could have seen it. Everyone was *together* in this amazing explosion of, just, honesty, and joy, and excitement about *life*—"

"Right, and having be-ins and dancing all night and traveling around." I'm hoping that she'll notice that I already know what's coming next.

She doesn't. "It was incredible. You would find people you *connected* with and just live like gypsies, on the road, exploring what it meant to be alive together when all the rules disintegrated and you were finally really, truly free. As free as a tree is, or a flower, or the wind. Free like human beings are *supposed* to be."

But instead, her first year of community college she slept with this older guy with a ponytail named Jeff who came into town playing bass in a rock band and then he took off on tour and then she had me. So no freedom-flower band of gypsies.

"Oh, Tess, I wanted to be part of it so bad. I wanted to find my tribe. I was just about to get out there—" And then suddenly she goes quiet, and gets that look like she's thinking something she doesn't want to say. "But. You know." And I do.

"But that's okay, Tess. We can make our *own* freedom. We really can. If we just quit searching for security and safety and all those stupid things that are just illusions anyway, then we can do it right now. Right here." She waits for me to say something, but I don't. "Right?"

And then she stops looking at the road and turns to me with shiny eyes, full of hope and trying to make it true, and I know I have to tell her, "Yes, we can."

She says we're here to make our freedom, but secretly I think we're here because of guys. We do a lot of things because of guys. Ever since my dad left for good when I was four, they've been parading in and out, and every one's eventually a Disappointment. There are the ones who wear a suit and take my mother to the Olive Garden and talk about their ex-wives all night, and the ones who tell dumb jokes to make me think they're cool and then sort of hit on me. The guys she meets in crystal healing workshops are all ugly and have stringy hair. Sometimes she finds a man who Follows His Bliss like her, which also means he Doesn't Know How to Commit. But her biggest weakness is the hunky guys who work at the lumberyard and think that she's Exotic. She'll toss her long brown hair at them and lean her hips forward and forget that in three weeks Exotic will start to mean Weird and she'll come to me crying, saying that no man will ever understand her and she might as well just give up.

The last time that happened, two months ago, she made us mugs of Lemon Zinger, pulled me onto the futon in her room, and said, "Tessa, let me tell you about men." Her eyes were red.

I picked at the tan and burgundy swirls of her Indian tapestry bedspread. I didn't want to talk to her when she was crying. "Mom, can't I just do my homework?"

But she was firm. "You're fourteen; it's time for you to know."

"Please, Mom, it's weird." I could feel her eyes on

me. I stared hard at the futon. "I'm only in ninth grade."

She shook her head. "Tess, you're a full being with your own consciousness. I don't buy into this whole 'shelter children from reality' thing. You're a person. And you need to know how it works."

And then she made me look at her and told me about how you can't ever count on men, how they never really value who you are inside, how they pretend to care because you're beautiful and then they lie and leave. Her voice choked up while she was telling me. I wished I could crawl under the blanket. Then she took my hand.

"But here's the good thing, Tessa. I've learned that all that bullshit drama isn't even necessary. Screw them. I've sworn off men. I'm focusing my attention inward." She held on to both my hands. "It's a whole new phase. You'll see."

That week, she switched from Tao of Relationships class to meditation group. Then she started waking up at five a.m. to say a Hindu prayer that lasted an hour. Then she quit her job.

So now we're on the way to this "ashram" place, her scarves and books and pottery piled into cardboard boxes, Rolling Stones in the tape player, and she's still talking about guys.

"You know, though, Tessa, I really should be thankful. I mean, Rick and Dan and all of them were disappointments, but at least they didn't abandon us like your dad."

I look out the window at the gas-food-lodging signs and pretend I'm not really listening, that I don't care about the things she's going to say. But my palms sweat and my fingernails dig little moons in them and I think: *Please.* Please tell me something that I've never heard before. Please tell me about my dad.

Here are the things I know: 1) His name is Jeff. 2) He is a bass player. 3) In 1971, he was in a band called Strawberry Express that toured Midwestern colleges, several of which were in Ohio, one of which was my mom's. 4) He stayed for four days. 5) He is currently in a band called The Green Tea Experience, which has recorded one album on a small record label called Honest Groove Records. 6) None of the letters I've written to his label have ever been answered.

I also know several other things about my dad, courtesy of my mom, but I'm not sure that I believe them. For example, he is an asshole. He's let her down too many times to count. The last time he came back, when I was four, they had a fight and her attempts to *just communicate* were thwarted so profoundly that she finally had to "approach him physically" so as to "wake him up" and then he shoved her. Hard. And this is unforgivable, so she's been telling me since I was eight and "old enough to know," and he is dead to us, and betrayed our family karma so profoundly that it cannot ever be resolved. That's what she tells me.

I wish that she would tell me other things: what he sounds like, where he lives, what it feels like when he looks at you. Every time I wait for her to do it, and every time she never does. But then I realize—she said we're going to the kind of place we've never gone before. A place that will finally be different. Maybe this could be the time I'll finally ask her and she'll finally answer.

·10.

My heart is beating really fast, which is kind of weird. I'm just sitting here.

"Mom?" It comes out kind of squeaky. "Can I ask you a question?"

She doesn't answer. I'm not sure she even heard me. So I try again: "What did Dad look like when you first met him at that concert at your school?" I repeat it to myself: *Please.* Please just tell me the story. Give me a picture I can carry in my head.

But her voice just toughens. "You know, Tessa, people like him, you can't want anything from them. Because you'll never get it."

I stare hard out the window, squint at the open space, grass and skinny trees and no one talking. I taste iron in my mouth and I realize I just bit my lip. And then

I feel: My cheeks are hot. And wet. I'm crying. Shit. I try to hide it, but she hears me sniffle.

"Tess." She takes her eyes off the road and looks at me. "Tess, what's wrong?" Her voice goes soft and she suddenly sounds like a mom. But in the good way.

"Nothing." I want to wipe my cheeks, but it feels embarrassing.

"Honey, c'mon. Something's wrong. Just tell me."

It feels good that she wants to know, but I wish she would've guessed. Because I can't tell her. I can't explain to her how all these parts of me need her to shut up about my dad, but just as many need her to keep talking. I don't know how to say that.

"Oh, Tess. I'm sorry," she says. My teeth stop clenching and I almost cry again from the feeling of *thank you*. Oh my god, she's finally going to realize I need her to stop hating him. She's saying sorry.

"I totally apologize. We're right at the start of an adventure and I'm being such a downer," she goes on. "You're totally right."

My heart sinks. "I didn't say that's why I—"

"I shouldn't be so negative. You don't need all those bad vibes about the past. You're right. It's about our future now."

She spots a road sign and slows down. "Listen," she says. "Let's stop for a second. Okay, Tess? And then we'll start again from scratch."

She pulls off the freeway into the rest stop and puts the car in park. An Ohio mom and dad with matching sky-blue baseball caps frown at us, but my mom doesn't notice. Her eyes are on me. Like I'm more important than anything else around her. Like she just remembered. Even though I'm still mad at her, I'm grateful.

She leans across the seat, clinking the little brass Buddhas that dangle on red cords from the rearview mirror. I stiffen against her, but she keeps holding on, and finally I let myself melt into it. "It's okay," she whispers in my ear, and then pulls back, ruffles my hair and smiles wide. "I'm such a dummy sometimes," she laughs. "Duh. What would I do without you to remind me, Tess? It's about our future," she says again, grinning into my eyes.

It's hard to stay mad at my mom when she's happy. When she turns her joy around on you it's like a waterfall, and no matter how hard you try to stay dry it floods over you fast, washing away everything that came before. I don't know if the future's going to be as beautiful as she says, but when she looks at me like that I don't care.

"Okay." I accept it. At least for now. "Okay. And you'll stay with me there? In the future?" I ask her. I don't mean literally; I mean stay with me like *this*.

"I will," she says. "I promise."

"All right," I tell her, meaning it.

"C'mon," she says, and puts the car in drive again. "Roll down the windows, Tess," she says, "all of them," and I do. She turns up the music, puts her foot to the gas, and we speed, faster and faster till wind floods the car and whips our hair into our faces, till the trucks blur and Ohio disappears, till everything melts away in motion and the world around us turns open and new.

Two

. . .

To know the bliss of universal solitude
is to touch the Absolute.

·14. After that she drives two hours without saying anything,
just singing along to her tape of the Rolling Stones.
When I try to talk to her, she just says, "Shh, Tess, I'm
really *in* the music right now." I simmer for a while, and
then at our second Exxon stop I announce I'm finishing
the trip in the way back, stretched out by myself.

"Come on, Tessa, stay up here with me," she says.

"The wind's making my eyes hurt."

"I'll roll the windows up—"

"Don't worry about it, okay? Just forget it."

"C'mon, Tess, we're on this trip together. It's for
both of us."

Then she asks what bands I want to listen to, and I
definitely do not want to talk to her about that at all. I
just say, "God. Would you just let me sit in the goddamn
backseat, please?" She gives me a look like she's annoyed

I said goddamn, but in our household there aren't any words that are inherently bad, so ha ha, she can't get me in trouble.

I dig into my backpack for my tapes. Most of them are mixed-together songs recorded off the radio, the DJ's voice coming in on the fade-out after some dumb song like *Manic Monday*. I never have money to buy much more and I'm also not sure what I'd like: at my last school I tried to figure it out by hanging around the guys that knew about different bands' histories, but when they started arguing about New Wave versus New Romantics all I could do was stand there mute and then they looked at me weird and I left. But when I heard *I Melt With You* and *Just Like Heaven* and *If You Leave* on the radio, I loved them so much I scrounged ten bucks from my mom's wallet to go and get the albums, and so now my collection is: The Cure, Modern English, John Cougar Mellencamp, and the "Pretty in Pink" sound-track. Plus one more.

In the middle of eighth grade I saw an ad in *Rolling Stone* for the most exhaustive catalog of music albums of all time ever. I decided to get the catalog, just to check, and halfway through the G's I found it. My dad's band, The Green Tea Experience. I wanted that tape more than anything I'd ever known. I didn't care about the stories my mom told me. I didn't care about it being a betrayal. I didn't care that she said he shoved her. He's my dad. I got home early to check the mailbox every day until it came, and then I got the record company's address from the liner notes, and then I wrapped the tape in a secret scarf inside a secret drawer to hide it away forever, as far as humanly possible from my mom.

She finally says fine, I can ride lying down in the back, on the express condition that I keep my feet off the defroster wires on the inside of the back window. They could break. So I put on Green Tea Experience and lie on my side, knees scrunched up to my chest, and strain to hear my dad's voice in the backup vocals.

Here is what it takes: thirteen hours of freeway, two hours of hills and woods and pine trees, forty-five minutes of deserted bungalow colonies with empty plastic swing sets that my mom says are for Jewish people in the summer. We are in the "Catskills," my mom says. "You know, historically, this land has been inhabited by Jewish people on vacation and by counterculturalists, like us."

I wonder what the Jewish people in the summer think of the swamis in their orange robes. I also note the names of the roads—Mount Hope Road, Butrick Way—that lead off toward Levner's River Cottages, in case I need to escape.

After Levner's, it's more trees. And then the gift shop. That's the first thing you see. The words "Atma

Lakshmi" are painted on wood out front, in big white cursive letters against a sloppy swirly blue background that can't decide whether it's supposed to look like the sky or the ocean, and so it winds up just looking like paint. On the front is a brilliantly colored transparent decal featuring a dolphin jumping over waves, underneath an arc of rainbow, which matches exactly the decal on my mom's car's rear window.

"Look, the universe is trying to tell us something. We're in the exact right place, Tess. We've come home," my mom says, pointing at the sticker. "It's a sign."

I don't mention that I've seen that exact transparent rainbow sticker at every New Age bookstore she's taken me to for the last three years. I just wiggle my socks up onto the rear window of our car, covering up the decal and the defroster wires around it. "Wow, that's cool," I say, so my mom will think I'm listening to her, and won't turn back and notice I'm touching the window where I'm not supposed to.

*

The ashram's driveway, so long it's more like a road, winds past the gift shop and the groves of pine trees before it spills out into a graveled area in front of the main building. It looks like the front of a motel, the part where you pull around and leave the car running while you find out if they have rooms available. And it's that big, too. Four floors of rooms lined up with numbers on the door plus a lobby in the front. Except that here the building is made out of wood instead of poured concrete, there's no fluorescent sign, and when you look through the window you see a spring-water cooler instead of a burned-out coffeepot. We sit in the car, idling by the entrance. I pray to myself that my mom won't ask me to go in alone and ask where we should park.

"Tess, would you run in and ask where we're supposed to park?"

I roll my eyes toward the back window so she won't see. The last thing I need is a conversation about why I'm rolling my eyes. "Yes, ma'am," I say, knowing she'll hate that, and slide out the car door, still in my socks.

I'm hoping that the ashram people will be annoyed I came in without my shoes on, but no one seems to care. They just stand there in the fancy lobby, as big as any of our apartments, staring, and then they all sort of smile, in a thin way that I don't quite believe. I shove my fists into my jeans pockets and glower back.

After a minute, a woman comes up. Her graying black hair is permed into the white-lady equivalent of an Afro, and her sweater is magenta with shoulder pads. Her name tag says "Ninyassa" and has a driver's license–looking picture on it next to a pink swan. "Welcome," she says, in this way that makes it sound like she's known me for a long time, except she hasn't. For a second I'm afraid she's going to give me a hug. "I'm Ninyassa." Behind her, other people are still staring. They're all old, like forty at least, and they're all wearing flowy cotton clothes.

"Um, where are we supposed to park?"

"Well, that depends. Are you here for the Weekend Intensive, or for Afternoon Chanting Practice, or for the Heart Awakening Retreat?"

I have never heard of any of those things. "I think we're just here to—to live here?"

"Well, nobody really *lives* here. Maybe you're here for Extended Retreat?"

"I guess."

"Okay, well, in that case you're going to want to come over here"—and she leads me to a pink marble desk, with tall lilies in a glass vase, and a zillion tiny framed pictures of this Indian guy with a long beard— "and check in with me. First you'll have your picture taken for your name tag. Birth name or spiritual name?"

"Huh?"

"Shall I put your *birth* name or your *spiritual* name down for your name tag?"

"I don't really know what—"

"You do have a spiritual name, don't you? If you're devoted to your practice, that's probably what you're going to want people to call you by. As a reminder."

"Um—could I get my mom?" She stops then for a second, and it seems like the first moment that she actually looks at me. I think she notices I'm fourteen. "She's outside, in the car. She doesn't know where to park."

"Well, we're still going to have to decide what name to put down for your name tag. But go ahead. Just make sure she doesn't park in the Heart Awakening section or the Dharma Lot."

To me, it just looks like a bunch of cars. But as we drive around in circles, I tell my mom, "You have to watch out for signs that say Heart Awakening section or Dharma Lot, and make sure not to park there." She looks happy that she's learning the rules, like when you get a good grade in math class.

The cars sit in haphazard rows: mostly station wagons like ours, a hatchback here and there, and more vans than you'd see normally, lots of them with bumper stickers that say stuff like YOU CAN'T HUG A CHILD WITH NUCLEAR ARMS and U.S. OUT OF EL SALVADOR. There are even a few of the old kind of VW buses, the ones that are yellow or purple or red and have a pop-up roof. I always thought those were the only really cool part of being a hippie, and secretly I wish we had one, but we've always just had a station wagon. My mom says the centers of gravity in VW buses are too high and they could tip.

After circling around a bunch of times, my mom says, "Screw it," and we pull into a random empty space. Gravel crunches and rearview Buddhas jingle as she puts our car in park. She turns to me, grinning. "You ready for the next big chapter, Tess?"

I am not ready for any sort of chapter. Mostly I want to go home, except there isn't any such thing. My mom puts on grape-flavored lip gloss in the rearview mirror, tosses her hair, slings her striped straw purse over her shoulder, and walks toward the entrance like she's leaving for a date.

Ninyassa's already waiting at the door. "Welcome," she tells my mom, in that same weird warm-but-not-warm way she said it to me, except she doesn't smile.

"Oh, we're so relieved to be here. It's been quite a journey!" my mom says. Ninyassa doesn't say anything back except she sort of frowns, and suddenly my mom doesn't look like she's going on a date anymore, she looks like she's standing at a party with no one to talk to. Ninyassa's white-lady Afro wobbles a little.

"You must be here for Extended Retreat."

"We are," my mom says. "The universe has been preparing us for quite a while now." She stands up straighter, nervous. I swear, she's like me on the first day of school or something. Ninyassa spends a long time looking at my mother's boobs and lip gloss. Then she glares.

"Okay, well, you'll need to come over here." Ninyassa walks over to the check-in counter too fast for us to follow behind. When we catch up she already has two blank rose-colored name tags out. She looks at me. "I don't believe you had decided which name you were using?" And she smiles.

"Uh, just Tessa." My mom looks at me like I should've answered something else, but what was I going to say? That's the only name I have.

Ninyassa's eyes flick over to my mom. "And you?"

"My name is Sarah," my mom tells her. "I mean, that's the name I was given by my parents. But it might be changing soon." She says it like there's a wink in it somewhere. Ninyassa just blinks. The thick knit ribs of her magenta cotton sweater move up and down with her breath.

"Okay, so Sarah. Come on over here and I'll take your photos."

I always loved Polaroids, the way you wave them in the air and gradually a picture is revealed that looks exactly like the room you're standing in, so you get to be inside the moment that you're in and look at that moment at the very same time. I don't so much love this Polaroid, though, because I have a double chin in it.

I don't normally have a double chin. It's just the way I was spazzy fake-smiling so my face scrunched into my neck. Normally my chin is fine. My whole face is fine: there's nothing wrong with it, except that there's nothing really right with it either. It's just there. Bluish-gray eyes, pale brown freckles, and dark brown hair, straight down to my shoulders. The hair used to be long, back when my mom got to decide. It got tangled and heavy and fell in my face, but when I'd complain, my mom would just say, "C'mere," settle in with the brush and start French braiding, tie it up in Princess Leia knots. We matched; she'd shake her hair and laugh and I'd copy her. When I was twelve I cut off my braid. After that I let it grow some, and since then it's been one length, blunt at my shoulders. My mom still tries to play with it, tie it back with silk and paisley scarves, but I don't let her. She can be beautiful enough for both of us.

Of course my mom looks gorgeous in her Polaroid, just like in real life—high cheekbones and white teeth that gleam, eyes warm and dark like molasses. Her long silver earrings nestle in her wavy hair. Ninyassa glares again. And then she says, "Wonderful," in her weird warm voice, and glues the Polaroids to our name tags, right next to the pink swans.

The weight of the milk crates bites down on my fingers; I know they'll leave nasty red marks when I finally put them down. This is our fifth trip up the stairs. I can't wait to get inside my room and shut the door and secretly start a letter to my dad.

The last few steps, I'm almost panting and I stink. This is the worst part of moving, when you've traveled all the way somewhere and all you want to do is stop, sit down, finally land, and instead you have to carry a thousand pounds of boxes until you're so tired you can barely even walk. I've done it a zillion times; I know. When we get to the top my mom hands me the keys. "Here," she says. "Just put that stuff inside; I'll get the last load." I wait till she turns before I open the door.

I don't know what I expected the room to look like, exactly. A lot of places we've lived have been small; in Big Sur we didn't even have walls, only tents. But I always had a place where I could close the door. Or the tent flap.

But here it's just one room for both of us, on one side a queen bed, a twin up against the other corner of the room. The tiny tiled bathroom tucks into a corner; the whole place seems small and old and cheap. Especially when you compare it to the pink marble entranceway, to what this place wants you to think it is.

I can't believe I'm going to live in a glorified motel room, with my mother, forever.

The latch clicks open behind me and my mom walks in. I hear her drop a suitcase or a box. "Tess?" she says. I don't turn around. She tries again, louder. "Tessa." I still don't turn around.

"This is it, huh? Well, it's nice enough," she says, and flops on the queen bed, kicking off her Birkenstocks. "Bed's good." I finally look at her then; she grins at me like we're on some kind of adventure. Except that we are not. We are in an imitation motel room with a gray tiled bathroom and brown scratchy carpet. I guess I scowl or something, because she says, "What's that look for?"

I just say, "What."

"That look. Like you swallowed something bad."

"I didn't swallow anything."

"Obviously I know you didn't swallow anything, I'm speaking metaphorically."

"Whatever."

And she says, "Don't 'whatever' me. What was that look for?" sharper and kind of mad-sounding, like she's actually expecting me to explain to her what I was thinking. "Tessa?" It's like she's trying to reach inside my brain or something.

I just walk into the tiny gray bathroom and lock the door.

I turn the water on and I don't care if it's environmentally wasteful, I let it run while I sit on the toilet so she won't hear me crying. After a minute I hear the front door click open, and I think, *Thank god maybe she left*, but then there's a knock on the bathroom door heavier and slower than my mom's.

Ninyassa's voice says, "Tessa? Time for Lice Check."

The fact that all kids that come to the ashram have to have a lice check isn't really comforting. Ninyassa seems to think it will be, because she keeps saying how it's a required part of admissions as she leads me back behind the main building and into the woods, down a trail made of wood chips to a little tan trailer marked "First Aid."

A skinny woman sits on the trailer steps, her long stringy blond hair exactly the same color as her skin. Between that and her beige leotard and drawstring pants, she blends completely into herself. "This is Jayita," Ninyassa says. Jayita motions for me to sit on the trailer steps in front of her, and goes through my hair with her fingers bit by bit. After about three minutes she says, "Oop," and pulls away. "White speck."

Ninyassa leans over and inspects it. My scalp doesn't itch at all, and when I lean over to see Jayita's finger I can definitely tell it's dandruff, but Ninyassa says, "Okay, Quarantine."

Jayita says, "You know, Ninyassa, I don't really think that's lice. It just looks like a little flake. We probably can send her back, I think—"

"Jayita, it's imperative that we take precautions. The last thing we need here is an outbreak. You know, I would think you'd be more thorough in your attention."

"Ninyassa, I'm plenty thorough. I just think there's no reason to isolate her when she's just gotten here, if it's so clear that it's not necessary."

"Yes, well, isolating one child for one single night is much less of a sacrifice than risking the serenity of the entire community."

Jayita rolls her eyes; Ninyassa scowls. "Ninyassa," Jayita says. "C'mon, it's really my call to make. Lice Check's my *seva*, right?"

"Right," Ninyassa snaps, "and my *seva* is to supervise and make sure everyone abides by the practices set out for us."

This is making me feel weird. First of all, I'm not a child. Secondly, I don't know what *seva* is, although it sounds kind of like a job. And third, the idea of people getting in an argument about who's in charge of a white speck on my head makes me feel like it's my fault.

"You guys, I'm pretty sure it's just dandruff—" I try to say, but Ninyassa interrupts me.

"Yes, well, you know, you're new to our ashram community, and you're not familiar with the rules yet. So Jayita and I will have to come to some agreement." And then she turns to Jayita again. "Respecting the rules is respecting the Guru, you know."

Jayita looks at Ninyassa like she's tolerating her, and then says, "Fine. Okay. How long?"

"Oh, I'd say Phase One," Ninyassa says, and smiles, smug. "Just follow Jayita"—and she looks at my name tag—"Tessa."

I definitely want to know what Phase One is before I follow anyone anywhere, especially because I am completely positive it's dandruff. If my mom would've bought Head and Shoulders like I asked her instead of Nature's Gate I wouldn't even have this problem. But before I can open my mouth, Jayita stands up and says,

"Come on."

"See you tomorrow," Ninyassa says, and marches off down the wood chip path.

The inside is a combination of a hippie cabin and the school nurse's office. There are vinyl upholstered benches, glass jars of tongue depressors and cotton gauze, but there are also Indian paisley tapestries and candles. And more photos of that same old bearded guy, who I guess is this "guru" they were talking about. Jayita pulls the curtain back and watches out the window as Ninyassa walks away.

"Ech, she can really be a drag. But we'll have a good time here, okay?" Then she goes over to a boom box and turns it on. The radio is playing George Michael.

Cause I gotta have a-faith, a-faith, a-faith. She smiles at me, sneaky.

"Sometimes the chanting gets a little old." She moves her shoulders to the beat, liquid and slouchy, like a dancer or a yoga person.

Then she pulls a stool up by a metal sink. "Okay, come on and have a seat. And change into this." She pulls out a T-shirt that says NUCLEAR MORATORIUM. I feel weird asking where I'm supposed to change, so I just turn my back to her, hunched over so she can't see my bra.

She reads some book while I take everything off and ball it all into a wad. "Okay," she says, and pats the seat of the stool. I try to sit up straight. Jayita laughs. "Lean back," she says. "I gotta wash your hair." She takes out a blue plastic bottle that says NIX in thick white letters.

"This should do the trick." She smiles; she reminds me of Janis from the Muppets, except paler. "Or at least it'll satisfy Ninyassa. For the moment, anyway." She rolls her eyes and laughs like *nothing ever really satisfies Ninyassa.*

I've decided that I like Jayita. When she starts rubbing my scalp I get this weird good goose-bumpy feeling and I want to close my eyes. She's just washing my hair like I do every morning, but somehow the fact that it's someone else's hands makes it feel way different and better than when it's just me.

After she combs my hair she says, "All right," and

puts the comb in a glass jar full of alcohol. "So you've gotta stay in here for the night. In the morning we'll shampoo one more time, and then you're good." The digital clock on the counter says 6:23. My stomach rumbles. I wonder 1) how I'm supposed to eat, and 2) what I'm supposed to do in here until 11:30, which is the earliest I can ever fall asleep. I didn't even bring a book.

There's a tinny knock on the thin door, and then it opens; all of a sudden, in one second, Jayita stops looking pale. This guy comes in, thirtyish, with a narrow face, kind eyes, and brown hair in tight curls. He's got a red V-neck T-shirt and peach drawstring pants. He's tall and skinny just like her; he looks like a yoga person, too.

"Hey," he says, slinging an arm around Jayita's waist. She beams at me like: *isn't that the most brilliant thing anyone ever said?*

"This is Chakradev," she says, unsticking from his side, going to clean up the sink. "Dev, we're just getting Tessa finished up here."

"Lice Check, huh?" Dev asks me.

"Yeah."

He nods, sympathetic to the experience of Lice Check.

"So you just got here today, huh? From where?" He asks like I'm a person, not a kid.

"Well, we drove here from Akron."

He squints at me like he's trying to see where Akron is.

"It's in Ohio?" I tell him.

"Right, right, Ohio," he says. "That where you're from?"

I'm not sure how to answer that; I'm not really *from* anywhere. "Well, that's the last place we lived." That sounds dumb. "We've lived a lot of places."

A smile cracks over his skinny face. "Aaah. Travelers, huh?"

"I guess."

"Yeah. Me too." Suddenly it's like we're in a secret club or something: the Association of Wandering Hippies. I don't tell him it's really my mom that's the member.

Jayita finishes with the bottles and jars and comes over, wiping her hands. "We're heading out, okay?" she says to me. "Do you want anything?" I can't exactly say Yes, I would like to go back to Akron with my mom, please; or failing that, I'd at least like you guys to stay here and talk to me. I just shake my head.

While they're gone I go through the cabinets to see if there is anything interesting, but there's just Q-Tips. And paper towels, and more pictures of that bearded guy. I'm starting to get curious about who this guy is, but I have this feeling that nobody is going to give me a straight answer.

After a while there's a knock on the door that sounds weirdly familiar, and then my mom comes in. She's holding a tray of tofu and bean sprouts and carrot salad with tahini dressing, and then she gives me a little travel toothbrush and some Tom's of Maine toothpaste. "Hey," she says. "I hear you're in Quarantine."

"Apparently," I say. "Ninyassa said I have to."

"Sorry." She frowns sympathetically. "But I guess they have to be careful about all the residents, you know. Lice can spread."

"Yeah," I say. "I don't think I have lice."

"Well, it's probably good to just make sure."

"Right." I wish my mom took Jayita's side and not Ninyassa's, but I guess she's too excited about learning all the rules.

"Listen," she says. "Here's a good meal, at least. And I'll come back to get you in the morning. You'll probably fall asleep pretty quick after you eat. Plus you're almost outside in this trailer, so it'll be easy to sleep with the dark and rise with the sun."

"Okay." I also wish she wouldn't use words like "rise." It's called "getting up." "Thanks for the food."

"No prob! Oh, Tess, tomorrow when you can walk around and see it here, you're gonna be so excited. It's so great." And then she breezes out the door.

I try the radio for company. The DJ screams to *CALL IN YOUR DEDICATIONS FOR THE TOP EIGHT AT EIGHT COUNTDOWN!!!* His voice is obnoxious. He talks and talks, reading out the dedications, Jenny for Bill and Bob for Rachel, and I start feeling like the only person on this earth who doesn't have someone like that to think about, someone to think about me. I switch it off.

The Guatemalan blanket scratches my thighs, heavy and too stiff to keep me warm. I could close the windows, but without at least the crickets, I think I'll feel so by myself that I won't be able to stand it. I hate this feeling. It's the same feeling I get when my mom stays out at night and leaves me home. She says the extra quiet will help me rest, but it's just the opposite; the air gets so still that every noise is deafening and I spend the night scared, tracking every creak and crack. I'm more used to it now, at least. When I was six or seven it used to keep me up all night and I would fall asleep in school.

I notice Jayita's paperback on the counter by the tongue depressors. It's called *The Supreme Journey*, and on the back is yet another picture of the bearded guy. I open to a random page. It says:

> *It is only by renouncing our own desires that we may destroy the illusion of our thoughts. Then we may*

achieve the true peace of solitude. Not separateness,
but the bliss of true connection with all the other
solitudes in the universe.

Then it goes on to say a bunch of other stuff in another language that I guess is Indian. I read the paragraph again. "Destroy the illusion of our thoughts?" I don't think my thoughts are an illusion. How else are you supposed to know anything besides by thinking about it? I *like* thinking about stuff. Understanding things makes me feel more connected to them, not less. Plus, "destroy" sounds awfully mean.

The solitude part I do get, though. I certainly can feel my universal solitude right now, trapped in this trailer, crickets creaking through the screens. I don't understand how that feeling would be something that anyone would want. To me it doesn't feel holy or sacred or peaceful, it just feels lonely. I think about Jayita and Dev, holding hands down the trail in the crickety dark, headed up the stairs to their room. I think about those people on the radio, liking each other enough to dedicate a song. I think about my mom, up late like me, in the huge soft yellow cotton T-shirt she always sleeps in, and I think about my dad, out there somewhere in the big open empty of America, wondering where I am, or maybe not. I fall asleep crying with nothing but the scratchy cot to hold me.

Three

. . .

Purity of Being is attained by delving wholeheartedly
into the community of seekers.

Jayita comes back at sunrise, hands me my clothes, and washes my hair again. When she finishes combing she pats me on the shoulder in her stoner-yoga way and says, "You're good. You can go ahead and meet your mom."

"Wasn't she going to come get me?"

"Oh, she was? I don't know, I guess maybe she was thinking she'd come later? But I gotta get First Aid cleaned up by eight. You can just head over to Sadhana Mandap to find her."

Everything has weird names here and everyone expects you to already know what they mean. I'm starting to suspect that the weird names exist just to make people who aren't part of it feel stupid, like the popular girls who make up their own words for stuff and speak it like a secret language and then laugh. "What's Sadhana Mandap?" I have to ask her.

She doesn't laugh, at least. "Oh, that's where meals are served. It's breakfast now. It's over in the main building; you can't miss it. Just don't forget your name tag." She nods to the counter where she left it last night, right next to *The Supreme Journey*. I hope she can't tell I was reading her book.

It rained during the night; the wood chips are damp deep dark reddish-brown. They crunch soft under my sneakers and the leaves glisten above, red and yellow and green all dotted with little silver drops. It's only sunrise. After a while the trees thin and the path keeps going, finally snaking around to the entrance. As I come up to the doorway I pray Ninyassa won't be there. She isn't, thank god or whoever, and I make it through the pink marble without having to talk to anyone.

The double doors swing open when I push them, like a saloon entrance in a TV Western. The room is huge, at least twice as big as the cafeteria at school. And it's filled with hundreds and hundreds of people. I don't know how Jayita thought I'm supposed to find my mom.

One of the guys from the lobby yesterday stops me at the entrance. He's bald, with a collarless shirt. Up close he looks like this guy Ed from the lumberyard that my mom used to go out with. He still isn't smiling. "Name tag?" he asks, peering at my chest. I hold the tag out from my body to show him, so at least he won't be looking at my boobs. Lumberyard Ed used to look at my boobs.

"Extended Retreat," he says. "Okay. Go on over to that line." I grab a tray and some silverware and shuffle toward the steam tables. Each of them is filled with a different kind of glop. There are little cards in front. One says "Amaranth," another, "Millet"; then there is "Sweet Cereal" and "Savory Cereal." Savory Cereal has flecks of stuff in it and smells like an Indian restaurant. I ask the lady with the ladle what it is. She says, "It's the Guru's special recipe. Try it!" I'm skeptical, but she seems so enthusiastic I let her scoop some into my bowl. It lands with a splat; a little gets on my shirt. I walk out into the sea of tables to look for my mom.

It really is kind of amazing how much like the school cafeteria it is: balancing a tray of food, trying to find a familiar face in a sea of chattering strangers where everyone knows each other except me. The only different thing is the huge painting of the beard guy surrounded by peacock feathers that takes up the entire back wall. Eventually I give up on my mom and settle for the next best thing, a table where there's extra space and people aren't talking to each other much. Just like school.

Nobody looks up when I sit down, which I guess is good. My Savory Cereal's cold by now; I can tell just by looking. Halfway through the first bite I am very sorry I didn't argue with the ladle lady. It's oatmeal, bland and thick, except with spices like Indian food, and no salt. It wants to be dinner but it can't stop being breakfast, and it is gross. Washing it down with orange juice sort of helps and sort of makes it worse.

I think maybe Savory Cereal will be more manageable with salt, and I know they won't have salt, so I ask the lady who's sitting nearest me, "Do you know if there's any soy sauce?" She jerks her head up fast, fixes me with a sharp look, then goes back to her amaranth.

I try the guy on my other side, a short-haired man with a checked collared shirt who looks like a normal person's dad. "Do you know where the soy sauce is?" He turns toward me slow and calm, takes three deep breaths, and then keeps eating.

So I lean across the table. "Excuse me," I say to a skinny woman with long hair and a longer face, dressed all in white. "Can you tell me where I'd find some soy sauce?" The lady next to me starts saying, *"Om namo Bhagavate"* over and over in an annoyed whisper. Long Face looks at Checked-Shirt Guy, lips pursed in a sort-of smile, and then she nods at a laminated card in the middle of the table. It says: THIS TABLE IS RESERVED FOR THOSE WHO WISH TO OBSERVE MEALS IN SILENCE. SAD GURUNATH MAHARAJ KI JAY! I am never going to get soy sauce. I hold my nose and eat my Savory Cereal in silence.

. . . . .

What I really want is my mom, but at least being around our stuff makes me feel a little better. I curl up with her yellow sleep shirt. I wish there was a TV I could watch like in a real motel, but on top of the dresser there's just an altar my mom set up with rocks and twigs from places that we've been, some crystals, a candle, and a soapstone statue of an elephant this blond kayaker guy Billy gave her in Big Sur. She worshipped that guy, till he took his kayak to Australia. She said they had a "soul connection." I always thought he was kind of a tool. ·39.

I tell myself what I always do: she has to come back eventually, all her stuff is here. I want to fall asleep so time will pass by faster, but my mind's too busy thinking. Even though our bedroom is silent and the window is closed, it's still noisy. Sometimes the quieter the room is, the louder it all seems inside your head.

I sit up, grab some paper, and start that letter to my dad. I tell him everything: getting pulled out of my school and then the road trip and the hamburger; Savory Cereal and Lice Check; Ninyassa and the Silent Table. I tell him that even though I'm completely pissed off at my mom for dragging me to this weird place and leaving me for breakfast and about a million other reasons, I still wish she was here right now so that I wouldn't be alone. I'm about to ask him if he ever feels that way when the doorknob turns and clicks.

I jump, crush the letter into a ball, and stuff it into my waistband, all in the split second before she opens the door. She would kill me. Oh my god she would kill me.

When I was twelve I asked her if I could visit him. If he ever said he missed me. If I could go to where he lived maybe for a summer sometime. I spent a week planning how I would bring it up and finally asked her at dinner one night, when she'd just gone out with this new guy named Bob and she was telling me how close she felt to me. We were having homemade hummus and she was drinking wine. It was way worse than when I asked her what he looked like yesterday in the car. That night she screamed at me that if I wanted to leave her behind to go and visit him, then maybe she should just leave me on his doorstep and let me experience his hostility and abandonment for myself and then I could go live on the streets because that's what he practically left her to do. Then she went in her room and locked the door, and the whole night I could hear her crying. I can still remember what it sounded like.

Now, in our bedroom, I squirm to hide the lump in my waistband that the letter makes. The paper scratches against my back. My heart thuds in my throat and my skin gets hot and when she asks what I was doing I just say "Nothing" and ask how she's feeling today.

It works: her suspicion melts away. I lean back against the wall, smush the letter flat.

"Oh, Tessa! It's so caring of you to ask. I am *wonderful*." She plops down beside me on the bed. "How was the rest of your night? I bet it was very peaceful." She pulls back and beams at me. "Tell me about your adventures!"

"Yeah, well, it wasn't really an adventure. I stayed in the trailer and after a while I fell asleep. I thought you were coming to get me this morning. Where were you?"

"Oh, Tess, I was gonna come right after breakfast—"

"I went to the cafeteria to look for you and I couldn't find you."

"You mean Sadhana Mandap?"

"Yes," I say, even though I mean "the cafeteria."

"Oh, well, there was a quick chant afterward in the meditation room down the hall. But I was coming after that."

"Oh. Well, at the cafeteria there was nobody to talk to. And my cereal was gross. And when I asked for soy sauce I couldn't get any, because I was apparently sitting at the Silent Table."

"Oh yes! Tebala Saanata!" she says, ignoring all the other things I just told her. "It's a powerful practice to take your meals in silence. What was your experience of that?"

"Uh—it kind of sucked?"

A few sparks fall from her eyes. "It sucked?"

"Well, I didn't know where the soy sauce was, and nobody would help me—"

"Oh!" The sparks light up again. "You had to face your attachment. Yes, that's part of taking silence. It's important to abide by the practices set out for us."

I don't know who took my mom away and replaced her with Ninyassa.

It's not that my mom has never said weird stuff before. She's always coming home from journaling workshop, movement class, Whole Food Cooking, with new favorite words she'll practice on me. "Process," "experience," "lacto-ovo," "emotional-word-picture." Some of them stick around and some don't; I'm used to that. But this isn't just words, it's entire sentences; a whole other way of talking, like a different person.

"I guess." I don't really want to talk about silence anymore.

"Well, do you want to hear what my adventures were?"

"Okay. I mean, if you feel like you need to talk about it."

It comes out in a burst, like the water has been storing up and she just turned the spigot on. "I met the Guru!"

"Cool," I say. Cool is a good word for when someone else is really excited by something and you don't know why but you don't want to hurt their feelings.

"Oh, Tessa, it was amazing. Last night after I left First Aid, they had a welcoming ceremony for new arrivals, but there were only a few of us, it was so intimate!" That word makes me feel sort of dirty and weird, like she's telling me too much about some date she had. "The swamis sang the most beautiful chant, and then he came in, and we all bowed, and he bopped each of us with a peacock feather, and the energy was so amazing! We all just started crying. And then I was laughing at the same time, and—oh, Tessa, I wish you could have been there."

"Cool."

I mean, I can see why she's excited by music and laughing and stuff, but I still don't get it. Why would everyone cry just because some guy hit them with a pea- cock feather? And if you were crying, why would you start laughing too? I don't really want to ask her, though; she's happy like she was in the car, that kind of happy that washes over you and wipes everything else away. If I make her explain, it might stop it. She just sits there on the bed with me and grins into my eyes, bright and shiny. "Oh, Tessa. I'm so glad we're finally here."

At ten, it's time for *seva*. I thought *seva* meant a real job, like the kind that you get paid for, but actually it means "selfless service," and is another word for chores. You do it from ten a.m. till five p.m., with an hour break for lunch. My mom got her *seva* assignment when I was at Lice Check, so for today I go with her, and tomorrow I will get my own. My mom's assignment is the kitchen, a huge stainless-steel universe behind the cafeteria in Sadhana Mandap. And guess what my job is once we get there.

Savory Cereal.

Turns out that that bald collarless-shirt guy is named Avtar, and he's in charge of kitchen prep. My mom doesn't seem to notice that Avtar looks like her ex-boyfriend Ed from the lumberyard. Which is fine with me. Once my mom and I went over to Ed's and he fed me Swanson Salisbury steak and droned on for an hour about his favorite TV show, which was *CHiPs*, while my mom put her hand on his leg beneath the table and he stared at me. All through dinner I was sure I was going to get in humongous trouble with my mom for eating meat. But she never said anything. Not even in the car afterward. It weirded me out.

Unlike Ed, however, Avtar is a vegetarian. He likes to bark things. "Ten tubs of turmeric!" "Three pounds of grated beets!" "Tahini! Tahini! Tahini!" After he sends my mom off with organic dandelion greens, he comes over to where I'm standing. "Savory Cereal!" he barks, thrusting a recipe card into my hand. I have to chase after him to ask where to find the ingredients. I tap on his linen-covered shoulder. "Excuse me?" He turns around. "Could you tell me where this stuff is?" I point at the card.

He says, "Yes, the walk-in freezers in the basement," like I'm supposed to already know. "Ah, where *everything* is?"

Here are the new things I experience at kitchen prep *seva*: standing in a huge refrigerator imagining the door locking me inside; industrial-size casks of flaxseed oil; meat cleavers (used on vegetables); sauteed mustard seeds; group chopping chants; silent chopping time; bleeding fingernails from peeling garlic; the importance of praying while you grate; cayenne in my eye; the names Avtar, Amrita, Chandi, Tikala, and Bhav; repetitive stress injury; how stirred liquid mimics the spiral pattern of universal DNA.

Most of the time that I'm experiencing, my mom is at the other end of the kitchen by the sinks, thrusting bunch after bunch of greens into tub after tub of water. When it's time for lunch she comes up grinning, humming the last chant through her teeth. She holds up her pruney hands like prizes.

Four

. . .

Through selfless service we discover our true destiny.

·46. The next morning, I have to get my *seva* assignment. My mom walks me to the office after breakfast, and then she leaves for kitchen prep. I watch her turn around and walk down the path, fingering a bracelet of mahogany wooden beads. She doesn't look back at me.

The office is in another beige trailer beside the lobby. Inside are houseplants, thin brown carpet, and a crappy desk. They have me fill out a questionnaire about my interests. The interests they list are weird, like: Social Growth, Organization, Nurturing, Finance, Manual Labor, and Nature. I check Nature because that's the only thing on there that doesn't sound completely lame.

When the *seva* coordinator calls me in, she gives me a stack of tattered textbooks. "We homeschool here, for kids your age," she says. "After junior high. So you'll need to take the practice tests in these books and hand them in, along with weekly reports on what you're learning from your *seva*. That's how school works here."

Then she informs me I've been placed on Grounds Crew. She hands me a special yellow vest and a piece of lavender notepaper where she's written the name of my supervisor. On the bottom of the paper it says "Smile At Your Destiny!"

The place I'm supposed to report to is called Darshana Gurunam, and it's basically a shed. Wheelbarrows, dirt and wood chips, flats of flower seedlings stacked on wooden shelves. It's tucked way behind the main building, through the woods, so you can't see it from anywhere else. No one's there. "Hello?" I call out, looking at the notepaper. "Devanand?" I sound out the name, voice echoing in the metal walls. I'm about to go and find my mom when I hear gravel crunch.

"That's me!" Devanand is string-bean thin and tall, in red running shorts with yellow piping, a tight sky-blue faded T-shirt that says JOGGING! and green Nikes with a yellow swoosh. He has a brown scraggly ponytail and a terry-cloth sweatband around his forehead and a gross, enormous beard. He's probably my mom's age, thirty-five or so, but she wouldn't think he's cute. He's not her type. His eyes blaze and laugh at once, which makes me think he's possibly a little crazy. His legs are very hairy, and his shorts are very short. "So what are we gonna do today?" he asks.

Weird: I thought he's supposed to tell me what to do. "Um—take care of the grounds?"

He laughs. "Well, yes, that is what we do here at Grounds Crew. But *specifically*, that is to say *particularly*, what are we going to do *today*, is what I mean, m'dear. It's up to you!"

I just stand there. I don't know anything about Grounds Crew or what the different jobs are, so I can't really answer. Plus, he is weird.

"Okay," he says. "Since you don't know, why don't I pick for ya. See those flats of asters over there?" He points. "They need to get planted. You know how to plant an aster?"

Two hours later, the wood chips finally break through the skin on my knees. I don't mind the dirt beneath my fingernails—I'm not one of those girls who acts dumb about that kind of stuff—but the wood chips actually hurt. Devanand gave me a wheelbarrow full of twenty flats of forty seedlings each, and scampered off like a tall, long-bearded rabbit. Grounds Crew doesn't seem to be much of a crew. It's just me.

· · · · ·

When I get to the back of the main lot, I spot a path leading through the trees. It opens up into another lot, which looks like it's for ashram vehicles. There are vans back there, and school bus shuttles; trash and tools and extra tires. Plus a red VW bus, the cool kind with the pop-up top. I don't see how anyone is going to notice asters back here, but I've got a lot left over, so I kneel down. It's hot; I take off the Grounds Crew vest and throw it in my wheelbarrow. No one's back here to see.

After an hour or so, somebody yells, "Hey!" I about jump out of my entire skin. I'm sure it'll be Devanand, busting me for not wearing my vest.

"Sorry, didn't mean to spook you." I turn around; it isn't Devanand. It's this guy with a wrench in his hand and grime smudged on his stubbly face, younger than Devanand but older than me. He's tallish and slouchy and cute, and he doesn't look like any of the other people at the ashram. He's got normal short brown hair, jeans, and a plain green T-shirt. Plus a little gold stud in his left ear, which I've only ever seen on rock stars. He doesn't have a name tag on. "How's the planting going?"

I shrug. I kind of want to tell him my knees hurt like crazy, quit digging and go sit over by his box of tools, but I just say, "Okay."

"Cool," he says, and grins at me. He squats down, crawls under a bus, and gets to work. The whole rest of the afternoon I can feel my back, knowing there's someone behind it. Through eight more flats of flowers, I want to turn around but don't.

The next morning when I wake up, my mom's gone. No note. Surprise. In the cafeteria I find a Silent Table so no one will notice I don't have anyone to talk to, and I finish writing to my dad. I tell him the names of the freeways we took here, Mount Hope Road and Butrick Way. And I tell him the hours when my mom's away at *seva*, and that I'm good at packing all my stuff up on last-minute notice. Just in case.

By the time I slip the finished letter in my pocket, the post-breakfast crowd is streaming out into the long hallway. This whole building is huge, dorm rooms and cafeteria and big marble lobby, plus a bunch of different rooms for meditation or chanting or who knows what. Not to mention I've seen other buildings we haven't even been in yet. I don't think I'll ever learn my way around. I slide into the gift shop—the fourth one I've seen so far—and buy some stamps.

Outside the gift shop there's a little slot in the wall to send mail, like at the post office. I open it, heart pounding, and drop in my letter care of Honest Groove Records. It's a huge relief to have it off me, out in the world, where she can never find it.

I'm wiping my hands on my jeans, wiping off the

sweat, when my mom comes around the corner and spots me. "Tessa!" She clips toward me past the long row of pay phones. "You're here so early!" she says, and hugs me. "Did you like the gift shop?" I stay stiff.

"Breakfast is over," I scowl.

She ignores that. "Guess what, Tessa! You're going to be so excited. No regular activities today—there's a special program at the Shanti Kutir. The entire ashram community will gather with music and chanting!" Too bad. I was almost kind of looking forward to *seva*.

The Shanti Kutir is a giant half-enclosed outdoor auditorium at the bottom of a hill. It's a hike to get there, through Sadhana Mandap and along a trail and through another building with glass walls and scarlet carpeting. Then you walk through a garden with statues of Gandhi and Jesus and some Hindu god that looks like an elephant, all of them with flower garlands piled on. My mom says there's a shuttle, but she wants me to experience the grounds.

At the top of the hill we walk by the shuttles pulling up, old school buses with speaker systems that play chanting tapes. I take note of them, where they stop, what they look like, so I can get around here on my own. I know I'll have to eventually, even if I don't know the way. The buses all have names of school districts on their sides in peeling paint; ancient, grumbling, belching smoke. On their last legs, all of them. I guess that lot is where they go when they break down. I teeter to stay steady as we flow down the hill in a river of people. I want to grab my mom's hand for balance, but she's already way ahead of me.

At the bottom is a huge wall of cubbies for shoes. My mom hands me a flat square purple cushion from a towering stack, and we pick our way barefoot through the hundreds of people sitting cross-legged on the cold floor.

When we take our places, my ankle bones clack against hard marble. We all face a big overstuffed chair surrounded by flowers. My mom leans over, grabs my hand, and whispers, "That's the Guru's chair." The lady next to us glares and breathes out loud. My mom shoots me an inside-joke look about how uptight she is. Her eyes spark like a Roman candle: there's that waterfall again.

A swami—bald, in orange robes—steps to the podium. The rustling in the room slows to silence. *"Sad gurunath maharaj ki jay!"* The crowd says it back to him, but I can't pronounce it.

The swami leans into the microphone. "It is a sacred practice to welcome one another," he reads in a sing-song voice. "Truly we are always being welcomed, and it is only our own limited vision, our own fear, that prevents us from seeing this. The walls of illusion we create in our own minds are all that prevent us from feeling welcomed into the ocean of love."

He thwacks his book shut; the words sit in my ears. I watch the swami stand there making peaceful faces down at us. A sting rises up inside my throat and suddenly I want to yell at everyone looking so serene with little smiles on their lips. Because it's a lie: they're not welcoming. They use weird words and act like you're supposed to know and don't talk to you and never ask your name.

But then I swallow the sting and think about what the swami said. How that feeling isn't really real. How if we choose to shift our perception it will change. And I start to wonder: am I maybe wrong? Maybe I *am* being welcomed all the time and I don't know it, because I'm busy making walls of illusion between myself and people. Maybe it's my own fault I feel so awful here.

The sureness of my anger dissolves. It kind of freaks me out. I never realized you could make up entire feelings, that my whole inside could tell me something's true when it's really just my mind making it up.

When they ring the meditation bell, I try to see inside my brain to figure out what's true and what isn't. Every thought I have ties a knot in there, though, and every time I try to untie one, the trying makes another. Till there's just a big tangle, like when I used to have long hair and never brushed it, and the only thing to do was take a scissors and cut the whole thing out. Except I don't really see how you could cut out your entire mind.

Then the drums start up. They're not like any other drums I've heard; they sound juicy and wet, each beat round and complete as it rolls into the next. The drummers sit on the floor, building walls of sound and rhythm; tambourine cymbals start shaking; and then a sitar comes in. I know what a sitar is because of the

Beatles. They plink out a melody; two men's voices pick it up, "*Jaya Jagatambe*," and then the whole room joins in, a sea of voices loud enough to swallow me. By the third time through I know the sounds of the syllables, and I sing too, and it washes away that knot inside my head, just like my mom does when she's happy. I don't know what I'm singing, what the words mean, how to spell them, but it's too big, too much like an ocean, and I'm too small to stand against the wave of it. I close my eyes and let it sweep me off.

When I open them, the beard guy is sitting in the overstuffed chair. He's got flower garlands around his neck: pink, orange, yellow, like in pictures of Hawaii, and he wears red robes. He's Indian and small; with his long gray hair and beard he looks a little like an old man and a little like an imp. He has a red dot between his eyebrows, and a burgundy ski cap on his head, which is kind of weird. He holds his hands up and out to the sides like he's holding up the music, eyes shut, rocking like Stevie Wonder.

Eventually his hands float down into his lap. The music fades and he opens his eyes. "Hello," he says in an Indian accent.

"Hello," the whole room says back like an ocean.

I've read the word *beatific* before in a book, but I never really got what it meant until now. That's the look on his face. Like beautiful, but more, and simpler. I hear fast loud breathing behind me, turn to see where it's coming from. Dirty looks dot the rows of people and someone puts their hand on my shoulder, firm. I guess you're not supposed to look at anyone. Before the hand turns me back around, though, I glimpse a long-haired guy collapsing into someone's arms behind him, panting. I sneak a glance at my mom, sideways, like cheating on a test. She looks beatific too.

After a long time the beard guy stands up and walks offstage. Then Swami Anantananda strides back to the microphone. "Blessings," he says. "Our Guruji has gifted us with *prasad* today! *Sad gurunath maharaj ki jay!* You may all line up at the top of the hill."

The mass exodus is like Christmas Eve at the mall, except everyone's barefoot and trying to find their shoes. Eventually we dig ours out of a pile and get in line. While we wait, I find out *prasad* means consecrated junk food. The beard guy says some kind of blessing over it, so then it's supposed to have his spiritual energy. To me, it just looks like Oreos, but maybe I'll feel something when I eat it.

Ahead of us somebody shouts, "I got your Oreo!" It's a kid's voice. I look up. The tall boy and the girl are brother and sister, definitely; pale and reedy, with curly nut-brown hair and distant eyes. Fifteen and fourteen, I bet. The third guy—the short one—you can't tell how old he is, because he hasn't gone through puberty; he could be anywhere from eleven to fourteen. Both the guys wear plaid madras short-sleeved button-down shirts; the girl wears calico like Laura Ingalls Wilder. I think for a second about saying hi. Not that they're going to ever be my friends, but it would be nice at least to talk to someone my own age. But the girl has her eyes closed, like I guess she's praying to herself, and when the short guy catches me staring he looks at me like I'm something rotten he just smelled, and then he pokes the other guy and they both laugh. So much for hi.

By the time we get to the front of the line, the aluminum pans are empty of everything but crumbs. One half of an Oreo is left. I put it in my mouth, waiting for the spiritual experience. I close my eyes. It just tastes like an Oreo without the creme.

FIVE

. . .

*Our loneliness exists only in the illusions
of our limited minds.*

Steam fills my lungs and after a few minutes I feel dizzy.
I don't care, though. I want the water all the way up hot.
I dig my fingernails into the Ivory, leaving half-moons in
the slippery white. My mom is in our room, getting
dressed for Evening Program, but with the door shut
and the water up I'm safe in the box of the bathroom. I
wonder if my knees will get used to wood chips, if me
and Devanand are the only ones on Grounds Crew. The
last few days, he made me weed all day near the main
entrance. I wonder if tomorrow will be the same, or if
instead he'll send me back to that junkyard parking lot
where the buses are again. I wonder if that guy is always
there.

Finally my head spins so much I'm about to fall
over, so I turn off the shower. I wrap myself in a towel
and crack the door; cool air floods in like ice water and

I gulp it down. Once I steady myself, I close the door again so my mom won't talk to me. I want privacy; I'm not sure why.

I look in the mirror at my sunburn. It makes my cheeks pink and my freckles come out. I kind of like it. I see T-shirt tan lines on my upper arms and make a note to wear a tank top next time.

Evening Program has a dress code: long skirts for women, buttoned shirts for men. Beyond that, you're just supposed to look "nice." I only have one skirt: when I was almost twelve, my mom wanted to talk to this guy selling hippie clothes out of his Venice boardwalk stall, so I got a skirt. It's paisley with a drawstring and a ton of flowing fabric, so even three years later it still fits. My mom says I look "attractive" in it and I should wear skirts more often. I don't like them: they make me feel too girly, sort of weirdly naked. She says I can borrow some of hers for Evening Program dress code. She has a lot.

I walk into the bedroom mopping off my face. "Jesus, Tessa, how much hot water did you use?" my mom says at the cloud billowing out behind me. I shrug. I had a long day. After a shift of telemarketing, my mom used to come home and say she needed a drink. I never had a job before now; I figure it's kind of the same thing.

She's putting on earrings in the mirror above the altar. Her long ones from Peru, green stones and brass that dangle down. She's got lipstick on, slicked red across her lips, and a turquoise dress. She looks girly, and also beautiful. I want to ask her what she did today, but I don't.

I want to ask about a lot of stuff. Like why we moved here in the first place. Like who the hell am I supposed to talk to, since she's away all day and there isn't even school. Like what is the beard guy, really, and how come everyone treats him like a different category of person, and some people make weird noises and fall down. Why does everybody have a name that's not their own? What's that bracelet of beads she keeps touching? And how come she knows so many new words all of a sudden? There's a lot of stuff that I don't understand.

I've never seen her this happy before, though, and I don't want to mess it up. She's always getting excited and joyful about stuff, workshops and classes and, of course, guys, but she's never settled into it like this: just come in, sat down in it, and stayed. Before, her eyes would dart around, flickering like butterfly wings, never staying all the way still. Even when she landed, she'd keep fluttering those wings, just enough to have momentum when it was time to pick up and go. There were always a couple cardboard boxes left in the corner. But now, we've only been here a few days and already she's unpacked it all and put it all away.

On the way out of Evening Program my mom and I hold

hands. The sweat from hers seeps into the cracks in my palms. We slide our shoes back on and she says, "Let's go for chai." Everyone stands around a plastic vat in the big open lobby, talking about meditation experiences and *seva* schedules and people whose names I don't know. They talk about Iran-Contra, because everyone hates Reagan, and someone makes a joke about televangelists and Tammy Faye Bakker. Jayita and Dev are there, loose and liquid, arms around each other; I want to say hi but they're too far away, so I stick to my mom's side. Or at least I try.

·60. It's not so easy; all the guys come up to her. Avtar and Bhav from kitchen prep, a blond guy named Rick, this guy with a beard named Gajendra. They cluster around, shouldering each other out. Everyone knows my mom's name. Nobody asks mine. Rick pushes me aside without even noticing and my mom laughs, sparkles up at him while she sips her chai. She sticks her chest out. Gajendra says something to her about "the sacred feminine," and I decide that he is gross.

Then a woman I haven't met, in dangly jewelry and a flowing skirt just like my mom's, comes up and touches my mom's shoulder. My mom squeals and they hug, ignoring Rick and Gajendra and Avtar and Bhav. My mom and the woman throw their heads back and laugh together, tinkling. They make all the men invisible: the guys just stand around, suddenly aimless.

I wish I could make that happen.

After a minute my mom remembers I'm there. "Oh! This is my daughter, Tessa." She points me toward the woman. "This is my friend Vrishti." Vrishti is a redhead. Almost as pretty as my mom.

We sleep hard, my mom in the queen bed, me in the corner on the twin. She stays in our room all night. I dream about Ohio—Roy Rogers and the grocery store. We go down the cereal aisle and my mom lets me pick out everything I want. I ride on the foot of the cart while she pushes me, fast and faster.

·61·

I wake up when her alarm goes off at four; lie still while she gets dressed and leaves for chanting. I watch the sky turn from navy blue to orange; stars fade and trees turn from silhouettes to real. I think: Akron doesn't have trees like this. I also think: Today I'm going back to Grounds Crew *seva*, and how can I get Devanand to send me to that back parking lot again.

I tell him I wasn't happy with the work I did on the flowers; I want to space them out more evenly. "Okay!" he exclaims with a grin, long gross beard jiggling. His T-shirt today says SRI CHINMOY 10K and has a bunch of people running down a mountain. "The work is for the Guru, so it's important you be happy with it. That's the essence of *seva!*"

When I get into the lot, I think maybe I made a mistake. The guy isn't here—nobody is, just bus parts and junk and my asters, which are spaced pretty evenly, to tell you the truth. I stay anyway, though, and start replanting; what else am I going to do?

Pretty soon I hear a clank behind me. When I turn around, there he is, beneath the bus again. I wonder how you're supposed to say hi to somebody when they're under a bus. Do you go up and kick their foot? Or yell at them? Or just stand and wait and hope eventually they'll notice that you're there?

I pick the final choice, big surprise. I've never known how to talk to someone if they didn't talk to me first. Not any kid at any school I've ever gone to, or grown-ups at parties, or even sometimes my mom. For example: we've been in this place a week already and I haven't even asked her why. It's like the law of inertia we learned last year in Lab Science. It's safer just to let things stay still; once you start, you never know when they'll stop moving.

I put my fingers in the dirt, dig up more flowers. The bus tugs at me like a magnet and my mouth wants to move, but I keep my eyes on the roots, try not to break them. Finally he must feel me thinking, because he comes out from under the bus.

"Hey there! You again!"

"How's it going," I say into my shirt.

"Huh?" he squints across the lot.

"How's it *going*." I enunciate a lot and lean forward, like I could cross the ten feet between us with my voice and my neck. It comes out too loud.

"Oh," he says, like he's surprised I actually asked. "Um, it's going pretty good. Almost done with this one, then I'm ready to move on to the VW. Engine needs a rebuild. You know."

"Yeah." I actually don't know. Pause.

"Okay, well, back to work." He wipes his hands on his jeans and crawls back under. I just stand there staring at the spot he stood in till I catch myself.

Six

...

You must shield the delicate web of inner silence
from the influences of the world.

·64.   By seven we're usually getting dressed for Evening
Program, but tonight my mom still isn't back. The sun
sinks outside the window. I wait till it's definitely too
late for Evening Program, and then I put on my sneakers and go out for a walk.

The path by the main building circles around and
tucks into the woods. The little lights along the sides
make it so you can still walk there at night. I've never
walked in the woods at night before. My eyes adjust and
I feel like a raccoon, pupils wide, watching things
through the black. The branches blur together into a
blanket above me, rustling, and for once I'm not scared
to be alone.

When the path pours me into open space again, I'm
almost sad. A country road cuts through the ashram
property; I look both ways. No cars for a long, long

time. I cross into the courtyard, with the statues of Jesus and Buddha and the elephant god. Little lamps around them cast shadows on their faces. Clumps of lilies and chrysanthemums hide them, so all you see is the light beams floating up from below. I think how everything is like that: you only see the shadows that the light makes, you never see what makes the light.

I sit there for a long time, in the courtyard surrounded by gods. Crickets are the only sound. After a while they blur together with my breathing, and I'd stay out here all night except that the truck pulling by on the road, too loud, snaps me out of it. By now it's probably ten; my mom will be worried, if she's back. I wander over to the glass-walls-red-rug building, try the door. Everything is always unlocked. I remember if you go through that building, out the other side is the shuttle stand.

I do, and there is, and I sit down on the bench beneath the canvas tent. Sure enough, after a minute a bus engine rumbles through the silence. The shuttle driver, a gray guy with a grizzly beard and tie-dyed baseball cap, raises his eyebrow, but I climb on without looking, just like going to school. In my seat I watch the woods out the window with my raccoon eyes. He turns up the tinny speakers and the chant spills out, *"Jaya Jagatambe,"* same as Evening Program. I hum along.

Back at the room, Mom is mad. I open the door and catch her mid-pace on the thin carpet. She whirls around. "Where were you?" Her eyes flash; underneath the angry is a scared red softness. I look away.

"Look at me, young lady!"

Young lady. Wooh. With my mom, you have to do a lot to get a "young lady."

My eyes are on her, but I'm trying to stay in my own head. I liked it out there, on the trail, in the courtyard, by myself. I don't want to let her in to mess it up.

"Where were you?"

I shrug. "I went for a walk."

She looks at me like it's incomprehensible I could put one foot in front of the other without her assistance or permission.

"What's wrong with that?" I ask her. I don't expect an answer; it just feels good to say it.

She paces toward me. "What's *wrong* with that, young lady, is that you are not to just run off unsupervised without telling me where you're going! You didn't even leave a note! And don't look at me that way."

"What way?" I'm not even looking at her, not really.

"You *know* the look I'm talking about. Don't play games with me." She's annoyed I'm getting her to answer my questions and not the other way around. Ha.

She glares at me and exhales really hard.

"Why are you even trying to sound all bossy like that anyway?" I say, half under my breath. "You sound stupid." I don't really want her to hear me, except I sort of do.

She hears me. "*What* did you say?"

Right now it's the part of the fight when I can back down and it's over, or keep going and it isn't. These last three years we argue often enough for me to chart the different moments that stay the same from fight to fight: where the exit hatches are, what buttons I can press to ratchet things up. I could say "nothing" right now and that would be it. I'd let her win, she'd leave me alone, and I could fold back inside myself where it's safe. But I don't. Instead I puff my chest up, make my face hard, square my shoulders. "I said, *Quit it.* Quit bossing me around."

"You don't tell me what to do! I will boss you around if I want to boss you around. I am your *mother.* That gives me certain rights. You think I *like* sitting here waiting for you and wondering where you are? You think it's fun? You're just so thoughtless. Jesus." She yells like she can force her viewpoint into my brain if she says it loud enough.

Secretly I know I could have left a note, but I don't care. I'm not going to say I'm sorry, and I'm not going to say I'll "do it different in the future." Even though that's what I'm supposed to say, and even though it might make the whole thing end, and even though it's sort of true.

Because it isn't fair.

"Why?" I ask her. "You don't ever leave a note. You always leave, and I sit there waiting, wondering where *you* are. That's what you did tonight!" I don't flinch. I want an answer. "Where were you?"

And then her chest deflates; her face relaxes. She folds her arms and shakes her hair. Her chin juts up. "I was with Vrishti." All of a sudden she's the teenager. "We went and had a chai."

I just look at her. She looks at me. It should make me feel better, her realizing that she did the same thing I did; but instead it scares me, seeing her look young that way. She's supposed to be the mom.

After a second she folds me into her arms like she forgives me. "Oh, Tessa, I'm just glad you're back." She squeezes my floppy arms against my sides; my elbows poke my ribs. I think about the crickets and the shadows and the trail, how good I felt until I came back here and she got mad. I want to be alone again, quiet and contained inside my skin, away from her yelling and her leaving and the red soft beneath them both. I wish I had a door to close, a room to go away to. I stand there and let her hug me.

The next morning I stop at the front desk on the way to *seva*. My heart thuds hard as I ask the lady if there's mail for me, harder when she goes in back to check. A little bright space opens up inside me in the moment before she comes back, a little space of *maybe*, and I have to remind myself not to let it open all the way wide to *yes*. Not yet.

When she comes back empty-handed, that space seals right back up, like a Ziploc baggie. On the way to *seva* I tell myself: It hasn't been that long. Maybe his record company hasn't sent it to him yet. Maybe he's on the road. I know how to say those things; it's what I always do. It opens up the seal a tiny bit, just enough so that little bit of hope won't suffocate.

Devanand's not at the shed, so I grab a trowel and some marigolds and head back to the lot, try to forget the letter and focus on my plan.

The guy's there again, beneath the bus. This time I go over and kick his boot. "Hey," I say, ignoring the law of inertia. He pulls out from under, looks up at me, surprised. For a second I hang there, wondering what

I've just done. But he's out now, staring up at me, and an object in motion will remain in motion, and I have to say *something*. "What're you doing?" I ask.

"I *was* fixing the transmission on this bus, till someone came up and kicked me."

My throat goes down into my stomach and I blush. I did the total wrong thing. I pissed him off. Why did I do that? Crap. Should have just stayed still. I'm about to turn around and go back to my stupid marigolds when he grins.

"Hey, I'm just joking."

"Oh." Right. Of course. Joking.

"I could use a break, actually. The air's kinda thick down here." He wipes his face with his arm to get the sweat off. A big black smudge smears his forehead. "What're you doing back here anyway? They got you on garden duty?"

"Yeah, I guess." I glance back at the flat of marigolds.

"Seems funny they'd waste 'em back here, there's nobody ever in this lot except me. But I suppose I should be flattered." Flattered why? It's hard to tell exactly what he means by things. At least he's not using any weird words, though. So far.

"I suppose."

He grins again. It's like he thinks I'm funny. "So where're you from?"

. . . . .

His name is Colin. We talk for almost a whole hour. He's
not an ashram person; he lives over by town. They bring
him in to fix the shuttles. He's good at fixing stuff. He's
twenty. He doesn't come here every day; only when
there's something broken. He has green eyes.

I've never had a crush before, not really. I mean, okay,
Erik Estrada from *ChiPs* when I was eight. And Almanzo
when he married Laura on *Little House on the Prairie*. But
those don't count. They're not real people. The only real
human person that's any kind of crush equivalent was
Randy Wishnick, and he doesn't count either because it
wasn't my idea, plus also because of how it turned out.
As far as I was concerned, Randy was just another nasty
dirtball boy at Volney Rogers Junior High when I showed
up there halfway through the seventh grade. I was used
to those boys: they wore jean jackets and had the short-
long haircut—short in the front and long in the back—
and freckles, little beady eyes. They weren't popular but
they were never nerds either; they had their own kind of
outcast power, and they were mean. Especially to new
kids, and to quiet girls who read too many books.

But Randy wasn't mean to me. Instead he came over
to my desk during fifth-period study hall and asked me,

"Whatcha readin?" It was sort of embarrassing because it was Judy Blume, but at least it was *Deenie* and not some book about periods like *Are You There God? It's Me, Margaret*. I showed him the cover and he said, "Cool." I could tell he'd never heard of it. After that he started trailing me through the hallway on the way to lunch. He'd strut around hyper in his Quiet Riot T-shirt, brag about shoplifting Nut Goodies from the Piggly Wiggly. I never really knew why he talked to me, except that he didn't have any other friends that I could see.

He kissed me for the first time on the hill behind the cafeteria, and it was nice. The tongue part was a little gross, but afterward he looked at me like I was someone who made him feel things. Up close I could see his hazel eyes had freckles in them, too, little flecks of green and gold. He leaned in and bumped my forehead with his, soft, and then this big grin spread across his skinny face and he started laughing, but not at me, and I started laughing too.

After that, lunch was always on that hill; he would give me half his Tater Tots so I could throw my six-grain sandwich away. Then we'd kiss. We both tasted like ketchup.

Then the second Friday he felt me up. He didn't even really kiss me first, just shot his bony hand up my shirt without asking and squeezed hard enough to hurt, pushing me back onto the ground with his weight. My eyes flew open but his stayed shut, and he made his tongue fill up my mouth and it got hard to breathe beneath him. All of a sudden his body felt like rocks pressing into my ribs, and I said, "Hey," but he didn't look at me or stop, and finally I pushed up on him and threw him off and stood up and headed down the hill. When I looked back he was standing up in his Motörhead T-shirt, wiping grass stains off his jeans and yelling, "What's your problem?" after me.

So that's what I had till now: Almanzo, Ponch, and Randy Wishnick. The good ones weren't real and the real one was mean. I was starting to think the whole "guy" thing was just for banana-clip chicks and girls on TV and my mom, given who was available to choose from. I never knew whether anything else was out there.

Now I know.

I leave *seva* early to go and take a shower. I'm not that dirty, but I want to do something to separate this afternoon from tonight. This afternoon in the parking lot with Colin was mine, like my walk the night before was mine, and I don't want them blurring together with my mom.

When I come out toweling my hair off, she's sitting on the bed. I see her see the cloud of steam, start to say something about wasting water, but she stops. She's trying to be nice. "Come on, get dressed; we're going to meet Vrishti for dinner." There's a lot of this Vrishti all of a sudden. She seemed okay the other night, but we'll see if she talks to me or just my mom.

At the dining hall, the two of them put exactly identical amounts of shredded zucchini and beets on their trays, identical tahini and identical sprouts. They also are the same height, both pretty, and both have long hair. One red and one brown. Like salt and pepper shakers. We come up to the table and everyone says hi to them.

Vrishti takes a chair on my left side and nods for my mom to sit on my right. She closes her eyes and says some long complicated chant before she eats; my mom does too. I don't know the words, so I just sit there between them and feel weird. But when they're done, Vrishti turns right to me and asks how old I am and what I think of the ashram. I just shrug. "It's cool." It would take way too long to really tell her. But I'm glad somebody asked.

My mom's never had a friend before. In Ohio the women were always scared of her, the other single ones who worked in offices and drank Tab and went to the bar on the weekends. She was so much weirder than even the "wild girls" who smoked pot and had affairs with Bill in Marketing; she was so much prettier that no one ever expected she'd be lonely. Dayton and Venice, Big Sur and Akron: all the women were just variations on the same weird mix of judgment and envy. The only people she ever had to talk to were her guys and me, and even I felt the same way as those office girls sometimes.

But the other women glare at Vrishti too. Just like my mom, she's lonely from too much attention, and the two of them stick to each other like magnets that finally entered each other's field.

Vrishti finishes her zucchini, and then she gives my mom a secret smile. My mom secret-smiles back. I watch back and forth like Ping-Pong. I wonder if they're going to let me in the game.

My mom says, "Sooo . . ."

Vrishti says, "Tessa . . ."

They secret-smile again.

"We have news."

"Okay," I say, with trepidation. I don't know what this news could be, but the possibility exists that it isn't good. Since we've gotten here, my mom's perception of what's good seems to have strayed away from mine, far enough that I'm starting to stop trusting that something is a good thing just because she thinks it is.

Vrishti squirms in her seat. "We've been invited to the Guru's kitchen!"

My mom beams into Vrishti's eyes. I have to say, I don't know what the big deal is.

"Cool."

"Tessa, it's an incredible honor," my mom explains. "I don't even know how they picked us or anything, they just came into the kitchen today—"

"And said," Vrishti chimes in—

"We would be honored to have your *seva* in the Guru's private kitchen!" they finish in unison. Then they actually giggle.

"So we'll be working up the hill, over at the Guru's quarters; we'll be helping with the prep for all his meals," my mom says. "It's such an incredible opportunity to be near the *shakti* of the Guru."

I've decided that if people use weird words around me, they're going to have to tell me what they mean. "What's *shakti*?"

"Oh, it means like spiritual energy?" Vrishti says. "The life force of the universe."

"Cool." I nod.

"After dinner, let's go celebrate!" my mom says.

"Yes!" Vrishti says.

Celebrate means have dessert at the Amrit, which means Snack Bar. At the regular cafeteria there's no dessert— apparently it's not yogic—but at the Amrit there is lots. Cobbler, cookies, cake, pie, all made with brown rice syrup and whole wheat pastry flour. I get a yogurt-granola parfait and we sit by the window. Vrishti has blueberry rhubarb crisp. My mom just gets a tea. Music pipes from tinny speakers like in the shuttle buses. My mom and Vrishti do a short version of their chant, holding both my hands, and then we eat.

As I'm scraping out the final dregs of yogurt, those kids tumble through the Amrit door. The brother and the sister and the other guy all laugh at something, stand near the jars of cookies, and pick some out. Peanut butter, from what I can tell. Vrishti nods toward them at my mom, small, like she thinks I won't be able to see. My mom nods back. I roll my eyes, but neither of them notices.

·77·

"Tessa," Vrishti stage-whispers, trying to be inaudible and failing, "do you know those kids?"

"No." I don't try to whisper.

She and my mom do their attempting-to-be-subtle nod at each other again. "Maybe you should go and say hello." Vrishti smiles.

My mom really likes that idea. "Tessa, I think that would be wonderful."

"Nah, it's okay."

"You can't have new adventures if you don't take risks!" She looks at Vrishti meaningfully.

"Really, I don't feel like it."

"Why? I'm sure they're perfectly nice."

I want to tell her that they're pale and weird and I

never know what they're laughing about, but I don't want Vrishti to think I'm mean. So I just shrug.

"It'd be great for you to meet some kids your age!" Vrishti chimes in.

"Yeah, Tessa, it really would." My mom gives her that nod again.

Oh, for Christ's sake. This is clearly going to end in disaster, but it doesn't look like I have a choice. I get up and go over to the peanut-butter-cookie jar. My heart is thunking and my cheeks are hot.

"Hi." I say it to the littler guy, the one who hasn't gone through puberty, forgetting that sometimes the little guys are the worst: they have stuff to prove. He raises his eyebrows at me like some kind of challenge. Brother and sis look at each other.

"I'm Tessa," I keep going. I don't know why. I really should have already turned around and gone back to my mom.

"Hi," the girl goes. "I'm Avinashi." She sucks on the side of her cookie till it's soggy. "That's Sanjit." She points at her brother. "And that's Meer." She points at the short guy. He raises his eyebrows again.

"Cool," I say. Neither of the guys says anything. They just stand there being weird and pale. "Okay, see you later," I say. When I turn around to walk away I hear them laugh. My face flushes redder.

Back at the table my mom and Vrishti titter like

popular girls, then stop and look like moms when they see me coming back. It's official: what my mom thinks is good or smart or fun has diverged permanently from the truth. Or at least from my experience of the truth. The swamis say that's all I've got anyway: there's no such thing as objective truth, at least not on the human perceptual plane. And who knows, maybe they're right.

SEVEN

. . .

To attain the new, you must abandon
old relationships and forms.

·80. Devanand gives me a stick with a spike at the end and tells me to pick up garbage. I can do it wherever I want.

When I get to the lot, Colin's finishing up the school bus. He must hear me crunching gravel because as soon as I'm in the lot he's up and out, wiping off his hands. His T-shirt says THUNDERCATS. "Hey!" he says. "You again!"

I blush.

"It's totally perfect you showed up."

I'm not sure what to say to that. "Cool."

"Are you busy? I could kind of use a hand with something."

"Okay." I don't even ask him what it is.

"Don't you want to know what it is?"

"Okay." What am I, a robot?

"Okay." He says it like I said it, and grins. He's laughing at me, but it doesn't seem mean. "So here's the deal. When I finish this bus here"—he points at the school bus—"I get to work on that one." He nods toward the red VW bus with white trim, the cool one. "The shuttle guys said if I fix it up I can use it during the week, and they'll just use it on the weekends when the extra people come. Sounds like a good deal, huh?"

I nod. "Sure."

"Yeah. Only problem is, 'fix it up' means rebuild the engine. I can do most of it myself, but there are parts where you gotta have two sets of hands. Think you'd be up for helping out a little?"

I've never done anything remotely mechanical in my entire life, and I normally have zero interest in that stuff, but he said "two sets of hands." That means: my hands and his hands. "Okay."

"Okay," he says again, and laughs. "Come on down here, and I'll show you about the tools."

Here is what I learn that afternoon: there is more than one kind of screwdriver. The oil pressure switch is located on the crankcase underneath the distributor. Gravel hurts your butt almost as much as your knees. Socket sets are kind of cool. Throttle positioners are fairly easy to remove. An engine is a complex organism.

It's hard to hold a flashlight steady when your hands are shaking.

The next day I don't even get marigolds or the trash spike or check the mail; I just grab my vest and head to the lot. Colin's under the bus, his jeans already smudged. He must hear me coming, because right away he comes out from under. Today it's a YES T-shirt. It has a space landscape with huge red polka-dotted mush-rooms. "Hey, it's my right-hand lady," he says. I blush.

First of all: "lady." And second of all: his.

He pats the gravel. We get to work removing the battery, and then the wires on the voltage regulator. For a while it's quiet, just birds and leaves rustling, squeak and clink of the engine parts. Just as I'm starting to wonder if I'm supposed to say something, he talks. "So how'd you get here, Tessa?"

"We drove."

He laughs at me again, in that same way that's not embarrassing, just funny. It makes me laugh too. "Duh, right?" I wipe black grease onto my jeans and start over explaining. "My mom wanted to come. I guess she went to some workshop or something and got into it." I won-der if I should explain about when she sat me on the futon and told me that she'd finally learned that you can't ever count on men. I wonder if I should explain about my dad. "She said it was a new chapter and an adventure."

"Well, definitely an adventure, huh?" The way he asks it makes me feel like he already understands everything I think about this place.

"Yeah, I guess so. It's pretty weird."

He raises his eyebrows. "Yeah?"

I snort. "Have you *met* any of these people? They like speak some whole other language." It comes out meaner than I meant it and as soon as it's out of my mouth I worry that he's maybe friends with them or something. I start to take it back, but he laughs.

"What, you mean after *seva* at the *Amrit* with the *Guru*?" His eyes sparkle at me and suddenly I stop feeling mean.

We laugh so much my stomach aches and by the time we pull out the last hose the trees are dark against the sky. The sun sinks down below the branches and everything turns orange and I might have missed dinner but I don't care.

The wind's speckling goose bumps on my arms when Colin stands up and stretches, grease-smeared T-shirt pulling across his chest so the space landscape mushrooms spread out wide like a fun-house mirror.

"See you tomorrow," he says, and for the first time since we got here I'm impatient for morning.

At Evening Program my mom pulls me past the pillow piles and the people searching for a seat, and we head straight for the front. On the way we pass the kids. My mom doesn't notice them, thank god. The sister, Avinashi, starts to smile at me and I start to smile back, but then Meer steps in front of her and glares. I can feel his mean prepubescent gaze stick to my back as my mom yanks me past them.

Three rows of people ring around the Guru's chair, a special section like the best seats at a concert. Vrishti smiles when she sees us, pats the cushion next to her for my mom to sit. The people up here are mostly all good-looking, with pulled-together clothes and fancy scarves, silk meditation cushions instead of canvas, beads made out of jade or amethyst. They all look at me like they know me already, though we haven't ever met. I only recognize one of them: Ninyassa. She glares at Vrishti and my mom.

It's like a special club up here. My seat's just half a space, wedged between two others, and I know it wouldn't be there if it weren't for my mom. It's weird being in a club that you know wouldn't invite you if you hadn't come attached to someone else. There's a line that separates this group from all the other people, and I'm inside the line and outside it at exactly the same time.

We're closer to the musicians here, though, and the drums thump in my stomach, liquidy and round. I breathe around the beats; my mom and Vrishti and Ninyassa go away and so do clubs, compartments, and special sections. The inside-outside line thins until it disappears, and I keep picturing space landscape mushrooms, red and white dots against a rainbow background that keeps stretching out and out and out.

Our room door creaks open; in the mirror I see myself jump. I slowly lock the bathroom door so she won't hear.

"Tessa?"

"Just a minute," I holler, turning on the water. Mascara sticks to my eyelashes like glue, and her lipstick leaves a pink stain on my mouth even when I wipe it hard enough to hurt. The soap tastes like incense but it gets things back to normal; when my face looks regular again I twist the faucet and come out.

Usually when my mom comes back from *seva* she takes off her clogs and earrings right away, but she's still wearing all her jewelry and her shoes. Her hair spills out from underneath a Guatemalan wool hat. "Grab a sweater," she says. "It's getting cool."

She takes me out and down the stairs, fast and wild, like on one of our road trips. She's always a few paces ahead of me, but she keeps turning back, scooping me up with her grin and pulling me along. It's nice, her turning back to check on me.

We make it through the lobby without her saying hi to anybody, even guys; then we barrel past the entrance and the courtyard to the woods. Tonight's the first night you know fall is coming, the way the air gives up the loose sprawl of summer, sharpens into the smell of cold and burning leaves. The sweatshirt I put on is enough, but barely. She keeps me moving fast enough to stand it, though, and we duck under the canopy of green and yellow. She points at a twisted tree at the entrance to the trail; its leaves are delicate like shadow puppets, red already, deep and rich. "Japanese maple," she says. "No leaves that color in Ohio, huh?"

Once we're on the path, she slows down. She keeps my fingers clutched inside hers; I wrap my sleeve over my other hand so it can stay warm too. We walk for a while, watching branches cast shadows on the forest floor, tangling till you can't see the spaces between them. It's a relief. I could walk like this for a long time, without weird words I haven't heard and places I don't know the names of and strange foods and rules. Without boyfriends or dates or skirts that I don't want, guys elbowing in front of me. I could walk like this for a long time, holding hands between the trees, quiet, me and my mom.

Pretty soon, though, she asks me what I did all day. I don't tell her how I almost peed my pants laughing at Colin's Devanand impersonation, how the quiet parts filled up with butterflies beating high up in my stomach, almost in my throat. I don't tell her about grease between my fingers and gravel in my back and how I kind of get it now when people talk about working with their hands. I don't tell her because she doesn't really want to know. I can tell by her voice that she's asking me about my day because she really wants to talk about hers, and so I say, "Nothing much, just *seva*. How about you?"

She breathes in deep like she's winding up, getting ready; then she turns to me. "Oh, Tessa," she says. When it's an Experience she always starts with "Oh, Tessa."

"Today at the end of lunch-cleaning *seva*, Swami Anantananda came in and told us all to find a place to sit down. Right in the Guru's kitchen! He said just sit on the floor or a counter or whatever, and once we all did they brought the Guru in. For *darshan*."

"What's *darshan*?" I was wondering how long it'd take for her to say a word I didn't know. Ten seconds.

"*Darshan* is when you spend a few moments together. Just you and the Guru and the energy between you. It means to share presence."

The new language makes us separate, a space of words I have to cross to get to her. But clearly she's not going to notice that or stop, so I have to find a way to deal. I decide to try to apply the words to normal things, like me and her taking a walk, or eating food, or talking. If I can do that, maybe they might not seem so weird.

"Like right now, are we having *darshan?*"

She laughs. "Oh no, Tess, this isn't *darshan. Darshan* is like a special audience with the Guru. It's not the same as just spending time with a regular person."

"Oh."

When I was little and she didn't have a boyfriend, my mom would play hooky from work and pin tapestries to the insides of our windows, pile up pillows and drape them with cloth till we were surrounded by the most amazing blanket fort in the whole entire world. We'd spend hours inside, ignoring the phone when work called, drinking strawberry-apple juice and laughing. It doesn't seem fair that that doesn't have a name, but there's a special word for the time she spends with this weird beard guy she's hardly even met.

I don't know how to explain that, though, so I just ask, "Then what happened?"

"It was so amazing. As soon as he walked in the room it was like my whole body turned into electricity." I feel kind of embarrassed, but I don't interrupt. "One by one he called us, and by the time it was my turn, there was so much energy running through me I was afraid to stand up. I thought I was going to fall down! My legs and my arms and my chest and everything, it was like there was this *light* in them, pressing out from the inside."

"Wow." I've never felt anything like that before.

"I was vibrating and vibrating and the swamis brought me up to the Guru, and I just fell at his feet. I can't even explain it. This incredible silence came over me. Bigger, and more, than any sound you ever heard. It was like . . ." There's no special word for it, so she's looking for her own. "It was like a *sea* of silence. Like an ocean. And I was the ocean, and at the same time just a teeny little dot in it. And the Guru was the ocean too."

She's got this look on her face, eager, like she wants me to say something, take a turn, tell a story to match hers. Like she wants me to understand. But I don't understand. When the beard guy walked into the room, all I saw was a little man with the face of a beatific imp and Hawaiian flower garlands. When I strained my eyes I could see how he was beautiful, okay, and the chanting makes me feel stuff; but not like my whole body being taken over by electricity, vibrating, when five minutes earlier I was chopping beans and wiping counters. Nothing that would make me fall at someone's feet.

She's still watching me and I stare down, shuffle gravel on the path. By now it's dark; the lights along the trail glow just enough to see three steps ahead. I want to ask her how you learn to feel all that stuff, but she already said she couldn't explain. And even if she could, it wouldn't make it cross over from her into me. It's not just all those new words that make that space between us; it's something happening to her, something I wish that I could feel.

She keeps looking at me, eyes wide and expectant, like I'm supposed to say something. It makes my ribs clench up; I want her to stop trying to get inside them. I feel hard toward her and too soft at the same time. I wish she'd just leave me alone.

·90·

Finally I let out a weird snort that's half a laugh. "So what'd he do next? Turn into Jim and Tammy Faye and ask you for your money? Praise the Lord!" I say the last part in a televangelist accent. It's supposed to be a joke, I guess, but I can see from the corner of my eye: her face scrunches up. For a second it looks like she might cry. I open my mouth to say something else, but I don't know what it is and it catches in my throat.

She drops my hand and turns around. "Come on, Tessa. I have to get up early to chant." We walk all the way back to our room without talking. But not the same way as before.

EIGHT

. . .

*The material world is but a creation of our consciousness,
composed of the stories we tell and are told.*

I can see through the trees to sky as I walk toward the parking lot; they look thinner in the daytime, less dense. I rub my lips together and blot my mouth on my hand, worrying I put on too much of her lipstick this morning. I wipe the extra red off on my jeans.

I'm almost to the lot when I spot the beard, and then the T-shirt. RUNNERS ARE SMILERS. It's been a while since I've seen Devanand, unless you count Colin's impersonations. He's wearing jogging shorts as small as underwear, even though it's fifty degrees. He strides right up and puts his skinny chest too close to my face.

"Where are *you* headed, m'lady?"

I just look up at him. I haven't done any *seva* in a week. Longer, probably.

"It's getting pretty close to frost; you must've finished planting those asters by now, huh?" He holds his crazy eyeballs on me for a second.

"Yeah, uh—" I stutter, then trail off. I haven't ever actually gotten in trouble before. When I think about it, I haven't ever actually even done anything I could get in trouble for, except forget my notebook or not finish all my kale. Well, that and writing to my dad. But I've gotten good at keeping that a secret.

I still haven't formed a sentence. Devanand is staring down at me, too hard. "Where's your vest?"

My vest is crumpled in the shed, behind a bag of wood chips. I hid it there so I wouldn't have to wear it in front of Colin like some kind of nerd badge. "Um."

Devanand is looking at me, arms crossed, like I have all the choice in the world. Like it's "my responsibility." And "my karma is my own." And I have "total freedom." Except I have to make the choice he wants me to or else all that freedom goes away; so really I don't have any at all.

I clear my throat, hunt between the stretched-out seconds for something to say. He shifts his weight. I'm screwed. And then, from who knows where inside my brain: "I thought I would gather some autumn leaves. As an offering. To the Guru." And the cherry on top: "There's a Japanese maple at the entrance to the trail."

Pause. Then Devanand raises his frizzy red eyebrows. "Japanese maple, huh?"

"Yes, it's beautiful. Have you seen it? It looks like shadow puppets."

"I do know that tree. It's a wild one!" Suddenly he's loose-limbed and jangly again. I've just made a discovery: I am a good liar.

"Yup. Just perfect for the Guru."

"Okeydokey then! Just take the leaves that have fallen to the earth already, 'kay? Wouldn't want to interrupt the life cycle."

"For sure," I say. "Would you like me to include a few from you?"

Colin's working on the throttle cable when I show up, fists full of red and orange leaves. I'm still buzzing from the lie. It was so easy. All I had to do was pretend it was the truth and it came out that way, slid from my mouth just like it was real. I didn't even blush. It sort of changes everything, knowing I can do that. It means I really *do* have "total freedom," or at least a lot more than I thought. All I have to do is tell a story.

I crouch down next to him; gravel presses up through the soles of my sneakers. "Hey."

"Hey." He looks over at me. My breath is still a little fast. "What're you so excited about?"

Now I blush. "Nothing."

He keeps looking at me. Not like Devanand, though. I'm not going to get in trouble with Colin. "Nothing, huh? I'm not sure I believe you." He smirks.

The only person here who can guess I'm not telling the truth is the only person I wouldn't want to lie to. "Well, okay, *something*." I tell him how Devanand intercepted me, make a whole story out of it, building up the suspense. I tell how as soon as I said, "offering to the Guru," Devanand got all reverent and enthusiastic. And how I threw in that detail about the Japanese maple, so he'd really think I'd been paying attention to the grounds.

"Smart," Colin says, and winks at me. "You're a smart kid."

I blush again.

I try an experiment: I tell *myself* a story. I figure it worked with Devanand, maybe it'll work with me. I tell myself I'm funny and beautiful and know how to say all the right stuff. That no one will ever want to leave me. That if I want something I can just say it; that I can find out the things I want to know.

Colin draws a diagram of the coil wiring before he starts taking it apart, so he'll know how to put it back together later. He scribbles with a stub of pencil, slips the paper in the pocket of his jeans. "So, Colin," I say. He looks up from the wiring. I tell myself: *You know what to say*. "Did you—did you always live here?"

Ech. That came out like the glasses guy in *Revenge of*

the Nerds. I reach for the socket set, ready to give up on my storytelling experiment, get back to work. Except: he answers me.

"I grew up about an hour away." I look at him from the corner of my eye. He seems to have missed my transformation into *Revenge of the Nerds* guy.

"Yeah?"

He smiles. "Yeah. Over near Narrowsburg? Delaware County. It's lame up there, pretty much. I've been around here the last couple years."

"Yeah?"

He looks at me like I'm funny, and then says, "Yeah," again. I feel like he's being nice to me on purpose. It makes me feel a little like a kid, but I don't mind. "I went to SCCC—"

Somehow it's easier to ask him what things mean than it is to ask my mom. "What's SCCC?"

"Sullivan County Community College? It's near here, kinda. I did a year there, and then I traveled around a little"—he says that part louder, like he's proud—"and then a friend of mine heard about this place down here that needed a caretaker, so, you know, free rent."

"Cool." I nod like I know all about free rent.

"Yeah, it is, mostly," he says. "It's one of those old bungalow places—used to be some summer camp or something in the sixties—and the guy doesn't want to give it up, even though no one ever goes there anymore.

He lives in Florida. So it's just me and fifteen cabins. Could even have a swimming pool, if I felt like cleaning out the leaves." He smiles. "But that's a lot of work. Doesn't seem worth it when there's a perfectly good creek in the backyard."

"Wow. You have your own creek?" I can't imagine having my own house, let alone fifteen of them, let alone a creek. I can hardly even remember having my own *room*.

"Well, it's not exactly mine. But close enough."

Suddenly I have this really strong urge to go swim-

ming. "That sounds amazing."

"Yeah, it's okay," he says. "Quiet. I kinda wish I was still traveling, though."

"Yeah." Again: like I know all about traveling. "Where did you go?"

"Oh, me and my buddies just hitched around up north for a while. You ever been to Maine?"

"No."

"It's beautiful. Imagine like it is here, but with woods ten times as thick, and pine trees. And ocean. People talk funny there, though." He does what I guess is an imitation of a Maine accent. Something about lobsters. He sounds ridiculous; I start laughing at him really hard. For a second I worry it's mean of me, but then he starts laughing too. "Lobstah," he says again, and then cracks up. It's contagious; we just sit there passing it back and forth until my stomach hurts. I don't even feel stupid when I snort.

He learned to be a mechanic from his uncle; thank god for that. The caretaking gig doesn't pay, so he's gotta do something part-time. Thank god for that. The last guy who fixed the shuttles at the ashram left to live on a yoga farm somewhere in California. Thank god for that too. I whisper it out loud on the way home as the sun starts to set: *Thank you, god, for adding up these things so that he is here right now.*
·97·

Usually when the alarm starts buzzing and beeping in the pitch-black dark I smush my head under my pillow and hide beneath the blankets till the door clicks shut and I can breathe again. But today, somehow my mother has talked me into waking up at four in the morning to go chant with her and Vrishti. She said the chant is "magical." She also says, "It's just about as far as you can get from those right-wing televangelists, young lady."

I'm so tired my brain hurts. On the way, she keeps trying to talk to me and I don't say anything; I just look at her. "Fine," she finally says, and walks the rest of the way three paces ahead of me, without looking back.

The chant doesn't have a tune, just a lot of really long words, lined up verse after verse. I don't know how to pronounce them, let alone what they mean. You read them out of a little hardcover navy blue book and I don't see what's so opposite from the televangelists; it reminds me exactly of the hymnals at my grandparents' Ohio church, except we're sitting on the floor. And speaking Sanskrit.

I wonder if the problem is me. My mom told me I should be "open" to the "energy" of the chant, "silence my mind so I can hear the song within it." Maybe if I were less closed off and noisy I would feel something besides bored and tired and backachy.

I decide to forget about trying to get the words right and see if I can "open myself up." I don't even know what that means, but for some reason it translates into concentrating on the middle of my chest. After a couple minutes of that I feel like I'm going to cry, or laugh, or both, which is weird because I'm not even thinking about anything. When I stop reading the words and turning the pages I can feel it more. I worry for a second that I'll get in trouble for stopping, but then I remember that it doesn't matter. I can always make up a story.

Colin comes into my head. It's not like I think of him. He's just part of the moment, which is a thing, and which includes: the feeling in my chest, the cry-and-laugh, the room we're in, none of it divided up at all.

But then my mind realizes it feels good to remember his T-shirt and coil-wiring diagram and the back-and-forth contagious laugh between us, and that feeling of all-at-once goes away, and it's just him there, and I don't know where we are in the chant, and I turn the pages trying to catch up.

But I keep thinking about him. It gets me through the drone of the half hour that's left, and it puts a little smile on my lips that must look a lot like Vrishti's and my mom's.

I'm still smiling when I slide my sneakers on, open the door into sunlight, when the path turns from asphalt to wood chips to gravel. I'm still smiling when I turn the corner toward the lot, eyes pointed toward the big, crisp blue sky, glad it's morning, that there's still so much day ahead of me. So much day to spend with him.

But then the path spills into open, and the bus is sitting there on woodblocks, engine half out, wires half clipped, bolts strewn around the tires like garbage—no tools beside it, no one beneath. I look around, quiet, wind ruffling the leaves like feathers. He's not here. *Maybe he's just late*, I tell myself. Maybe he overslept, or took too long making breakfast. Maybe he had to clean one of his cabins. I'm used to waiting. *I'll just wait.*

I sit there forever, cross-legged, gravel poking my

butt, and wish I brought a book. I think about doing some work on the engine, but I have no idea what. I try to trace the branches underneath the half-fallen leaves. They look like nerves, or veins. I count them, tree to tree. I'm still bored.

There's this other thing too, a kind of antsy jump in my throat, the opposite of the one-thing-ness I felt earlier. Everything is broken up into little shards of worry, thoughts circling each other like hungry birds and swooping down to peck at me. It's like when I was younger and my mom would leave me overnight without telling me when she'd be home. I used to comb through everything I'd done the days before, searching for the thing that I'd done wrong, that made her mad, the thing that would explain why she was gone. Now I wonder if Colin secretly did feel bad when I laughed at him for that Maine accent, or was annoyed at me for asking all those questions. If he's bored with me, or thinks that I'm a stupid kid.

The sun gets stronger in the sky and I tell myself, *That's dumb, it's not your fault, he likes you fine.* I tell myself something must have come up, something I don't know about; that he has a life full of things I've never heard of that don't have anything to do with me. When I do that with my dad it usually makes me feel better. I just tell myself there's just some reason I don't know about, and then keep hoping.

But with Colin, it weirdly makes it worse. Because I realize: I don't like thinking there are parts of Colin I don't know about. I don't like thinking he's a mystery outside our parking lot, and that I don't really know him at all. He could even have a girlfriend. Everyone keeps all these secrets from me, these places in themselves held back and separate; it's like nobody wants me to really know them, not for real, not all the way.

I know how to tell when someone's not coming. It's been two hours already, almost. He's not just late. If I go ask Devanand for a new assignment, he'll ask what I've been doing all morning, and my mind's too tired from ·101. worrying to make up something good. My mom's at Guru's quarters, cooking. There isn't anybody else. The day stretches out in front of me, wide and empty, alone.

Gravel leaves its achy imprint on my thighs when I stand up. I don't know where I'm going, but I can't sit here anymore.

There's a tiny opening off the edge of the lot, so small it almost isn't there, and I duck in, branches scratching my shoulders. The path snakes through woods, behind the kitchen, plastic soy-oil vats stacked up by the Dumpsters, stainless steel equipment and old sinks. A pair of arms thrusts out the back door to throw a bucket of scraped carrots on the steaming compost heap, and I hurry by.

It's trees again and then the First Aid trailer, rickety steps and yellowing white paint. I think of going back in there, wrapping myself in the scratchy Guatemalan blanket, turning on the radio, picking up Jayita's book about the bliss of true universal aloneness. I wonder if I would get it now. I get up close and squint through the shades, trying to see if she's in there, smiling up at Chakradev. I wouldn't mind. They're the only ashram people who have ever been nice to me. I stand for a minute, listen-

ing for Jayita's stoner-yoga voice, but it's just quiet. I get back on the trail.

The woods go on and on and I start to worry that I'm lost. If I am, I'll be screwed—it's the country here, no pay phones anywhere, and anyway we don't even have a number for me to call. Ahead I see daylight and when I get closer, the road. Across it are falling-down houses, pale blue and yellow and tan, one with a rusted-out car in the front yard, another with a dog. The lawns in front of them are patchy, half green, half brown. I stay on my side of the street.

I remember the letter I sent to my dad, the names of the highways and routes, and for a minute I imagine his van chugging over the hill to scoop me up, take me off on tour, tell me stories that I haven't heard. When a pickup truck whizzes by, fast and rickety, my heart jumps a little, even though I know there's no reason in the world it would be him. It's stupid even to think it. The pickup fades into the distance, and then there's nothing for a long long time.

There's no real shoulder, just a seam where road meets grass, crumbling asphalt bleeding into green and dust. I kick my feet along it, step after step. I wonder if I'm going to have to hitchhike to get back. My mom used to hitchhike some, in Big Sur when we didn't have a car. She'd catch a ride up Highway 1, go off and meet Billy the kayaker while I stayed back in our tent. I always wondered why he didn't just come pick her up; he had a truck. But she liked catching rides, she said, and she always came back bearing food and stories. She never hitched with me there, though, and she always told me: Never ever hitchhike. It's dangerous and just for grown-ups. You never know who's driving.

The dog by the tan house barks loud and I jump. It's probably been forty-five minutes already, but I decide to walk a little longer before I stick my thumb out.

It's two miles at least before the woods let up. On my right I spot a smooth, wide opening, grass trimmed and thick and green, white-and-purple-spotted lilies growing on the sides of it like someone planted them. My sneakers squish in the moist ground as I turn in. A big old oak with a NO TRESSPASSING sign marks the start of the path, more lilies sprouting from the tangle of its roots. Nervous, I wonder if a rich person lives here, someone with a burglar alarm, but then I see another oak tree with another sign. In rose-colored paint is a big "om" symbol inside a purple circle, flanked on either side by swans. Underneath it says THE GURU'S DWELLING.

Another ten steps in you can see the big white mansion. It reminds me of my fourth-grade field trip to the state capitol. The house is sprawling and square, and even though it's fall, flowers spring up everywhere in perfect clumps. Allium, asters, anemone: almost the entire "A" section from my alphabetized field guide to flowers. I used to page through those pictures for hours, wondering how all those different shapes got made, so many, all of them so beautiful. Here, they sprawl out like a map of all the different kinds of perfect in the world.

I hug the side of the mansion, follow it around to the back. Behind, I find a smaller concrete building, whitewashed to match the main house. Another garden stretches out, wrapped in chicken wire, fat squash resting on dirt, the last of the tomatoes slowly reddening on the vine. A thin strand of barbed wire tracks the top of the fence, keeping out the deer; plastic tubs for trash line up by a small back door, each one with a chain and a lock. Past that—a big uncovered window.

I keep myself small, sneak close enough to peer in. Inside, the kitchen is all stainless steel, garlands of flowers crisscrossing the ceiling, just out of reach of clouds of rising steam. It's a hive in there, *sevites* buzzing around, carting tubs of dirty dishes, sweet potatoes, squash; chopping stems off purple blossoms; mincing herbs. They cross paths and then clear, and I can see the stove. Stirring a big steel pot and sweating, hair tied in a blue bandanna, is my mom. Her cheeks flush pink from steam and she looks like a picture of a peasant girl in Italy a zillion years ago, or some angelic hippie on a sixties Arizona commune. She grins at someone I can't see and her teeth flash. Then she turns back to the pot, singing to herself. I have an impulse to say, *Mom! Hi!* My ·105. knuckles clench up to knock on the window before I even think. But then I remember that NO TRESSPASSING sign technically refers to me, and I put my hands back in my pockets.

Past the whitewashed kitchen building is the back of the mansion. No gardens, just a row of fall crocuses along the wall, beneath leaded glass windows. Curtains hang inside, white silk and gold embroidery like a sari, almost see-through but not quite. A bird twitters on my right and I startle. I stop walking a minute, hold still. Nothing but quiet around me.

When I turn the corner I catch a flash of movement in the middle of the white. A curtain's pulled. The window's high up; I have to stand on tiptoe.

The room is the color of rose quartz. Everything,

walls and carpet and pillows, silk-covered altars and the big soft velvet chair. The beard guy is sitting in it, dressed all in red. He's watching TV.

I can't believe it. One television in this whole huge ashram and it belongs to the beard guy? He's supposed to be the purest one here, and he's got *cable*. I turn to see what he's watching. *Mr. Belvedere.* George and Mr. Belvedere are having an argument. I can't hear what it's about. Then the TV shuts off; the door to the room cracks open, and all of a sudden the beard guy's face looks mad.

I crane my neck to see who he's glaring at. It's Jayita, dressed in a beige shawl to match her skin and hair. The beard guy says something to her, some kind of command it looks like, and she nods. She looks sad. She lifts her head to say something back, pleading, it looks like, and he just shakes his head. *No*, I see his mouth say, sharp.

The window's old heavy glass and I can't hear through it, even with my ear up close. But there's a tiny crack along the frame. If I can pry it open, I can lift the window. I find a stick and jam it between. It makes a creak. I duck down fast, heart pounding in my ears, blood rushing to my face. *Shit*. I imagine them stop talking and turn toward me, count the time it'd take for the Guru to get up and walk to the window to look. I wait even a little longer than that.

Slowly I stand up, back stiff from hunching, lift up

to look again. They're still arguing. They didn't notice. I stick my finger in the gap and push. This time the window doesn't creak, it just cracks open.

Indian accents are usually lilty, smooth, and up-and-down like music, but his is clipped and hard. "You will understand it as a test," the Guru says. "In time. Right now, your perception is not sufficiently refined to see that this relationship is harmful, so you must trust the Guru's guidance."

She's trying to make her voice sound calm, but you can hear the quavering underneath. "But aren't we sup- posed to follow our hearts? I can't just end a relationship with someone I love—"

"Ah," he says like she's a child, "but there are realities more powerful than the minor attachments you call *love*. Sometimes we must give up our desires in order to know a larger truth." And then he pauses, and he looks down at her boobs. She doesn't notice.

"But it just feels wrong—"

He interrupts her. "That's enough. There is no arguing. Serious spiritual work requires sacrifice, and this place is not for anybody but the serious. So let me make it very clear to you: If you do not give up your attachment, you will have to leave."

"*Leave?*" She sounds shocked, and even mad. Then she catches herself. "I'm sorry. I just don't understand."

"It's not important that you understand," he says.

"It's important that you follow the practices laid out for you. You've made your own choice to commit to the path of surrender. If you diverge from that path now, you will find that it becomes strewn with obstacles beyond that which you had previously imagined." It's weird; it sounds like a warning.

Fear flicks across her face. Her eyes fill with questions, and it reminds me of that first night at Special Program, when I couldn't tell the difference between the truth and the illusions of my mind, and all of a sudden everything I was sure of crumbled and I didn't know how I was supposed to know anything at all.

"So—this is my karma?" she asks tentatively, like she's setting one foot on an icy lake to make sure it won't break beneath her.

He stares down at her and gives a tiny nod.

"The divine consciousness is testing me?"

He nods again.

"Okay," she finally says quietly. "Okay. It's a lesson. It always hurts to let go of your attachments." She sounds like she's trying to convince herself.

"So you will end this—*thing* with Chakradev?" the beard guy asks her, his voice like a stick, poking.

Her eyes fill up. "I will."

His face softens and he leans toward her. "Good," he says. "This is good." He reaches out to touch her face, brushes his fingers down the side of her cheek. Gravity pulls his hand down past her chin and it grazes her chest. It stays there too long. She flinches. And he says, "Go."

I remember that night at First Aid, how Jayita lit up all sparkly when Chakradev walked into the room; how she got all sassy with Ninyassa and danced to the radio even though we weren't supposed to. Now she looks like a different person. She slinks out the door, her body like a bent piece of grass, stepped on and limp.

When the door clicks shut, the beard guy sits up straighter in his chair. I'm mad at him, and also I'm confused. Jayita and Dev were nicer to each other than anyone else I've seen here. They made each other happy. Why would he want to stop that? And why would he get to decide in the first place? That seems more like a boss or a dad than a teacher. And that touch at the end—that was creepy.

Then there's music from inside. Bells, and voices singing Sanskrit words. Four women in saris walk in, waving incense in circles. One of them is my mom. Another one is Vrishti. Behind the incense circlers, another two women, almost as beautiful but not quite, come in with platters of food heaped up and surrounded by flower blossoms. It looks gourmet.

The women bow down in front of him. All of a sudden the beard guy's face is reassuring and warm, like a good dad playing with a toddler. The opposite of how it was with Jayita. My mom touches her head to his feet.

NINE

· · ·

Surrender to the guru is the birth of enlightenment;
the truth and the teacher are one and the same.

·110. I stayed there watching till the sun sank down and the
sky turned white with just a bottom rim of gold. More
cooking, more cleaning, more beard guy sitting in his
chair. I wondered what he thought about when he was
alone. Did he watch the red bars of the digital clock and
think, "Ah! Time for pretty incense ladies to come in!"
Or "Almost time for *Love Boat!*" Or did he worry
whether he was right to make Jayita leave her boyfriend?
What was it like to have a thousand people plan their
lives and feelings based on just the way he looked at
them? If that were me, I think I'd spend every single second freaking out about every single flicker of my eyes.

That night my mom didn't come back until super late,
and I was glad. It took an hour just to get the mud out of
my sneakers. And I didn't want to talk to anyone, especially
her. I had a secret that I didn't ask for. Not like Colin, not

even like the letters to my dad. This wasn't a secret that I chose. It got forced on me, and knowing it felt dirty.

There wasn't any reason for Jayita to break up with Chakradev. The Guru was making her do it just because he felt like it, and she was doing it because he said. Even though she didn't want to. Like she was a little kid, except she's not. It scared me to see it. And it scared me even more to see him touch her after.

And I wondered: did the beard guy get to say what everyone here was supposed to do about every person in their lives? What if he told my mom it was better for her karma to get rid of me, leave me alone forever? Would she be strong and tell him no, or would she crumple like a stepped-on blade of grass?

I practically hold my breath all the way to the lot. I make myself imagine it empty so I won't be disappointed; I squeeze shut that little space of maybe from the start. The hope pushes at me, but I steel myself against it. When Colin's face pops into my head I shove it away, picture a plain gray stretch of gravel, no one there.

When I come around the bend the yes rushes in so fast I almost make a sound. His Converse sneakers are sticking out from underneath the bus. And then his jeans. And then the bottom of his shirt. He hears me coming, swivels out from under.

"Hey!" he says, and grins. And I start crying.

All of yesterday swells up inside me like a water balloon, and his face is the pin that pricks me. I'm so relieved to see him it just gushes out. I can't believe what an asshole I am and I try to hide it—laugh over the tears just to cover them with *something*, then choke it all back into my throat as fast as I can. It doesn't work very well. I think I might actually look crazy.

"Hey," he says again, his voice softer, worried. He sits up straight. "Hey, what's wrong?"

Snot is streaming from my nose; my cheeks are hot and damp. I shake my head, my face tucked down. I can't look at him like this. My chest hitches and I breathe in hard and slow, try to get a grip.

It seems like forever till the tears slow down, but I know it's not even a minute. I wipe my face on my T-shirt and look up. His eyes are soft and worried like his voice.

"Sorry," I say.

"Don't be sorry."

"Okay. Sorry." It's a reflex.

I almost do it again but he stops me, smiling. "Are you okay?"

He didn't say, *Is everything okay. Are* things *okay.* He said, *Are* you *okay.* Somehow that difference matters. I open my mouth to say, *Yeah*—another reflex—but it won't come out. I shake my head again.

He pats the gravel beside him. I crouch down, and he wipes off his hands with a rag. I don't know how to start, and he doesn't ask me any questions. Just sits there, leaned up against the side of the bus, next to me.

Finally I ask him: "Have you ever had a secret that you didn't want?"

He says, "Sure." He doesn't tell me what it is.

The quiet yawns between us. He stands at the edge of it on purpose, waiting, and finally I dive in. I tell him about pillars and marble, steel pots and NO TRESSPASSING, white silk and gold. I tell him how I watched my mom through thick heavy windows, didn't knock. And then ·113· about Jayita and the beard guy.

His eyebrows knit; he curls his lip. "That's fucked up," he says, and it makes me so relieved to hear it. "Nobody has the right to tell someone else who they can be with."

Be with. "Yeah," I say, shaky. "Yeah," I say again, surer.

We work for a while, quiet, tools clinking on metal, grease smearing on hands. When the sun's high in the sky he stops, flips the top off a gallon jug of water, drinks. He squints at me. "What were you doing walking all that way, anyway? That entrance must be four or five miles up the road at least. That's way more than an hour even if you go pretty fast."

So much stuff happened since yesterday morning that I almost forgot about that part, but now it comes right back. I went because he wasn't here. I went because he has a whole life I don't know about, and all I've got is this lot. I waited and I freaked out and all I could do was walk, away and fast, get to someplace different, far from here. How am I supposed to say that stuff?

"Um, I was bored, I guess."

"Yeah?"

"Yeah." I stick to my story. "Just bored."

He leans back. "Bored, huh?" He thinks something, but I can't tell what. All of a sudden I feel like he's looking at me through a lens. Like a magnifying glass. I feel like a bug on the hot ground.

"Well, you weren't here, so—"

"Ahh." He cuts me off. "Ah. I see." His eyes spark; the corner of his mouth twitches up. I'm not sure if I'm supposed to smile back. I'm not sure I could, though, regardless. I hardly explained anything, but somehow I said too much.

Colin sits there twinkling at me for a second, stretching things out so I'll have to say something. My cheeks are hot. I know they're red. I feel like a naked baby bird. He isn't being mean, just teasing me. It should be no big deal. At school people made fun of my almond-butter sandwiches and the dolphin stickers on mom's car, and it always bounced right off my skin; I never cared. Now I do.

My eyes well up again. Ridiculous. Just a little, but come on. I try to fake like I'm gazing thoughtfully into the distance, but he sees.

"Wait," he says. "Hang on. Are you crying?"

I have to look at him to answer. I shake my head no, but a tear spills out of one eye, streaks down my cheek.

"You are. God, I'm sorry—"

"It's okay—" I start to say.

"I wasn't laughing at you. You know that, right?"

I nod, small.

"I really wasn't. Okay? I just thought it was—Crap. Sorry."

Another tear drips on my nose.

"Oh, Christ," he says. "Come here," and he leans over and puts his arms around my shoulders. We're sitting down, so it's a weird halfway kind of hug. Still, this shudder of electricity goes into my shoulders and down my spine. His T-shirt is soft under my palms, and past that is his skin, and muscle underneath. I hang on.

I hung on a long time, till it was almost weird. The funny thing is, he did too.

I think. Maybe he was just waiting for me to end it, the way you do when you don't know how long the hug's supposed to last and you don't want to hurt the person's feelings. But usually you can feel the question in the other person's fingers: they loosen their grip, hold on halfway till you let go. But he didn't pull away.

Finally I had to. I was starting to blush hard and even sweat. I moved back, and he tilted his head, thinking something. I couldn't tell what. After a second he said, "C'mon," picked up the socket, and got back to work.

Now six hours later, hair washed, dinner eaten, and mail fruitlessly checked and checked again, I sit in Evening Program. I can't look at my mom; I feel like she'll know that I know things I'm not supposed to, things that *she* doesn't even know. And I don't want to tell her. Just because it's in my head doesn't give her the right to know it. I want to keep it for myself.

Jayita's up in front now too, closer even than my mom and Vrishti. She has a red dot on her forehead. Chakradev is nowhere to be seen. It's weird to me that she's still here. I mean, the beard guy said that if she didn't want to dump Dev, she could leave. Well, he told her she would *have* to leave, but still. If that was me and I had someone that I loved, I wouldn't let anybody split us up. I guess she loves the Guru more than Chakradev. Except it didn't really seem like love.

I watch Jayita sway, eyes closed, off inside her head

somewhere. I can't tell if she's blissed out or she's really sad. She must miss Dev, I know. And I wonder if she misses herself, too. I stare at her hard, hoping she'll feel my eyes and open hers and meet them. I want to see inside her. I want to know if she's still there.

A swami strides up to the podium and I stop watching her. "Welcome!" he says. "We have a very, very special gift for you tonight," he says. "The Guru will grant *darshan*." *Darshan*: that thing that made my mom feel like an electric ocean. Sharing presence with the Guru. This means I'm going to have to look him in the face.

After the murmurs of excitement, the room fills ·117. with the low thunder of mass rustling. "Please line up in a centered and orderly manner," the swami says into the mic. I try to keep my eyes on Jayita, to see what happens to her when she gets up close to him again, but she just disappears into a mass of paisley skirts and patterned shawls and drawstring pants.

It's ten minutes till we get to the head of the line. Two swamis stand between us and the beard guy like bodyguards, nodding when the next person has permission to go.

"Go ahead," a lady swami finally says, and nods at me.

I don't want to bow. I'd have my doubts even if it weren't for yesterday, but when you add that to it too, my knees are locked, like my legs are made of long, unjointed bones and if I try to bend, they'll break. Everyone is staring at me. Some of them are glaring. I cannot bow down to this guy. Finally my mom puts her hand between my shoulder blades and shoves, hard enough that if I don't go in the direction she's pushing me I'll fall. *Fuck you*, I think at her hand, and fold over.

When I look back up, the beard guy's beaming down at me. Up close you can see all his pores. He stares like he can see all the way through my clothes to my skin, and through my skin to my bones. I want to cover up my insides, but there's no blanket that could do that. His eyes are lasers. I feel hot.

"You have a new friend," he says. I don't know what he's talking about, except I kind of do. How would he know that, though?

We're there for a long minute; I can't move. Finally he lifts his gaze off me and it's like cool air floods in, like a door opened in an overheated room. He turns to the lady swami, says something underneath his breath that I can't hear. She nods and walks behind his chair, bends down. When she comes back she's holding out a red-and-pink stuffed teddy bear, the kind you get for five dollars at the drugstore for Valentine's Day. On its stomach is stitched, *Someone Loves You!*

I feel gross taking it, but I wonder if it's some kind of sign.

. . . . .

On the way out of Evening Program, Mom and Vrishti want to see my teddy bear. It's like they're cheerleaders at school and the bear is from some football jock. I hate cheerleaders.

Mom and Vrishti want to have girl talk, except about the Guru. Who did he look at and for how long, who got special gifts and *You are so lucky he gave you that.* It's just a drugstore stuffed animal from an out-of-date holiday, made in China and thin at the seams, but their eyes light up like it's a diamond.

"It holds the Guru's energy," Vrishti says. "Now you can keep his spirit with you at all times!" I don't want to keep the Guru's spirit with me at all times. I don't think I want it with me ever. But he knew I had a new friend; the bear says someone loves me. If there's even any chance at all that it's true, I have to hold on to it.

"It means you're special, you know," says Vrishti. "He recognizes something in you." She and my mom both look at me, jealous. I clutch the bear tighter to my chest.

TEN

. . .

As you progress, all desires transform;
what was bitter becomes sweet; what was sweet, bitter.

·120. Monday I go over to the *seva* office like it's school, and turn my homework in. I drop the papers on the fake wood desk between the spider plants and head for the front desk. Still no mail. The lady there is starting to look at me funny. I head for the lot.

I wonder the whole way there if Colin will be weird, but as soon as I see his face I can tell that he's not. "Hey." He grins. "Fancy meeting you here." I smile back. I wonder if he can tell how many times I've thought about our hug since Friday.

"So today's a big work day, Tess. We're almost done. If we work hard I bet we can pull the engine before it gets dark."

We keep going through lunch, take apart the starter and remove the heating cables, disconnect the fuel lines. When the sun starts to sink, Colin gets out the jack and a big wooden board; we slide them underneath the bus. My thighs burn with the weight. It feels satisfying, all the way down to my bones. I can smell both our sweat. I'm working too hard to be embarrassed, though. Finally we get the jack cranked up; Colin undoes a bunch of bolts with his socket and then we use all our strength to wiggle the engine around till it slides out, metal scraping metal, heavy as a boulder.

There's a big gaping hole in the back of the bus where the engine was. I beam at the steel hulk sitting on the gravel, smudged black grease on the pale wood board. I'm smeared too: my cheeks, my hands, my jeans; my hair's a mess. Colin has motor oil on his eyelid. I've never accomplished something like this before. It's like getting a baby out, or an egg, or putting up a wall. Rumpled and dirty, we breathe heavily and grin at each other, proud.

"Good job," Colin says, and wipes his brow. Then he hugs me again.

He's gonna be gone a couple days; he has to take the engine into town to the machine shop so they can do the pistons and the rods and cylinders. The way he tells me is careful and kind. He explains exactly what he has to do, just how long he thinks it'll take. "Don't worry if it's a little longer, though, okay? The shop can be a little flaky. It might be an extra day or two, but I'll be back." He looks me straight in the eye when he says that last part. "I'll be back." Nobody's ever done that before.

I want to look away, but I don't. I stay right there. "Okay."

I'm reading my mom's copy of *Whole Earth Review* when our doorknob turns and the door clicks open; I'm still reading when she comes in and dumps three big plastic shopping bags onto the bed. I've got my Walkman on, *Kiss Me, Kiss Me, Kiss Me* by the Cure. "Just Like Heaven."

"Tessa?" my mom says, twice. I pretend not to hear her. *Show me show me show me how you do that trick.*

"Hel-*lo?*" she says again, loud and close. I wish she'd shut up; I love this song—*The one that makes me scream, she said.* I finish reading the paragraph, then act like I just noticed that she's there.

"Don't roll your eyes at me," she says as I take my headphones off. "And don't give me that look."

I don't think I rolled my eyes or gave her any kind of look, but I don't feel like arguing. "Whatever."

She raises her eyebrows like she's going to hand me down another *don't*, but I raise my eyebrows back and she decides against it. "Fine," she says. "Anyway, I didn't come back here to argue. I came to show you something!"

Hooray. I can't wait.

She goes over to the bed and shakes her plastic bags empty, one by one. Mounds of clothes spill onto the coverlet. All white. "What, did you do laundry or something?" I ask. It's not that I *want* to be snarky; it's that I don't seem to really have a choice.

"No, I didn't *do laundry*," she says like I'm stupid. "It's a *tapasya*."

"Oh, right, a *tapasya*." Pause. She doesn't answer, though. So I say it like *she's* stupid: "What's a *tapasya*, Mom?"

"It's an austerity. A step on the spiritual path? I'm going to be wearing all white now. Giving up my attachment to adornment and dress."

I think it's pretty weird that giving up your attachment to adornment and dress involves getting a whole new wardrobe. "Ah."

"You're a teenager, so dress and adornment are probably more important to you right now. But I'm in a different place."

It's funny she should say that: I'm the one with three pairs of identical jeans and the same red Nikes I've had through four shoe sizes. I'm the one with T-shirts and mousy straight hair to my shoulders. The only makeup I've ever worn is hers; the only earrings, thieved from her jewelry box. She's the beauty: lip gloss, purses, dripping gypsy jewels.

"Congratulations."

We stand there and look at each other. These days there's so many pauses between my mom and me, all filled with annoyed facial expressions.

She huffs and stuffs the white clothes back into their bags. "Yes, well, I was thinking I would offer some of my clothes to you, Tessa, as a gift. But if you're not interested, that's okay. I'm sure someone else can use them."

"Wait, no," I say. Secretly I've been starting to get sick of red sneakers and identical jeans. "What are you getting rid of?"

"Oh, so you *are* interested?"

Here is how much I want to show it: just enough that she'll hand over the clothes, and not enough to give her any satisfaction whatsoever. "Sure."

"Okay, then." She heads over to the dresser, starts pulling out stacks, shirts and skirts and leg warmers mixed together, folded up. They're organized by color: orange swimming into red pouring into magenta, then purple, then blue. One by one she shakes them out and lays them down. "Whichever ones you want," she says. "They're yours."

I pile up her T-shirts first: LIVE SIMPLY THAT OTHERS MAY SIMPLY LIVE, ESPRIT, a drawing of a watermelon slice. Then her baggy purple silk Tibetan tunic, beige eyelet skirt with a *Little House on the Prairie* ruffle at the hem.

"Tess, try on the leotards," she says. "I bet they'd look great with jeans."

I'm skeptical but I pick one up, royal blue with aqua stripes, long-sleeved. In the bathroom I put it on and slide my jeans back up. It cuts into my butt but when I look in the mirror I can't believe what I see. I look amazing: like a woman, sort of. I pull the sleeves up, snap the scooped neck against my collarbone. The elastic gather in the front makes my boobs kind of huge. It's weird how a different shape of shirt can make you look like an entirely different person.

"Let's see!" she hollers. I'm embarrassed leaving the fluorescent cocoon of the bathroom, but she giggles like a girl and says, "Woo-hoo!"

"Yeah?" I ask.

"Tessa, what a babe! You look great."

"I do?"

"You totally do."

"Thanks." I stand there with my hands in my pockets. I've never looked great before.

"We gotta find more stuff that fits you like that. C'mon over here." She starts rooting through piles, pulling out tops and holding them up, squinting. When she's been through them all, she hands over a heap and says, "Here. Go try these on."

The lame part about leotards is you have to take off your pants to take your shirt off. Between that and the annoying butt thing, the jury's still out on whether leotards are worth it. Luckily, though, she's handed me mostly regular shirts, stretchy and tight but comfortable. I pull on a long-sleeved T-shirt with batik tulips. She hollers.

"Lemme see!"

I come out and show her. "Awesome!" A little like she's trying to be cool, but I let it pass. "Next!"

She calls me out of the bathroom between every one, and each time says how fabulous I look. By the fifth outfit I'm spinning around, faking that I'm Christie Brinkley on the catwalk, and we're cracking up. At the end we both flop down on the bed, heaps of clothes soft like a backyard leaf pile. She rolls over on her side toward me, loose and smiling, close enough for me to feel her breath. "Maybe tomorrow I can skip chanting and we can go to the Amrit for breakfast, huh? I heard they're making yogurt coffee cake."

"Sure." I smile back. "Sounds good."

"It's a deal. I'll wake you up. Hey, Tess?"

"Yeah?"

"Love you, you know."

For the first time in forever I don't feel embarrassed when she says it.

"Love you too."

We sleep in her bed that night, curled up together in the soft warm dark. By the time the light seeps in at sunrise, her side is empty. I rub my eyes and see the note on the table: *Off to chanting! Don't forget to clean up the clothes, Tess. All of them, please.* A smiley face and a little "om" symbol at the bottom, and *P.S. We'll get coffee cake next week.*

I listen to Green Tea Experience, twice through, the bass ·127. turned up. I can only play it when my mom's gone, but she's gone enough lately that I've learned every note by heart. I study his photo for angles that match mine. I've memorized the liner notes, especially the special thanks. It doesn't have my name or my mom's, but at the end it says "Thanks to my two angels," and I always imagine that it's us.

After a while, Green Tea Experience starts sounding old and sad, reminding me of times when I was younger than I am. I don't want to be younger anymore. I want to be something different, but I don't quite know what that is.

I switch off my dad, put in Modern English, turn it loud. I look in the mirror and see myself in stolen lipstick with my Walkman on, new batik tulip T-shirt tight across my boobs, *I Melt with You* playing, and I imagine that I am the video. That the song has its own world, a place where you could actually go, and I'm in it. The batik shirt makes it easier for me to imagine myself there.

The future's—open—wide. A knock startles me out of my video, back into the room. When I open the door there's this short, squat woman with a baggy dress and a bucket full of cleaning stuff. "Hey," I say.

"Hi there. Main office sent me. Is this Sarah Walker's room?"

"Yeah, that's my mom."

"Well, she's on the Guru's private staff? They sent me up to clean her room."

"Clean it?" I'm confused.

"It's like a gift. A special privilege. The Guru must be happy with her."

"Oh. Okay. Cool." She shoulders past me into our room, ready to get to work, I guess. I scrounge a five from the dresser, put my headphones back on, and leave her there to pick up my mom's clothes.

At the Amrit, they're almost out of coffee cake. I get the last piece—the corner one, crusty—and an apricot juice, and settle at the window to watch the rain streak down.

I take out my notebook, open it to a blank page.

Dear dad, I listened to your tape today. And then I don't know what else to write. Which is weird. I've always known what to write to him. I write secrets, things that I can't tell my mom. I ask him questions that I always want to know: Where is he and what's the road like, what did he think when I was born. What really happened with my mom when I was four. I tell him he can tell me, that he doesn't have to worry I'll take mom's side, that I know he has a story too. I tell him it's okay, and then I wait for him to answer. And the waiting fills the quiet till my mom gets back from wherever she is, and I know that whenever I get too lonely I will always have the hope of him.

But that hope is starting to wear down, thinner than it used to be, like a patch of carpet that you've walked over and over for years. And I can't explain to my dad about being the girl in the video, and how my boobs look in the tulips shirt, and how that weirdly makes me feel like a new person and strong. And I can't tell him that when it's quiet I'm starting to think about Colin instead of him.

I close my notebook without writing any more.

I'm about to head back to my room and try on leotards when those kids show up. The boys are immersed in a plastic fork battle, but Avinashi spots me right away and makes a beeline for my table. She's chewing on her braid.

"Hey," she says when she's close enough.

"Hey," I say back.

She sucks spit through her hair. She's got that thing where it seems like she has something specific to say but then she doesn't, so you just wait there and she waits there too, and it's weird.

"You got the last piece," she says, pointing.

"Yeah." What do you say to such a statement of the obvious? *Yes, you have made a correct observation, pale creepy braid-eater.*

"We're on break from Crafts."

"That's cool."

"At Crafts we're making bread dough sculptures of the deities. Then we're painting them with tempera. I'm working on Ganesh."

"Great." Rain slides down the glass, making the green greener, the ground wetter. I wish I was out there in it.

"Sanjit's almost finished Kali Ma, soon as he paints the skulls. Meer was doing Hanuman, but he broke it, so he has to start over. The Guru wants us to make the full pantheon of deities. So we can't skip Hanuman."

"Cool." Is there a reason she's telling me all this?

"Well, are you going to come to Crafts? Because it doesn't look like you have another *seva* today."

"Um, I don't think I'll come to Crafts," I say. "But thanks."

"Really? We're about to start on the aspects of Vishnu and we could use some help. Guruji says little hands are best kept busy, you know." She raises her eyebrows like a baby Ninyassa, except the *Addams Family* version.

"Well, I've got some other stuff I have to do."

She squints. I can tell she doesn't believe me.

I pop open my apricot juice and take a swig. I don't talk. Finally she gets impatient; she drops her Ninyassa eyebrows and her face goes weak and mushy. "What is it? What do you have to do?" It comes out sudden and whiny.

I can't think of anything good. "Just stuff."

"Well, don't you want to come hang out with us?" The whine gets louder, like she wants me to be her friend or something. It's the opposite of school, where I'm always getting shut out for eating kale and sprouted chickpeas, wearing hand-me-downs, not having a TV. Not now.

Now I'm the one who gets to say no.

Even if that means I wind up by myself, it's worth it.

ELEVEN

...

Risk throws open the doors of fear and habit
so that the Divine may enter.

·132. When you're alone a long time, awake blurs into sleep the same way light blurs into dark: slow, without you noticing. I don't hear my mom come in at night, and I don't hear her leave again the next morning. In the too-quiet dawn I brush my teeth and put the batik tulips back on. And lipstick.

Colin said *a couple days*, but he also said *maybe*. I grab my Walkman, get a chai from the dining hall, head out to the parking lot to warm my fingers and wait. It's my fifth time in two days listening to *If You Leave*.

Tires thunder on the gravel and I look up. A truck pulls up, rust eating blue paint on its doors, Colin in the cab with the driver. Colin hops out, and then the driver, wrinkled and leathery, comes around and helps him heave out the engine. It's wrapped in grimy green towels.

"You sure you can get this back in single-handed?" asks the driver.

"Oh, I'm not single-handed," Colin answers. "I've got Tessa." He shoots me a grin. The driver eyes us skeptically, looking at my lipstick. I push up my sleeves to show him I don't mind getting dirty.

They set the engine on a plank behind the bus. The driver hitches his pants. "Alrighty," he says in the kind of plainspoken guy way I recognize from Ohio, and holds out his hand.

"Thanks, man." Colin shakes. They speak the same language—masculine, simple, mysterious. All of a sud- ·133. den I stand back and see: *I have a friend who is a man.*

Then the driver pulls away and Colin is a kid again, or something like it. "C'mon," he says. "Let's get this baby in."

It takes half the day, lifting and lining up. Finally it's in; my batik's smudged with black like the bumper and his jeans. He offers me a swig of his Sunkist orange soda. Then he says, "Hop in. Let's test her out."

I don't know if he means test-*start* it or test-*drive* it. And I don't know which one I want him to mean. My heart pounds in my throat. It would be like jumping off a cliff to go with him. I don't know my way around out here, how to get back, how to drive. And I'd be in massive shit if we got caught. But if he wants to take me for a ride? I can't not go.

"C'mon," he says, cocking his head. *Maybe he just wants to turn the key.* I unstick my feet, unlock my knees, loop around to the passenger side and step up into the seat.

He smiles at me; the engine turns over, coughs, settles into a hum. "See what we did?"

The seat is scratchy. I nod, hoping he can't hear my heart pound through my chest. It's so loud I think he must be able to. He just sits there for a second, watching me, and I almost feel relieved: This is it, we're not going anywhere, I'm not going to have to make a choice.

And then he presses on the gas and we lurch forward.

We make it off the gravel onto pavement, past the lobby and Atma Lakshmi. No one sees. We turn off ashram property, hit the road and speed up, half-naked trees whizzing by, fields stretching out and out and out with no people to clutter them. Cool air floods in through the window. I'm glad I didn't stop us leaving. I feel like I can breathe.

Colin reaches for a backpack at his feet. He has to bend down for it. He keeps a hand on the wheel, but I'm terrified we're going to veer off the road. I sit up straight, keep a sharp eye out for oncoming cars. He unzips the bag, fumbles around, pulls out a tape. "Violent Femmes," he says. "You ever heard 'em?"

"No," I tell him.

"Pop it in."

He hands it to me, sits back up and puts both hands on the wheel. I exhale. The cover has a picture of a little girl in a lace dress looking through a window. You can't see her face.

I jump as bass jangles through the speakers, then a snare drum, then guitar. The singer's voice is tinny, nasal. *When I'm walking, I strut my stuff, and I'm so strung out.* The tune is bouncy but there's something dark, a little scary about the singer and the words. It's not like any songs I've ever heard on the radio or on my tapes: not about loving someone and then they go away and you want them back, please don't leave, how you will never forget. The next song has this talk-sing count-down thing about loneliness and lost causes and pills, and the chorus tells the world, *You can all just kiss off into the air.* Colin sings along. It's like he's saying it back to the whole world, everyone who ever gave him trouble, and I wish I knew the words well enough to sing too.

Fields give way to houses, houses to storefronts, that song to the next one; Colin asks me, "You want Dairy Queen?" It's cold out, almost time for DQ to close for winter, but I tell him yes. We take a turn and drive past crumbling brick buildings, 1950s drugstore signs, papered-over windows. Scraggly trees poke up through pavement, black scratch marks against the white sky. Shaindy's Girls-Boys Fashions and Sruly's Bakery look like they've been locked for years: everything's out-of-date, faded, full of dust. Trash blows by like tumbleweeds.

He gets a Butterfinger Blizzard; I order a vanilla cone with cherry dip. He pays.

Ice cream gives me goose bumps in the late fall air, so we get back in the bus. The silence suddenly feels huge, but Colin just looks out the window, relaxed, jiggles his knee to some tune inside his head like he doesn't even notice.

Finally he sucks his straw noisily and turns the key, pulls out of the lot. The Violent Femmes guy comes back on, loud and sudden, singing, *Why can't I get, just one kiss.* Then *Why can't I get, just one screw*, and then *Why can't I get just one*—Colin pops out the tape. His ears are red. I concentrate really hard on my cherry dip. Out of the corner of my eye I see him lean down, pick another from his bag. He rewinds bit by bit, furrowing his brow. While the tape's whirring backward, he asks, "You know Neil Young?"

Thank god he finally talked. I shake my head no. This look comes over his face like he can't believe it.

"You never heard of *Neil Young?*"

I shake my head again.

"Wow," he says. "Crazy." Then he thinks for a second. "There's a lotta stuff you need to get introduced to."

I don't know what to say to that. "Okay."

"Okay. So this album is called 'Harvest.' Neil Young recorded it in 1971, right after Crosby, Stills, Nash, and Young split up. You do know them, right?"

I know Crosby, Stills, and Nash from my mom. I never heard the "Young" part, but I fake it. "Yeah, I know them."

"Cool. Okay. So CSNY is breaking up, and Neil recruits this country band called the Stray Gators and they hole up and record this album. It was the only one he ever did with them, but it's a classic."

"Cool."

He finds the beginning of the song: some acoustic chords, then a harmonica. I start to ask about more Neil Young history, but he says, "Shh. Listen."

Another nasal voice comes in, this one warmer or more soft or something. It doesn't sound dark like the Violent Femmes guy, just a little ragged. *I wanna live, I wanna give, I've been a miner for a heart of gold.* Even though Colin and I aren't talking, I feel somehow connected to him, like the song's a string between us. We pass through the rest of town, back into fields and hills, farther and farther from the ashram. I see the sign for Levner's River Cottages and realize that I sort of know where we are, even though we're in a place I haven't really been before.

Out the smudgy window I watch the half-bare trees dangle their last leaves. The song builds to its end, *Keeps me searching and I'm growing old*, and I get this weird sad feeling, like missing something I haven't even felt yet. When the song ends, Colin turns the volume down. "Beautiful, huh?" he asks, and I say yeah.

We drive for a minute, quiet, that string still stretched between us even though the music's over. Then he asks, "So whaddya think, Tessa?"

What do I think? "What do you mean, what do I think?"

"That's what I mean. What do you think?"

"About what?"

"I don't know," he says. "About anything."

It's funny how when you're allowed to say anything at all you can't ever think of something; when a big space stretches out in front of you, it's hard to find your place in it. It's always easier when there are lines drawn, limits traced around the ground you're standing on. I can't find one thing to pick, but I want to tell him something more than *I don't know*.

"I think . . . the trees look sort of sad, like they're about to miss their leaves, and I think that's kind of how I feel about Neil Young, and I think I'm glad we got the engine built, and I think . . . um."

He looks at me, waiting for more.

"Um, I think the ashram is weird? And that that cherry dip was good? And I'm kind of wondering where we're going, but I kind of don't really care at the same time." That came out sounding maybe snarky. "I mean, not in a bad way."

"No, I know what you mean," he says.

"Why?" I ask him, stepping out on a limb. "What do you think?"

He smiles. "Hmm. Let's see, Tessa." It's just my name, but it feels like something real when he says it. "I ·139. think . . . I know exactly what you mean about Neil Young, and about the ashram too. I mean, who *are* those people, right?" He gives a little laugh. "I think it's good for you to get out of there sometimes, 'cause you're smarter than they are. Know what I mean?"

I don't want to seem conceited, but secretly, I do agree. I nod.

He nods back. "Yeah. Like everyone's living in this little pretend world they've constructed, ants in an ant farm, pouring themselves into some mold and copying each other and thinking that's the only way to live, when you can think of so many other ways to be but no one will let you do it. Right?"

I nod again.

"Yeah, I kind of know how that feels." He almost

looks sad when he says it. Then he washes over it with that grin. "Oh, and I also think there's a ton of bands you really need to learn about, immediately." He turns Neil Young back up. The song says, *Old man, look at my life; I'm a lot like you were.*

Past Mount Hope Road and Butrick Way, Colin turns off Route 51. The trees thicken as the road gets narrower, sunshine-yellow leaves making overlapping shadows on the ground. When I was little and my mom and I were on the road, I'd watch the woods go by out the window, in love with the half-dark stretching out and out, roots webbing the wreckage of fallen trees, every inch of forest holding some kind of story. I don't even know what I thought went on in there, just *something*, many things, all different from anything I knew. My mom would drive, wrapped up in her music, and I'd slip out the window, disappear into the woods, imagining myself someplace new.

Now it's different, though, because I could really go there. I could ask Colin to pull over if I saw a path to walk down, and I think he would. He makes a left and then another left, the road getting rougher, narrower; then it opens up. A field stretches out on both sides of us, green hills pouring down into a valley, at the base of it a huge old oak tree reaching out and up.

"Wanna see my favorite tree?" Colin asks. As soon as I nod yes he stops the car, climbs out, and takes off down the hill.

He's like a kid out here, tumbling down the hill, goofy and hollering, and the wind hits my open laughing mouth as I run to catch up. Suddenly I'm not scared, and I'm not worried that he'll run too far ahead; I'm not embarrassed or anxious or shy. I'm just running, eyes watering from the wind, and when I tumble onto flat ground at the bottom of the hill, breathing hard, he's there, grinning that grin by the trunk of the tree, and my feet keep moving forward and I stumble into him and lift my face and plant my mouth on his.

This kiss has nothing to do with Randy Wishnick. No ketchup, no fish flopping around in my mouth, no cafeteria background noise or Quiet Riot T-shirts. Randy Wishnick was a kid, like me, and then he turned into just another kid who didn't really like me.

This is a completely other kind of kiss.

At the end of it, Colin wraps his arms around my waist, strong like the tree we're standing under. I can feel his whole body press against my stomach and my shoulders and my chest. He looks at me. "Wow," he says. "Where'd you learn to do that?"

The last thing I want to do is bring Randy Wishnick

into it. So I just tell Colin, "I don't know," shrug and smile, stay there in his arms.

"Wow," he says again. He shakes his head like he's trying to clear it. "So. What was *that* all about?"

He keeps asking me these questions like I have all the answers. Funny, it's usually the other way around. I don't know what to tell him so I just kiss him again.

We stay till it starts to get dark. When I get cold, Colin gives me his flannel shirt; it's plaid and soft and the best
thing I have ever worn in my life. We sit leaned up against the tree, my head on his shoulder, his arm around mine. My heart stops beating so hard; the feeling of him slows down in me, leaves my throat and settles in my chest.

When I lift my head up I catch him watching me. I can't tell what's going on in his mind, but I feel like I can ask. I squint my eyes at him. "So, what do you think?"

He does a double take, then laughs to himself. Then he says, "Nothing."

But I can tell he's thinking something. "Nothing? Really?"

"Okay. Not *really* nothing." He takes a pause. "I mean—you sure that you're okay with that? That wasn't weird?"

"No," I tell him. "No. It wasn't weird at all."

· · · · ·

On the drive back, Colin's quiet, eyes on the road, hands on the wheel. That free feeling running down the hill is gone, and now the silence makes me nervous. When he asked if it was weird, my *no* came out so clear and strong, the crossed currents I always feel about everything washing out of me like water. But now that we're driving and it's dark and he isn't saying anything, I start to wonder if he asked me that because *he* thought it was weird. I start worrying that maybe it actually was. I mean, he is twenty.

He's not talking, I'm not talking, so finally I do like he did when Violent Femmes got embarrassing and dig in the backpack for a tape. I have a feeling Colin will always want to talk about music. I wonder if he ever heard of Green Tea Experience.

The first tape I find says "Pink Floyd The Wall." I heard some dirtball boys talk about the movie of that once. Apparently there's some intense scene where the guy freaks out on drugs and shaves his nipples off or something. I was always kind of curious. I put in side two and ask about the story of the band.

I was right: immediately he quits being quiet. "Oh man, 'The Wall.' This album is *historical*," he says. "It's a concept album. You know what a concept album is?"

I shake my head. I don't really care what a concept

album is. I just want him to talk to me.

"It's an album where the whole thing is a story, not just a bunch of songs? Anyway, it's about this guy named Pink, and his parents oppress him and everyone at school tries to stifle who he is and mold and twist him to fit into society, and no one understands him? So he builds this wall, like a literal wall, around himself, like to protect him."

"Wow."

"Yeah. But eventually he becomes this big rock star, and the wall drives him crazy, 'cause he's totally lonely and isolated from everyone else, know what I mean?"

·144.

"Yeah."

"And by the end of the album his conscience, like, puts him on trial, and the judge, which is really just him, tells him he has to tear down his wall and open himself back up to other people."

"Wow."

"It's kind of deep," he says.

"Yeah."

This song called *Hey You* comes on and he reaches over and holds my hand on the gearshift. It doesn't bother me when he gets quiet again.

Twelve

· · ·

Surrender all desires, for they are the only root
of misery and suffering.

When I show up at the lot in the morning, he's already there beneath a yellow school bus, socket set catching the early morning sun by his feet. I consider kicking his boot like before, but I decide that it's a bad idea. Sure, yesterday each time that I got nervous, he was perfect, holding my hand on the gearshift, saying just the exact right things. But between then and now there was a night. What if he spent it thinking, She's boring, she's fourteen, she's just a kid. What if he even thought that it was wrong? I don't want to act like I expect everything to be okay, just in case it isn't.

I say his name.

He comes out from under the bus wiping grease off his forehead, and I almost die at how gorgeous he is. Of course I always knew it, but before, it was distant, like a mountain or a statue, something far off and amazing.

Yesterday I saw it close: dirty hair, scar running through his eyebrow, pores dotting his cheek, all the perfect imperfections that make a person just exactly them. Not the beautiful that comes from far away; the beautiful that comes from real.

He sets down his wrench. "Hey," he says. "I wanted to talk to you."

"Okay," I sit down on the gravel. He looks at the ground. I can tell he's planned something out; he looks nervous.

"I, um—I want you to know I didn't take you out there intending for anything to happen. It's important to me that you know that."

"Okay."

"It's not like I had some plan to put the moves on you or something."

My cheeks get hot. "I know."

"And it's okay that it happened, but at the same time. . ." He trails off.

I can't believe he is going to trail off right in the middle of that very sentence. "At the same time *what?*"

"Well, at the same time, Tessa, I really value our friendship."

Crap.

"It's not that I don't want to hang out with you; it's actually the total opposite. I do want to hang out with you, I want to *keep* hanging out with you, and

I don't want anything to get in the way of that."

My eyes are starting to sting. I keep them on the gravel. I can't look at him.

"And, you know, I'm kind of a lot older than you."

What does he think I am, stupid? "I know."

"And it really wasn't my plan for that to happen yesterday."

"Yeah, you said that." He doesn't have to rub it in.

"And so I think it's a good idea if it doesn't ever happen again. Ever."

I'm trying to keep my eyes closed enough to hold the tears in and not so tight that I squeeze them out. ·147.

"Know what I mean, Tess?" He cranes his face closer to mine, trying to get me to look at him. He waits. I can't believe he is trying to get me to look at him. I can't believe he's making me talk.

"Yeah, I know what you mean." It comes out choky, catching on the phlegm in my throat. If I say one extra word, I will start to really cry.

"Okay. Because I really like you, you know. I really do."

And for some reason that one nice thing at the end of all the horrible things makes my chest crumple and I do cry, not a few tears like the day after he was gone, but hard, with noise and everything. I sound like a horse. It is officially awful, but I can't stop; everyone always leaves me, and my chest is hitching on its own.

He just watches. His eyes crinkle down at the

corners like he feels bad, which makes me cry harder. He fidgets and sits on his hands. He opens his mouth like he's going to talk, but nothing comes out. He looks away, and then back at me again. Then he says, "Fuck it," leans in fast and hugs me.

I wish I had a wall to put around me like the Pink Floyd guy so I didn't feel so naked, but Colin's shoulder is the closest thing there is. I get snot on his Led Zeppelin T-shirt. I can feel his neck next to my wet face, his arms tight around me. For a long time, I cry there and he doesn't move.

·148· And then he does. When my sobs slow down he pulls back partway, hands on my shoulders, eyes pointing into mine. It's hard to stay locked into his gaze, but impossible to look away. I can't even imagine how I look to him right now, the snot and the red and the blood-shot. But he doesn't flinch.

He tilts his head; this look crosses his face, part shaky, part sure; and then he leans back in.

His lips are on my eyelids, then my forehead, then my cheeks. Then my nose, which is kind of funny; then my chin. It's like he's making a skin of tiny kisses on my face, thin and delicate but strong enough to cover up the raw, sewing me back together so the tears dry and the hurt stops. I stay there, still, barely even breathing.

I almost jump when his lips touch my mouth.

I don't understand what he's doing—five minutes

ago it was *That can never happen again ever*—but I don't want to stop to ask. Who knows, this might be my last chance. The back-and-forth of yesterday, then today, now this, yanks me in opposite directions till I don't know what the rules are: there's nothing to expect, nothing's coming next; all I can do is be inside this, right this second, now.

Now keeps going for a long time. Finally Colin pulls away. I get scared he's going to take it back again, but he doesn't. Instead he looks at me and says, "Oh boy." He raises his eyebrows and shakes his head, then leans in for one more kiss. After it: "Boy, oh boy." And then he says, "I told this guy in town I'd check out his car at ten. It's got a rattle."

"Okay," I say, even though I don't want him to go. We get up, but he's still near me, close enough that I can feel the sliver of air between our stomachs like something solid. I imagine it's a rubber band, pulling taut between us, keeping us connected even as he starts to back away.

Then something bright and moving catches my eye over Colin's shoulder.

Devanand.

He's close enough that I can see his T-shirt says HARMONIC CONVERGENCE, AUGUST 15, 1987 in turquoise and magenta letters.

What I should do is pull back. What I should do is

pull back so Colin and I are far apart, reconstruct the safe space of air between us. Instead I make myself very very still, like a rabbit staring at a fox. Devanand keeps walking, just a hundred feet away, watching his feet. I hardly blink. If Colin notices me move, he'll turn around; then Devanand will notice back, and what happens next could tip things in the entire wrong direction. The last thing I want in the whole universe is Devanand coming in and scaring Colin off again.

I lose my balance; my sneaker scuffles on the gravel. Just a second, just an inch, but it's enough to make a tiny noise. Across the trees, Devanand quits staring at his socks-and-sandals toes and his eyes lock directly into mine. Shit shit shit. I freeze again. For a second there's a question. Then he pieces the picture together like a puzzle, and then his whole face focuses in on the space between my chest and Colin's. His brows knit and he tracks back to my face again, his eyes telling me: *I see you guys. I see.*

I know these ashram people say, "There's no such thing as duality," that "opposites like *good* and *evil* are just illusions of the ego," but I can tell you: *good* is thin veils of kisses, close-together chests with rubber bands between them, and *evil* is Devanand's eyebrows condemning my entire being in the parking lot. They are exact and total opposites. I don't care what they say about the essential sameness of the universe.

They duke it out inside my head all day. I'll be turning that last kiss over and over in my mind, and then Devanand pokes his face into my imagination. My afternoon becomes an epic battle between the warm ocean of the happiest I've ever felt and the terrifying knowledge that it could be destroyed at any moment by a gross-bearded hippie with jogging shorts and an anti-authoritarian authority complex.

When we're filing out from Evening Program, I spot Devanand's ratty auburn ponytail above the crowd. I'm sandwiched between Vrishti and my mom like vegetarian lunch meat; their skirts swish at my ankles as we inch toward the lobby. My chest thunks hard and I think, *Please please please don't let Devanand ever ever meet my mom.* If he meets her, he'll tell, and if that happens, she will break us up. I'm fourteen years old and Colin is twenty. I'm not stupid. I know what that means. But I also know that he is the only good thing that has ever happened to me, the only thing I have ever had that's mine. I can't let them take him away.

In the lobby, I hold the Styrofoam cup to my mouth and blow to cool the chai. It burns my upper lip, but I don't mind. Finally Devanand is out of sight and I can think about trees and hands on the gearshift and what worn T-shirts feel like under fingers.

Around me people talk, bangles jangling on gesturing wrists, voices loud. They all speak the same weirdly formal language that's not quite theirs; it makes them the same on the surface, like cliques of kids at school. They're discussing some new rule the Guru made, something about separating men and women for meditation. There seems to be some controversy. Gajendra says that *he*, for one, is extremely concerned men won't have access to sacred feminine energies, and what are the women supposed to do to reconnect with the warrior archetype?

My mom steps forward from the guys clustered around her; puts down her chai and jumps down his throat in front of everyone. "I really think it's inappropriate to question him, Gajendra." She sounds like she's talking to me, not an adult her own age. It's weird to me how adamant she is. "Don't you think that it's maybe a bit presumptuous? I mean, think about the layers of desire clouding and obscuring our perceptions. Think about all the things that we don't know or understand. Aren't you grateful he can see so clearly?"

Gajendra looks at my mom like she is wildly stupid. "Well, *Sarah*, of course I'm grateful for his clear perception. But that doesn't mean you give up your free will and right to question. That's just naïve."

Everyone is listening.

"For example, have you actually considered how your own practice might benefit from this decree?"

"Well, the Guru says—"

"Yes, we all know what the Guru says. But what do *you* feel, Sarah?"

"Well—" my mom stammers. For a second she teeters, too far out on a limb and wobbly, like when one of her old boyfriends stopped pretending to listen but she hadn't stopped wanting to talk. I know that face— the scared-deer look in her big brown eyes, the flutter in her lips. I kind of want to link my arm through my mom's, tell Gajendra he's being an asshole, but at the same time I kind of don't.

Then she pulls herself up straight, fixes her eyes on him, strong. "You know what? What I feel, Gajendra, is what an incredible relief it is to finally simply *trust* someone, without argument or questioning or worry. What I feel is the joy of surrender." Her feet are planted on the floor, her voice calmer and steadier than I've ever heard. Nods and "hmms" of Deep-Realization-Agreement come from the clutch of people around us. "*Surrender,*" she repeats, rolling the syllables in her mouth like something sweet, and there's nothing he can say.

The air has the crisp bite of almost-November. Outside the dorms, Mom and Vrishti hug good night. Vrishti looks into her eyes and says, "That was beautiful tonight, Sarah," and means it.

Normally I'd expect my mom to puff up proud, but she just shrugs, bashful. "It's just the truth."

They look into each other's eyes like real friends, hands clasped in the cold air; then Vrishti squeezes and lets go. "Night, Sarah. Night, Tessa too." She blows a kiss and jingles down the path.

Alone with my mom, I'm afraid she'll find out about Colin. I'm scared she'll hear my thoughts; she'll look at me and somehow see it on my skin. And I can't let her. I can't take the chance. I have to distract her. Just like I'm sure Colin will always want to talk about music, I'm sure my mom will always want to talk about the Guru, and so I lead her down that path.

"So, is there some kind of new rule about men and women at the ashram?"

She looks at me, surprised. "Well yes, Tessa, there is." Pause. Crickets. "Did you want to hear about it?"

"Sure."

Her face lights up. "Oh! Well, the Guru gave us a big new teaching today. You know how usually men and women are all mixed together here, just like in the outside world?"

"Yeah." That's weird: *outside world.*

"But Guruji says we've been progressing very rapidly, so it's time to begin to live in a more disciplined way. More like monks or swamis, sort of."

"Oh, yeah?" What does she mean, everyone has to be celibate or something? I'm not about to ask *that*, though.

"Yeah. I mean, not *literally*." She looks at me meaningfully. That answers that. "But for meditation, you know, any kind of practice, men and women will sit on opposite sides of the room. It's an austerity. He wants us householders to move closer to renunciation."

"Huh." Footsteps. Breathing. Voices in the distance. "So what does that mean, householder?"

"Oh." She laughs. "Right." Like she just remembered I don't know, and it's somehow funny. "Householder . . . ·155. is a phase of the spiritual path? Like first you're a child, and then you're a student; after that you're a householder. Householder's like when you have a family and your focus is on your relationships with them and all that stuff. Then the final stage is *sannyas*, when you give everything up to merge with the Divine. Normal people take years to get through each stage. But if you're really dedicated, you can speed it up."

"So he's trying to speed you up?"

"Yeah, isn't it cool?" She grins at me. "He says if we willfully leave behind the householder stage and move quickly toward *sannyas*, we can accelerate our liberation!"

What I don't get is that the "householder stage" she's so excited to leave behind sounds a lot like "Mom."

Thirteen

. . .

The universe is a secret.

· 1 5 6 . "Come on," Colin says, "let's get out of here," and grabs my hand. Thank god.

"Where are we going?" It feels so good to just let him decide.

"I dunno." He grins. "On a walk."

We stay off the main paths so no one will see us, tracing trails to who knows where. We could technically get lost, but I'm not scared. When we pass the First Aid trailer I see lights behind the gauzy curtains. I don't think Jayita'd get me in trouble, but just in case I drop Colin's hand until we're past.

Finally we wind our way through the woods till you can't see buildings, backs of trailers or the open air of parking lots. Just gray branches, naked like nerves, crosshatching till they're thick enough to shade out the sky, and I know their edges and angles will keep us safe from the world past the woods. I stop walking and turn to Colin. He stops and turns to me. And then my back is against one of those trees, bark scratchy and hard through my sweater, and he's pressed up against the front of me, warm and human and alive.

Every day that week it's like that. Lost and found, cold and warm, risky and safe.

It's the happiest I've ever been in my entire life.

I'm at the Amrit, waiting to go meet Colin at the lot. The sound track is this Yaz tape he lent me, "Upstairs at Eric's," which, in the first fifteen minutes, is giving Green Tea Experience a run for its money. This song *Only You* is playing, so beautiful and perfect it's making my eyes start to water, and then Avinashi walks through the Amrit door. Ugh. The last thing I want is Avinashi to interrupt this song, and the *last* last thing I want is for her to see me tearing up. Her rust-colored turtleneck is pilly, braids brittle at the ends like paintbrushes where she's been sucking on them. I watch from the corners of my eyes as she moves through the line, picking things out and putting them back, finally settling on a yogurt. Then she sees me.

Crap.

"Hey." She comes over, big empty tray holding one little tiny yogurt cup.

I don't look at her or talk, just try my best to stay inside the song. *All I needed was the love you gave, all I needed for another day.*

"*Hey*," she says again, almost yelling. The cashier looks up. I press PAUSE and pull my headphones off.

It's funny. Two months ago Avinashi looked about my age. Now, suddenly, with me in my striped leotard and lipstick, her in spit-soaked braids, it's like I'm the teenager and she's the kid. It's crazy how fast you can cross that line, a million invisible changes adding up till you just tip over the edge into a whole different category. In school I used to see it with guys, their familiar soft high voices suddenly shifting down, turning them overnight into strange, large, clumsy creatures more like my mom's boyfriends than like me. Now it's weird: I can see it in myself.

She doesn't say anything, just stands there with her tray, ignoring my refusal to invite her to sit down. I remain silent. I may be doomed to abandon "Upstairs at Eric's," but I am not going to ask this girl to be my friend.

Finally she breaks the impasse and sits down, avoiding my eyes. She peels the lid off her yogurt. She stirs slowly and much longer than is actually required to mix in the black cherry flavor, waiting to see if I'll talk to her.

"Hi," I say, just so I don't have to feel her waiting anymore. She looks up at me expectantly.

I feel kind of bad just ignoring her, but I don't know what there is to say to this girl. She's made up of everything I don't want to be: the know-it-all Ninyassa talk; fake Hindi words my mom and everyone insist on using; Addams Family skin and the remnants of an unwiped runny nose. And underneath all that she reminds me too much of myself, a version of me that I'm trying to escape: the girl who does everything that grown-ups tell her to, who thinks and thinks and finally settles on something as boring as *yogurt*, the girl with big lonely eyes and no one to talk to in the cafeteria.

Avinashi swallows a bite of yogurt and leans forward like she's finally going to talk, but before her mouth can make words I pick up my Walkman, press PLAY, and walk away, leaving my crumpled muffin wrapper on the table.

Colin's waiting in the VW, drumming his fingers on the dashboard to some song I can't hear. As soon as I see him, my cheeks stretch into a grin and I feel like the me I want to be again, the me that I'm becoming, the me that I am around him. I climb into the bus, shaking my hair out from where my headphones were. "That tape is awesome."

"I knew you'd like it. I think you have a taste for the New Wave, my dear."

"Cool." Colin knows enough about the world that he can tell me what my own tastes are. I love that it's possible for someone to know things about you that you haven't even found out yet.

He looks side to side, broad and funny, like a bank robber in a Charlie Chaplin movie; then leans in and pecks me on the cheek. I laugh. He revs the engine.

"I'm hungry. You hungry?"

I nod yes.

Colin doesn't seem scared about getting caught, but I duck down, heart pounding, till we're safely off the grounds. We drive over hills, through woods, across highways; finally we pull into McDonald's off the interstate. We inch up toward the red-and-yellow drive-thru menu and Colin says, "So what'll it be? Happy Meal? Quarter Pounder with cheese? My treat."

I think about the last hamburger I had, the revenge burger on the way to the ashram. It definitely made my top ten list of best meals ever, but I have to admit I was green for at least four hours afterward. I don't want to risk throwing up in front of Colin, or much worse: gas.

"Um, I'll just have fries."

"You sure?"

"Yeah, I'm good. A large one, though."

The girl at the window is Colin's age. I can tell she thinks he's cute the way she smiles through her freckles, lingers just a little too long with the grease-stained paper bag. Then she eyeballs me: scans from my legs up to my face, then back at him. She can tell how old I am. I feel like saying, "I know. He picked *me*." But I don't. I just say, "Thank you!" really loud and cheerful, brushing Colin's chest when I lean across to take the bag from her.

The parking lot stretches pretty far, and we sit in the bus at the very end of it. Colin lets the engine run so we can listen to the Allman Brothers while we eat. "Man, I love the Allmans," he says, mouth full of Big Mac. He watches me eat my fries. "You a vegetarian or something?"

I blush, a little nervous that he'll think it's weird. But I don't want to ever lie to him. "Yeah."

"That your decision?" he asks me like he already knows the answer.

I roll my eyes. "What do *you* think?"

He bursts out laughing. I didn't mean it as a joke but I crack up too, enough to barely escape snarfing a half-chewed french fry.

Finally I choke it down. "Ah, *not* exactly my decision. I was vegetarian in the womb."

"Wow, your whole life, huh?"

"Yup."

"So you've never had a steak?"

"I've never had a steak."

"Man. We're gonna have to remedy that. I mean, if you want to."

Aside from my brief moments of rebellion-via-hamburger, which were mostly only satisfying because they made my mother mad, I've never had the chance to really think about it. I don't even know *what* I want. Given the choice to do whatever I wanted—totally outside of my mom—what would I do?

"Is it good?"

"Steak? Yeah. Steak is super good. You ever had a burger?" He holds out his half-eaten Big Mac, shedding special sauce and lettuce out the sides.

"Yeah, I've had hamburgers. Thanks." I laugh. "I mean, I've eaten meat a little. But not much. My mom always gets pissed."

"That is weird, man. Anyone ever tell you that your mom is weird?"

And you know what? I realize: nobody has ever told me that my mom is weird. They've only ever told me *I* am. All the stuff I've always gotten shit for—hijiki, kale, and six-grain bread, hand-me-downs and no TV, "emotional word pictures" and "processing" and Hindu chants—that's all her. None of it is me.

"Nope. No one's ever told me that she's weird."

"Really?" he says, surprised. "Well, I'm here to let you know."

He grins. I laugh. And finally exhale.

After we've been kissing for a while, necks craned across the space between our seats, I start to get a little sore. I guess he does too, because he reaches for my waist and pulls at me. I stumble, clumsy. He doesn't notice. Finally I tumble over onto him, smushed against the steering wheel, straddling his lap. I'm afraid my butt's going to accidentally honk the horn, but then he shifts his seat ·163· backward and I settle in, one leg by the gearshift, the other squeezed between the driver's seat and the door.

This whole last week it was always sweet, and soft. He'd rest a hand between my ribs, his kiss saying, *Shh, it's okay, you're safe.* Suddenly it's like safe stopped mattering. To him, at least. Even though we just finished eating, he seems hungry, grabbing my hips. He kisses me like he's looking for something inside my mouth. I press down against him, bite his lip. When my hips hit the steering wheel and honk the horn we both laugh, and then we grab at each other again.

We drive back full and happy, listening to XTC. Tomorrow is my birthday. This is the best fifteenth-birthday present I could get, better than anything you could wrap or hold.

"It's my birthday tomorrow," I tell him. I'm not saying it so he'll do something special; I just feel like he should know. I don't remind him of how old I'm turning.

"Really?" he says, surprised. "Man, aw, crap!"

"What?"

"I've got a job tomorrow, working on some cars in town."

"That's okay." It really is.

"You sure? You should've told me earlier, I would've done something. Man, I feel bad."

"No, no, don't. It's cool. I'm sure my mom will want to hang out anyway."

"Right." He pauses, squints at me, remembering I'm a kid. I don't want him to remember that. I want to make him forget. I try to sound cooler.

"I totally have plans."

He stops squinting. "Okay. You sure?"

"Yeah."

"Okay. I'll be back to pick you up day after," he says. "Promise."

I like the sound of that word.

It's practically night when we pull into the ashram. Headlights cut through dusty air and the dark makes Colin brave or careless, because he pulls all the way up to the main entrance and kisses me before the stereo's even off.

"Happy birthday, Tess." He smirks into my eyes like it's still part of the kiss, and a shiver goes all the way down my spine into my toes.

Back in our room, I'm supposed to be sleeping, but Colin lent me his Dire Straits T-shirt and it rubs the thought of him against my skin, keeping me awake. My mom just sits on her bed, oblivious. The world inside my head is so alive and big; I can't believe the only thing keeping it from leaking out into this room is the closed seam of my mouth.

I'll get a lecture about silence if I listen to tapes, so I just lie there and wonder if my mom's going to say anything about my birthday. She usually starts talking about it the night before, counting down to midnight. But she just scribbles in her red silk journal in the glow of her bedside light, blankets pulled over her lap. Her mouth twitches at the corners as she writes, smiling at some secret tucked inside the envelope of her. The expression on her face feels familiar. For a second I don't know why, and then I realize: her face looks how I feel about Colin.

After a while I hear the scribbling stop, her notebook close. I slit my eyes and watch her through a screen of lashes. She looks over at me, furtive, studying my face to make sure that I'm asleep. I slow my breathing, make the rhythm even; I heard once that how fast you breathe is how someone can tell whether or not you're really sleeping. When she's finally satisfied I'm not going to wake up, she pulls the covers off, stands up, and slips her sandals on. She's not in her pajamas. She's wearing this fancy silk dress that clings to her, all white, embroidered at the hems. I've never seen that dress before. She switches off the light and leaves the room.

·166.

It's weird she didn't say anything about my birthday. And it's even weirder that she just snuck out. It makes me itchy, anxious like ants on my skin, and I suddenly remember all these things. Like waking up at four a.m. because of thunder and walking down our hall and she wasn't there. Like waiting on the sidewalk after school until the sun sank and it started getting cold. Like getting yelled at for complaining that she was leaving overnight to take a crystal healing workshop, and how I stayed up in our empty house that weekend, afraid to go to sleep alone. If I knew Colin's number I'd go straight to the pay phone by the dining hall and let it ring till he woke up. He'd answer bleary, and I'd say, *I need you; come and get me in the bus.* It'd be okay. She isn't here. She wouldn't notice I was gone.

. . . . .

Sleep finally floods in, thick dark liquid filling up the spaces. But daylight opens them again and I wake up with a hole in my ribs. Her bed is empty, but I hear the shower running. Anger rises in my throat.

I want to tell her. I want to tell her I saw her and ask her why she left without explaining. I want to say I know she's keeping secrets, breaking rules; that she can't just leave me here and go someplace she's not supposed to go. I sit up, blood flooding my veins, ready to turn the tables on her.

But then I realize—she could say all those same things back to me, and they'd all be true. If I want to keep my own secrets, I can't get too close to hers. So I make a vow: I will pretend everything is normal, and I will take all the spaces that she makes in me and fill them up with Colin. I won't ask her anything. She'll come out of the shower and say happy birthday and ask me how it feels to turn fifteen, and that is all we'll talk about.

"Howdja sleep, Tess?" she asks, stepping out of the steam.

I wait for the *happy birthday* part.

It doesn't come.

I look down at my sheets and tell her, "Great."

"Cool." She smiles.

And that's it.

She forgot. I can't believe she forgot. She has never forgotten before, not ever. Granted, there aren't calendars at the ashram, but how can your *own mom* forget your birthday? My eyes sting and fill up. Forget it. I'm not going to wait around for her to remember, and I'm certainly not going to remind her myself. I swear, the next time I see Colin I am asking for his phone number and tattooing it on my leg.

Fourteen

. . .

At a certain point the path will break you open.
There is nothing to do but give way.

She never remembered my birthday. After a few days, I
got tired of waiting and decided to just forget it.
Nothing came from my dad either. Of course.

Now she rushes into the room, breathless, hair
loose around her face. "Tessa!" she exclaims. I close my
notebook, tuck my pencil in the spiral. There is clearly
going to be a conversation; I'm not going to have a
choice.

She plops down on the bed across from me. I raise
my eyebrows. "Yes?"

"Tessa, guess what!" she barrels on.

I wish she'd just spit whatever it is out and get it
over with, instead of making me ask what. "What?"

"I got a name!"

Great.

"Cool, Mom, what's your name?" It's like there

is some kind of script of everything I'm supposed to say, and somehow I've memorized it without even noticing.

"Guhahita Prapati!"

I knew it would be weird, but that is over the top. "Guha-what?"

"*Guhahita Prapati*," she says, stressing all the syllables like I don't speak English. Or Sanskrit. Which I don't, but you know what I mean.

Pause.

"Well, do you want to know what it means?"

"Sure." Of course, I don't want to know what it means. I wish she would quit making me act like I'm interested; it obviously doesn't matter to her whether or not I actually am.

"It means 'total surrender, in a secret place in the heart.'" She beams like the football captain asked her to the prom or something.

"*Awesome*." That's what the banana-clip girls say about the prom.

"I know, isn't it?" She giggles. "So that's what you can call me!"

"What?" Now I really *am* asking.

"You can call me it! You know, instead of Mom."

"Wait. You want me to stop calling you Mom?"

She looks at me like, *Duh*. "Well, yeah!"

"Um, no."

That stops her. Her face drops. "What do you mean, *no?*" she asks, like she can't believe it.

"I mean no," I say, like it's completely obvious, which it is.

She just stares at me.

"I'm not calling you *Guhahita Prapati.*"

Her cheeks turn pink. "Why not?"

"Because, *Mom*, you're my mom! That's why! And anyway, it's not even your real name."

She's trying to sit on her rapidly increasing irritation, but I know that flicker in her eyes. "Tessa," she says, holding up a mask of calm and condescension, "that is, in fact, my real name now. In *fact*," she says again, "it's *more* real than the name of Sarah. It's my *spiritual* name. That means it's actually always been my name. The Guru gave it to me."

"Yeah? Well, how has it always been your name if the Guru just gave it to you?"

She looks at me like I'm stupid. "The Guru didn't make it up, Tessa, he just *recognized* it. On the spiritual plane, it's been my name since the first moment of this incarnation."

"That doesn't even make sense, *Mom*. A name is just what people call you. It's not *you*. If nobody called you that, it wasn't your name."

"That's not true!"

I just look at her.

"Okay, you see that tree?" She points out the window. "That's *actually* an elm tree. That's what it is. If someone accidentally called it an oak tree, that wouldn't make it an oak tree, would it?"

"No, but someone calling it an elm tree doesn't make it an elm tree either. It just is what it is, no matter what anybody calls it. You're not *Guhahita Prapati*. You're just you."

"Look, Tessa," she says, exasperated, "I'm not going to argue philosophical points with you. The truth is on a totally different plane from conceptual debates, so there isn't even any point. Just call me Guhahita, please." She says *please* like a command.

I am not going to give in on this, though. It's too much. I'm sick of feeling like she wants to be someone else besides my mom. Like the entire fact that I exist makes her somehow not herself.

"No, Mom, I won't. It's fucking weird." There. I said it.

She stares at me, shocked. I take advantage of the opening and barrel through.

"It's fucking weird, this whole *thing* is fucking weird, this place and the white clothes and all the Sanskrit words, what is that about, you don't even *speak* Sanskrit! We came here and all of a sudden you're like a totally different person." It feels good to finally get it out, and hurts at the same time.

She's upset, so much going on in her face that it looks like it might start throbbing, but she tries to cover over it with calm. "Tessa, I *am* a different person. Before we came here, I was lost. I was miserable. I didn't know who I was."

"Before we came here you were my *mom*. Remember that? Remember when you used to take me places and make me breakfast and come get me after school? Remember when I used to go to school? You never asked me if I wanted to stop! You never asked me if I wanted to come here. You just picked me up and dragged me here and then ran off and left me by myself." I'm not really by myself, not anymore, but I leave that part out; that's *mine*, not hers, and I swear I will never ever let her know. "Like you always fucking do. And now you want me to call you some stupid fucking name I can't even pronounce? No *way*. Fucking forget it."

She inhales deep, on purpose: her chest goes up and down, her nostrils flare. Then she starts saying some mantra to herself, under her breath. It's like she's trying to show me I'm pissing her off without just coming out and admitting it. Like, *Look how hard you're making me work to keep my spiritual composure.*

"Just quit it, Mom. You're not fooling anyone." I roll my eyes.

And then the mantra stops, and the deep breathing. "God *damnit*, Tessa, who the hell do you think you are?

You think it's fun doing telemarketing in Akron to pay for your food when your father won't even send a *dime*? You think it's easy buying the groceries and paying the rent and getting you back and forth to school every single day totally alone? Excuse me if I try to have my own *identity*. Excuse me if I try, against the wishes of the whole goddamn world, to be *happy*."

Now I'm crying. "I'm sorry it's so *hard* for you to be my mom. I'm sorry I'm such a big giant drag. What am I supposed to do? Buy our food myself? Go get a job so you can go on a road trip with gypsies? I'm your *kid*."

She hurtles forward like she didn't even hear me. "You know, Tessa, you are just so cruel. After *fourteen years* I finally get us someplace where I can finally be happy. And you just want to spit all over it."

"Fifteen," I say.

"*What?*"

"Fifteen. It's fifteen years. Last week was my birthday."

Her face falls. "Oh, Tessa—"

But I don't want her to feel bad and say sorry and make me forgive her. I want to stay mad. "Right. Did you ever think about maybe the whole goddamn world doesn't revolve around *you*? Do you ever even think about whether *I'm* happy? I didn't want to come here on your fucking stupid spiritual journey. I didn't want to hear all about your boyfriends or hang out with that stupid kayaker in Big Sur or switch schools a million times. I didn't want to go on the road or live in a tent full of mosquitoes. I wish I could live with *Dad*."

And now the sorry leaves her eyes; she's mad.

Good.

"You do, huh?" Her face flushes hot; tears shine her cheeks. It sort of disgusts me. I feel like neither of us has any skin. "Well guess what, Tessa. Your father doesn't want to live with *you*."

I feel like someone kicked me in the gut, but I don't let her see. I clench my jaw so tight my teeth grate, and I think: *I hate you.*

·175.

"He doesn't want us, Tessa, okay? *He's* not here. I am. I bought the gas. I paid for your room and your food and your goddamn running water. You better learn a little gratitude, lady. Or else you just take your judgments and your attitude and you see how you do on your own, without someone devoting their entire goddamn life to taking care of you."

Something stronger than blood is coursing through my veins. My fingers are pulsing with it. So are my feet. They need to move. I need to move. Now.

"*Fine.*" I rip away from her, hurl myself out of the room. The crack of the door slamming echoes down the hall behind me, interrupting everybody's morning meditation.

. . . . .

I tumble down the back stairs so fast the concrete is a blur, shove the fire door open and run out. Gravel slides under my feet but I don't think about falling, I just run. People cluster, queuing up for breakfast, but my tears are too thick to see who they are, and I don't stop to look. All I can think is one thing: *Be here please be here please be here.*

He is. He's hunched over the hood of a school bus and I don't care who hears me, I yell his name from twenty feet away. He turns and sees me crying. Worry takes over his face, soft fills up his green eyes, and that's the look, that was the look I wanted, the one that says: *I see you.* I run right into his arms. "Let's go," I say. "I don't care where. Just get me out of here."

He's nervous driving me out during the middle of breakfast, crowds clutched around the entrance, everyone awake in early morning. He puts his hand between my shoulder blades to push me below the passenger window. I press back, stay sitting up. I don't care who sees.

I find the Violent Femmes tape, and once we pass Atma Lakshmi I turn it up loud. The jangly chords match my nerves, the energy of my body reaching through the air to meet the music. I move my head hard to the snare drum beat and suddenly understand heavy metal headbangers. Colin just watches me and drives.

They hurt me bad, but I don't mind; they hurt me bad,

they do it all the time. I know the words now and I sing along, face pointed out the open window, wind biting my teeth. By the time *Please Do Not Go* comes on, my breathing's even, tears dried sticky on my cheeks. I lower the volume. Colin turns to me.

"What happened, Tess?"

I don't even know where to start.

"Mom?" he starts for me. Thank god.

"Yeah."

"What'd she do now?"

"She's just so . . ." Frustration curls around my words, catches them before they can get to my mouth. ·177· I push them out. "She's just so *selfish.*"

He nods.

"It's like—Okay." I shift in my seat, dig in for the story. "It's enough that she forgot my birthday. But now she comes home with a new name, right? They all get new names from the Guru. In Sanskrit or whatever. Fine. But she wants me to call her it."

He makes a sympathetic face of *ugh.*

"I know! And it's like *Guhahita Prapati* or something. I'm not going to call her that. It's ridiculous."

"So what'd you tell her?"

"I told her I'm not calling her that."

"And?"

I'm a little hesitant to admit it, not sure if he'll think it's cool or mean of me. "I told her it's bullshit."

"Wow." He raises his eyebrows, impressed. "Really?"

"Yeah, I did," speeding up, relieved he doesn't think it's mean. "And I told her these people are all fucking freaks and they're full of shit."

His eyebrows go up even higher. "*Wow.*" Then he laughs. "Good for you."

I feel better, so much my skin can hardly hold it in. He said *good for you*. I stood up and said the truth and for the first time in my life I didn't wind up by myself. I feel big, and free, and strong. Maybe there's a little part tucked way down deep that aches when I think about my mom's red eyes. A part that's terrified it's true my dad has never wanted me. A part that knows that's why I don't tell Colin about him. But those parts are all tiny.

Mostly I feel strong.

We drive and drive and listen to the Violent Femmes and finally he says, *Where are we going, Tessa?* I swallow hard, look at the sky, remind myself of that strong free feeling, and I tell him, *We are going to your house.*

Finally we pull around a bendy road and he slows down. There's a wood post with a paint-peeled sign that says "Dee's Cottages" in almost-chipped-off blue; it swings as we drive by. The tires churn up dust and the trees thin out as we pull into a clearing. Colin shuts the engine off.

My heart is pounding in my throat.

The cabins were all white once upon a time, but they've peeled so much that you can see the wood; their roofs are red with little clumps of moss. They ring around a patch of brown grass with picnic tables and a rusty swing set. Colin takes his seat belt off and says, "So, you wanna see my place?"

I am so nervous I think that I might die. My palms have little geysers in them, and when he takes my hand to hold it I almost slip out of his grasp. He hangs on, though.

We cross the patch of grass, past thin screen doors and concrete doorsteps, to the big cabin at the back of the circle. He nods toward the woods. "That's the path down to the creek. I'll take you down there later."

"Cool."

The screen is ripped, the door unlocked. "Don't you worry about burglars and stuff?"

"Nah," he says. "Nobody comes around here. Anyways, there's not much to steal."

It's true: jeans and T-shirts sprawl out on a wire-frame bed; posters spell "Led Zeppelin" and "Dark Side of the Moon" on wood-paneled walls; dim light hits the stucco ceiling when he flips the switch. On the nightstand, he has a book called *Siddhartha* stacked on top of X-Men comic books. Clouded windows peek out from olive-green wool curtains beside the hot plate and the mini-fridge. It looks like a cross between camp and a teenage boy's room on TV. It's the most beautiful thing I've ever seen.

He goes over to the dresser where his boom box is, sifts through a crate of tapes with no cases. "So what's our soundtrack, Tess?"

"Um." I get distracted for a minute, looking at his nightstand. There's a box of condoms on it. I stare. He doesn't notice.

"Here, lemme give you some options." He sifts some more. "J. Geils Band. Police. Ummm . . . the Kinks. Pretenders. REM. Oh! How 'bout early Aerosmith? 'Toys in the Attic?'"

I yank my gaze off his nightstand, try to come up with an answer. All I know about Aerosmith is that *Walk This Way* song that was on the radio last year. It was sort of rap. "Are they rap?"

Colin laughs. "No. They're not rap. Here, listen."

He presses PLAY; it picks up in the middle of a song, all loud guitars and bluesy beats. "I saw them, you know."

"Wow, really?" I'm sitting on the bed. There's no place else to sit.

He nods. "'Back in the Saddle' tour, 1984. Joe

Perry—the guitarist? He was on some crazy drugs, but they *rocked*."

"Wow."

"Yeah. Me and my buddies Clint and Bennett camped out for two days for those tickets. You'll meet them. Clint and Bennett."

"Oh." He wants me to meet his friends. I'm at his house. I'm sitting on his bed.

"That okay with you?" He chuckles.

"Yeah." I say, blushing and half mute. "Yeah, of course it's okay. I'd love to."

"Cool." He plops down next to me. A new song comes on. "Oh *man! Sweet Emotion.* They did this for the encore. It's a serious classic."

The bass line thumps a long intro. He leans in and kisses me. The singer comes in, stretching it out as long as he can, *Sweeeeeeet emohhhhtion*, till it finally gives way to the guitar like an avalanche or a roof caving in, and he opens my lips with his tongue, and I drop into him and the song. His hands are on my back, beneath my shirt, on my bra hook, and it comes undone with one snap, and then his hands are around the front of me and a shiver goes through my entire body and all I can do is fall back onto the bed.

The pillow smells like him and half-clean laundry. He lies down beside me, slides a hand up my shirt. My eyes are open, looking into his. Guitars get louder. He leans in and kisses me again, and when I lift my face he hoists himself up and over, onto me, his corduroy thigh pressing my blue jean legs apart.

These last few weeks it's always been by a tree or in a car or at the corner of the parking lot: someplace exposed and temporary. We've never been really *alone*. Now it's different. Now I am lying on his bed inside his room with the door closed, and there's nobody to knock or walk in, no one even knows where I am; there's no net of getting-in-trouble to catch me, and I can jump as far and as deep as I want. He presses against me. My body shudders. I have never felt like this.

"Let's do it," I whisper to him with my eyes open.

All movement skids to a halt and he pulls back to look at me.

"What?"

He stares hard into my eyes, not judging or mean, more like, *Where did you come from?* and *Are you telling me the truth?* I could back away, say, *Nothing, forget it*, just kiss him again like we've been kissing all month, but I don't want to. I want to jump.

"Let's do it," I tell him again.

He tilts his head to the side. "Tessa."

I don't say anything.

"Tessa, are you sure?"

And now my heart starts thumping hard, because suddenly I'm not. Suddenly the fact that he doubts it makes me think that maybe I should too. Maybe it's wrong; maybe I'm not ready; maybe doing it will take us down a different road I can't even picture or imagine. Maybe it's not safe, or he'll freak out and get uncomfortable, or leave after two months of it like all my mother's boyfriends. Maybe it actually matters that he's twenty and technically it's illegal. I start to panic: *What did I just say?*

Except then he takes his hand and runs it down my cheek, and somehow the soft of his skin wipes away all those maybes. My heart doesn't slow down, my breath doesn't get smooth, I don't stop being scared, but I ·183· know. They always say you're ready when you love someone, and we've never said it but I know that this is love. His smell on the pillow, his hair on my lips, his hand on my back; the familiar when he laughs, the safe in his van with his hand clutched in mine. It doesn't matter if anyone else wants me but Colin. This is it. I will never be back in this moment again. I gulp in air and tell him, *Yes.*

Afterward, you're supposed to feel like a different person. You're supposed to feel like a woman or something, suddenly adult—all the little-kid hitches gone, transformed into a new, more finished version of yourself. But lying on his bed, sheets swirled around, I still feel like the regular me. Except naked, which is weird, because he's naked too. I haven't been in the vicinity of another naked person since my mom and a bunch of her friends took me to a nude beach when I was six, and even then I wore my bathing suit. And anyway, the two experiences don't exactly compare.

He lies there, sprawled on the pillow like it's totally normal. The sheet's pulled halfway up his stomach so I can see his chest, the muscles of it, dark hairs against pale skin looking bare and animal. He looks like a man. He's smiling. The fact that he's a naked animal doesn't seem to bother him at all. He props himself up on his elbow, turns to me.

"Hey, Tess," he says, his eyes a mixture of sweet and amused.

I feel tender and shaky, like all of me is on the outside. "Hey," I say.

He drags one finger down my side. "You feel okay?"

"Yeah," I tell him.

"It didn't hurt too much?"

I shake my head no.

Right at the doorstep of doing it, he said, *This is your first time, right? You didn't tell me but I know.* Like him knowing in the van that I had a big fight with my mom. Like him knowing what music I would like without me saying, before I even knew myself. My mom is always telling me I'll understand things when I have more life experience, and I've always thought that was kind of a crock, but now I know what she means. Colin has life experience; it makes him know things before you tell him. It makes him know me better than I know myself. Maybe that's what they mean when they say "wise."

He said, *This might hurt a little,* and it did, but I didn't flinch. My eyes welled up but I squeezed them shut, and anyway his face was over my shoulder by then, pressed into the pillow, in his own world. The hurt bled into the whole of it, him moving over me, closer than I'd ever been to anyone, closer than I'd ever even been to myself. I thought I might crack open, but I just hung on, memorizing the smell of the skin of his neck, and when it stopped hurting enough to open my eyes, I counted the million freckles sprawling out across his shoulders, each one a tiny miracle.

"Do you feel different?" he asks, and I don't know how to do anything but tell the truth.

"Not really."

There's a pause.

"Is that weird?" I ask.

"That's not weird," he says, and cracks that grin again.

"Good," I say. "I was worried it was weird." When I hear it come out of my mouth I realize how funny it is to worry things are weird when you're with another person who's not hiding even a little tiny part of himself. And I realize that's the whole point: to be together and not hiding any parts. No secrets. Nothing held back. That's the whole entire point. The shaky feeling melts away and suddenly I do feel different.

We lie in bed forever, talking, and when we finally start to get restless he lends me his sweater to go outside. I watch him get dressed, cross the room without his shirt on, dig through laundry for his clothes. His sides slant toward his waist in a V, sloped in from his strong shoulders, and I think: That's what a man looks like.

He pulls on a flannel and jeans, and when we walk onto the stoop, the sky's already pink. Winter's close, I guess, and night comes early, but still, I can't believe the whole day just swallowed itself inside his room. It makes my body feel confused, like when you lie down for a nap in sunlight and wake up when it's dark.

The air smells cold; his hand's warm around mine. "Wanna see the creek before we head back?"

Now that I saw how dark it is, I'm getting anxious, but I say, "Sure," and remind myself nobody's going to notice that I'm gone.

Light floods out through the windows of Main Building, all the ashram people laughing through the glass. You can't hear what they're saying, but you can see them in there like a diorama, their own little enclosed world. I used to walk by other people's houses, right at dusk and after, when my mom was out on dates. One by one I'd peek in all the windows, see a tiny universe in every home, like dollhouses but real. Sometimes there'd be an old guy having a TV dinner, but mostly it was families clustered up in twos and threes and fives, boxed in by four safe walls, everybody home. I'd watch them from outside, wishing that one of those worlds would hold my mom and dad and me, TV on while we ate meat loaf, cleared the table, got some milk. Our apartment always seemed too empty when I went home afterward, dark even when I turned on all the lamps.

I sit with Colin in the van, dim light above the windshield circling us in our own private glow. And I realize: This van is my world. My light. I'm not outside anymore; I'm one of the people that I used to watch.

Colin kisses me good night.

"You're beautiful, Tessa," he says, and I believe him.

FIFTEEN

. . .

Resistance, like fear, is not to be heeded;
you must push past discomfort to know the bliss
that lies beyond.

·188. I haven't seen Jayita since that night of *darshan,* and I
was almost hoping she'd left. I was hoping she'd decided
to do the thing she really wanted to, not the thing she
was supposed to. Even if it was hard.

But now she's right here in the cafeteria, standing
up and arguing with a table full of people. She's lost a
bunch of weight; even through her flowy skirt you can
see the angles of her bones. Her eyes look jumpy and
scared, like a hungry animal's. I move a few steps closer,
just enough to make out what she's saying. "Prapati" is
the first word I hear. I'm trying to figure out why that
sounds familiar when I realize it's my mom's name.

Avtar and Bhav and Gajendra all sit around their
table. "Jayita," Gajendra says, "we're all entitled to our
questions, but come on. Don't you think what you're
implying is a little—rash?"

"No, but I mean it, I think I saw something really upsetting going on up there." Her voice is high and loud; she seems almost panicky. "We're supposed to be pure here, there are rules, and he's supposed to be the purest one of all, and it's—"

Avtar cuts her off, sharp. "Perhaps we should all just take a breath and refocus our intentions."

"It isn't about intentions, Avtar." She's yelling now. People at other tables are starting to look. "I'm really trying to ask a question! I really think he's—"

Now Gajendra interrupts. "That's enough, Jayita." He shoots Avtar this tiny smirk, like Jayita's just a kid having a tantrum.

She gives up on them and scans the dining hall, like she's searching for anyone else who'll listen, but everyone who was watching her just turns back to their food. I slide behind a pillar; I don't want Jayita to see me. For some reason, I really don't want her to tell me what she thinks is going on.

She turns back to the table. "Why won't anybody listen to me?" she pleads. She does kind of sound like a kid. A really scared one.

"Look, Jayita," Bhav jumps in with a pretend-soothing voice. "You've had to work on an attachment that was very strong for you. It must've certainly been difficult when Chakradev left the ashram, especially since he said all those awful things about you and about

Guruji. And we're very proud of you for maintaining your devotion through that process. But couldn't it be possible that what you think you're sensing is only a product of your own emotion?"

She gets that look again, the one I saw that day at Guru's quarters, like the ground is going soft beneath her feet and she doesn't know what the truth is. "I don't think so, but—"

"Right. That's right," Bhav says. "What is that 'but'? Maybe that 'but' is actually the voice of your inner knowing. The voice that knows that suspicion and doubt are only obstacles that rise up as we progress, and rather than spread that doubt to others, we need to learn to get beyond it."

Jayita looks at him, eyes wide, and scared, and open. "But I don't know—"

"Exactly!" Avtar jumps in. "*None* of us know. 'Knowing' is just an illusion of our limited egos. That's why we have to trust the Guru." He smiles. It's kind of creepy that he's smiling at her when she's so upset.

Jayita looks to Gajendra, unsure, like, *Is what they're saying really true?* "It's true." Gajendra nods. "Doubt is just another manifestation of fear. And our work here is to overcome our fear."

"Okay," Jayita finally says, but she doesn't look any less afraid.

. . . . .

I leave the dining hall without eating. For some reason that whole thing made my stomach nervous. Jayita seemed really scared about something, for real; I don't understand what it was and I don't know why those guys wouldn't let her say it. But I know that she said my mom's name. That means my mom is part of whatever Jayita was talking about. It makes me panicked. I don't even want to talk to my mom, but for some reason all of a sudden I just really need to know where she is.

I go up to our room, then comb the gift shops and the lobby, the garden by the Gandhi statue. She isn't any- where. Finally I find the road that leads to the Guru's quarters. That's the only place that's left.

At the NO TRESSPASSING sign, I turn in. The flowers are gone, the last few red and orange leaves fluttering off naked branches; you can see the rocks and dirt. I tuck around the whitewashed kitchen build-ing, crane my neck toward the bustle of steam and pots and vegetables. I watch everyone in the kitchen chant in unison while I pick through the faces for my mom. She isn't there.

She isn't in the next room I look in either, or the next. I take the long way around, passing six colors of sari curtains, till I get to the room the Guru brought Jayita to. Its white curtains are half drawn; I squint through them.

She's in there. And so is he.

She's kneeling at his feet, like Jayita was, but closer. Their eyes are locked. My mom's are wider than I've ever seen them, like Alice in Wonderland. Like a little girl. She looks younger than me; it sort of scares me. Tears stream down my mother's cheeks and I can't tell if she's happy or sad or afraid or all of them at once. Seeing it makes me feel dirty, like I'm watching something nobody's supposed to see. I've never seen her look like that, and I think, *That's where all the love is going. That's what she looks like when she loves someone.* It makes me furious.

Finally the beard guy kisses her forehead for too long. She gets off her knees and leaves the room. He turns the TV on. I stand there on tiptoe, watching through the window, trying to hear. I don't even think about getting caught. I don't even notice when the Guru hears my sneakers slip on the gravel and perks up his ears. I don't notice when he rustles in his seat, gathers his robe to stand up. I don't see him till he's walking toward the window, toward me, and it is way too late for me to run away.

A million thoughts run through my mind. This is way worse than Devanand, way worse than Ninyassa or my mom. All of a sudden I can see every little paint chip on that NO TRESSPASSING sign, and my mind says, *Why the hell didn't you listen to it?* There is no story I can make up to get myself out of this one. He strides to the window, black brow furrowed, slips his hands under the wood frame of the window, and hoists it up on its track like it's a feather. I don't know how someone that small could be so strong. I'm imagining my bones snapping like twigs when he reaches down and grabs my arm.

His grip is hard; his hand is hot. Hotter than any skin I've ever felt, in fact. It feels like it might burn. Heat floods through my shoulder to my neck. He says, "Come on," and pulls me up. There's nothing to do but go along. This little tiny elfin man, two hands gripping one of my arms, is somehow able to pull me off the ground and up five feet into the window. I try to brace my sneakers against the side of the house; he keeps pulling and I keep wriggling, and soon I am sitting in a pile on the rose quartz–colored rug.

"Ha," he says, looking me over. "The one with the friend."

I don't know how he remembers me from six weeks ago at *darshan*, but that has to be what he means.

"You still have the bear?" he asks. I nod. And then I realize: if he remembers who I am, that means he probably knows who my mom is, and she's probably still in the next room. Shit. *Do not go get her*, I say to him in my head. *Please please please do not go get her.*

"Don't worry. I won't," he says.

"What?" I say, confused. Did I say that out loud?

"I won't call your mother."

I didn't say that out loud. He just read my mind. Goose bumps prick my skin.

"Sit," he says.

"Huh?"

"*Sit*," he says again, sharp, and points at a couch near his chair.

"Okay," I say, and scurry over.

He watches me cross my legs, appraising something. Then he strides over.

"We will watch," he says.

·194. I have no idea what he's talking about, but I say, "Okay."

He switches on the TV. The Southern guy comes on again, and I recognize him: it's Jimmy Swaggart, one of the televangelists like Jim and Tammy Faye. My mom's always talking about what repressive hypocrites those televangelists are, how they're just out to steal poor naïve sad people's money in the name of god.

Jimmy Swaggart is doing an interview with Larry King. They show a picture of Jim and Tammy Faye, and then another of this redheaded woman who looks kind of slutty. Jimmy Swaggart starts talking about Jim Bakker's sinful adultery with the redhead, and the beard guy turns to me.

"They are more fragile than they think, no?"

On TV, Jimmy Swaggart says Jim Bakker is a cancer on the body of Christ. The beard guy laughs.

"You see, that is the problem."

He looks at me like I'm supposed to ask him what he means.

"What do you mean?"

"They think one man can hurt the body of Christ. So much pride. One man's actions only ripple out into the ocean of divine bliss and disappear."

"Ah." So it doesn't matter what any of us ever does? That doesn't really make sense. I want to ask him what he means again, but he's not looking at me anymore.

Eyes on Larry King, he drops his hand onto the couch, between the outside of my leg and the edge of his robe. His knuckles graze the edge of my thigh. I squirm away, shifting my weight, but his hand comes with me, sending a burn up my leg into my waist and ribs. His touch is so slight, the couch so narrow, that I can't say for sure he's doing it on purpose. If I told him to quit it, he'd be shocked, and I'd be wrong, and I'd just end up feeling guilty and embarrassed. But I sort of feel like I want to throw up.

He turns his face toward the TV and chuckles at the televangelists.

When *Larry King* ends, the beard guy tells me to leave. Somehow I seem to have gotten through this entire experience without getting yelled at, but if my mother's anywhere nearby, that's going to end the second I step out that door.

"You are afraid, no?"

I exhale a little. Maybe he'll take it easy on me. "Yes."

"Well." His eyes flash. "We must push past our fear." He turns the knob and shoves me forward.

At the end of the hall is a fire door. It says EMER-GENCY EXIT—ALARM WILL SOUND in big red letters, but I don't care. I run, stumbling on the carpet; too fast, I hope, for anyone to see. The rug's like sand slowing my feet down but I push through and slam into the door and the alarm shrieks behind me, getting quieter and quieter as I run past the kitchen across the perfect lawns onto the road.

By the time I get to the lot my feet are sore and my head's spinning. The sky stretches out white, wind rattling spindly branches. My knuckles sting with cold. I don't feel any better about Jayita and my mom.

Colin's sitting on the ground, leaned up against the side of a bus, reading *Zen and the Art of Motorcycle Maintenance*.

"Hey you." His eyes crinkle when he sees me.

"Hey." I go straight to him, fold into his jean-jacketed arms. I don't have to ask for permission anymore.

We don't go to his house. It's too far, too late already; I have to be back for Evening Program. We just drive the van a little off the grounds and park.

It's weird how once you've done it one time, it's just assumed you will again. It's like there's a threshold and every step leading up to it is a question, but then you cross that line and all the questions disappear. Dissolve into the ocean of divine bliss. Or something like that.

He goes right for my bra and then my zipper, takes everything off fast, pushes forward. Inside I want to say, *Wait, don't I get to decide again?* The deciding was part of it, the *Are you sure?* and *Do you want to?* and the saying *Yes,* and it doesn't seem quite right that that's just over now. Last time I knew I wanted to; this time, I'm not so sure. But he's not asking anymore and I can't find a space to say, *Stop*; there's nothing I can do but let it happen. The Allman Brothers blare through the speakers, guitars fast and jangly, weaving into interminable jams as my head spins out, his mouth pressing into mine, my head pressing into the wool-upholstered mattress in the van. It all happens too quick for my body to catch up; there's so much of everything so fast that it's hard for me to feel. The song stretches out and eventually he stops kissing me and closes his eyes.

I tell myself that it's enough that we're this close. I don't need to feel what he does; I don't need to always feel safe. It's enough that it's me in the back of his van, me he comes to pick up every day, me between him and the mattress. It's enough that he gives me all of him, and that he doesn't leave. The feeling of making him feel fills me up and I just concentrate on that, let it grow till he finishes and lowers down onto his elbows, sweaty and grinning. I made him do that. I can make someone feel things. That's all I have to do to make him stay.

When the tape ends and he pulls apart the green plaid wool curtains, it's dark again. Something about sex makes time work different, and I wonder if that's what they mean when they talk about timelessness, how past and future disappear and so do second hands, minute hands, hours, till all there is is one big giant *now* stretching out in all directions. "We better go," I say.

This time he stops short of the main entrance and thank god, because not only Ninyassa but Devanand are standing by the door. I keep my head forward as I walk toward them, acutely aware of my skin beneath my clothes. Ninyassa nods at me half distracted and turns back to her conversation. Devanand, in leggings and a turquoise turtleneck that swallows the beginnings of his beard, keeps his eyes fixed right on me. I want to flinch, look down, but I know I can't.

"Hey, Tessa," he says in that too-enthusiastic way of

his. There's something sharp beneath it. "How's Grounds Crew *seva* going? Not so easy when the soil's frozen over, huh?"

I shake my head, spine straight, eyes up. I know I have to tell a story with the way I move and look; I have to act like I believe it. "It's okay."

"Well, I guess you're finding stuff to do. You're a resourceful one. Always looking for new ways to serve!" He smiles crooked, a flash of something flinty in his eyes. My pulse races.

"Yup," I say. "Well, I better get some rest."

I breeze past them through the front door, Devanand's eyes hot on my back as I head for the stairs.

At Evening Program my mom acts weirdly formal. The last few days all she talks about is food and scheduling, what I'm wearing, where we'll sit. She doesn't talk about our fight, or look at me.

The beard guy comes in and sits down silently. I watch his face, my eyes open in a sea of closed ones. I don't know what he is, and I can't tell if he's real or not. This afternoon he was just a person, watching Jimmy Swaggart on the couch, like my grandparents in Ohio. Except his hands made my entire body break out sweating, and when he touched me I wanted to throw up, and he could read my mind.

My mom loves him, though. More than she loves me. I turn my head and look at her, next to me on her cushion in an entirely different world. She can't tell what I've done, and I won't tell her. And there are just as many things, I think, that she's not telling me. Car trips and blanket forts, strawberry juice and hand-me-downs and mugs of tea: all that stuff seems like fifty years ago, even though I've only been alive fifteen. The gap between that life and my new one widens, empty and filled up with silence, till finally I spin off into the music, cut loose, on my own.

Sixteen

· · ·

There are worlds beyond our limited "reality."
Go there and roam.

These days he meets me up near Atma Lakshmi: the gift shop's closed for winter and I'm not risking the front entrance again. His house is far, so mostly we park and keep the heat on, off Route 9 or behind the multiplex; no one goes to movies in the middle of a weekday. We play the Allmans and REM and XTC, sometimes the Cure, and afterward we go to McDonald's and I eat meat.

It feels regular now, this secret life that I have: regular, adult, and mine. I know what I'm supposed to do with my hands; I know how to make my own decisions and pick my own tapes. I know all the words to the Violent Femmes and half of Aerosmith. We don't talk as much as before we had sex, but sex is sort of like talking. In a different way.

When Colin picks me up to go to Clint's, the first snow is clinging to the browned grass, wiping everything clean. I haven't met Clint before, or Bennett either, though I've been hearing about them for at least a month. Clint's the hard-core prog-rock fan—King Crimson, Rush, and Yes. Bennett listens exclusively to the Grateful Dead, except when Clint and Colin force him not to. They grew up together, skinned knees and Tonka trucks, dirt and *Super Friends*. Colin and Bennett finished high school, Clint dropped out; Bennett and Colin went to SCCC, then they all hitchhiked to Maine. I can't imagine what it's like to have a real friend, let alone two, let alone for fifteen years. That's as long as I've been alive.

"Prepare yourself for the prog-rock onslaught," Colin says as we wind through the bare hills on the way to Clint's place. I've heard a little Yes before, so it's okay.

Clint lives right outside town, in a vinyl-sided house that's divided into apartments. It reminds me of some of the places my mom and I have lived. In the driveway there is an enormous ancient rusted Chevy van. "The Spacemobile," Colin says, and points to the space landscape mushroom stickers coating the back windows.

Clint answers the door, a big translucent purple plastic tube in his hand, half full with water. Before he says anything he exhales a giant cloud of weird-smelling smoke into our faces. I think it's pot. "Hey, man," Clint says to Colin, and then squints at my boobs. "Hey, manna," he says to me, and laughs.

Clint has slitty weasel eyes and a strawberry blond mullet, and also freckles. He's skinny and tall and wears a worn, black Jethro Tull shirt. He looks like a rat.

"C'mon in, folks," he says. "*Entree la casa.*"

His apartment is one room, filthy yellow linoleum kitchen in a corner, and then a brown plaid couch, a *Star Wars* blanket–covered bed, and about a zillion record albums. The walls have black light posters and a gigantic Canadian flag. "In tribute to Rush," Clint says when he sees me staring at it. I look at him, confused.

"They're *Canadian?*" he says like it's extremely obvious.

"Ah," I say.

He looks at me another beat, then laughs again.

Colin plops down on the bed. I want to sit with him, but I wonder if it's too weird for us to both be on the bed. I don't want to sit next to Clint, though.

"Well, have a seat," he says. I decide on the bed. Clint laughs. "Hot and heavy, huh, you two?" I blush.

Clint goes to the stereo and picks up an album. "Here. Some Canadian education for the young lady."

"The prog-rock assault begins," Colin says to me conspiratorially. Very complicated music comes on the stereo, with intense bass lines and a singer with a high, nasal voice.

"The great Geddy Lee," Clint says, handing the purple plastic tube to Colin. Colin pulls a Zippo from his pocket and lights a little bowl on the outside of the tube, pulling smoke up through the water. The tube clouds till it looks almost solid. Finally he pulls the bowl out, sucks the smoke in fast, and immediately starts coughing hard.

"Harsh!" Clint says, dissolving in laughter. Through the coughing, Colin cracks up too. It's definitely pot.

I've never seen pot, but when I was a really little kid I used to smell it. My dad would come and visit and they'd shut the door, tell me to stay outside and draw. I'd hear them laugh, and then it would get quiet. Other times the laughter would turn into yelling, and I couldn't tell what was a joke and what was really scary. After my dad stopped visiting for good, my mom quit smoking pot and started drinking wine. My mom said pot impeded her self-actualization. I was six when she told me that, so I just nodded.

Colin hands the purple thing back to Clint. Clint raises his eyebrows. "Aren't you skipping someone?" He looks at me.

"Oh," Colin says, like he hadn't even thought of it. He looks at me too. "Right."

"Did you—did you want some, Tess?" His voice is half gentle, half embarrassed to be gentle; it comes out sounding stiff.

Clint ping-pongs between the two of us, landing on me. "Wait. Dude. Have you never gotten high before?"

I shake my head.

"Well *I'll be*," Clint says in a fake redneck-y accent.

"We have ourselves a virgin on our hands," he says to Colin, leering. Immediately I feel very weird.

Colin inches close, leans in like Clint's not there, and makes that moment go away. In my head I say, *Thank you thank you thank you.*

"Tess, do you want some? You don't have to."

Somehow the fact that I don't have to do it makes me kind of want to.

"No, I'll have some. Sure."

Right away Colin gets excited like a kid. "Awe-*some.* Okay. Lesson number one. You hold the bong"—he hands me the purple tube—"and you light the bowl, and put your lips inside and pull as hard as you can without inhaling. Then you pull the bowl out and suck it all in at exactly the same moment. Got that?"

I look at him like, *Uh, not really, but I'll try.*

"Here, I'll light it for you."

I balance it on my knees and suck in while he lights.

"Pull, pull, pull," he says. "And"—he snaps the lighter off and pulls the bowl out—"Suck!" My lungs fill up with so much smoke, it's like they'll overflow, and I start coughing.

"Harsh!" Clint yells again, and it is. My lungs burn like crazy. Colin hands me his Mountain Dew. I gulp down the cold liquid sugar and let out a huge burp. Instead of being embarrassed, I crack up. So do they.

"You feel anything, Tessa?" Colin asks.

"Sometimes you don't feel it the first time," Clint says. "The THC's gotta build up in your system."

I search myself to see if I feel anything. I don't know. "Lemme try again," I say.

This time it doesn't hurt my lungs. Afterward I check myself for signs of feeling it. They watch me like a science experiment. Everyone in the room wants to know what's happening to me. It's kind of cool.

"How do I know if I feel it?"

"Look at the bedspread," Clint says, pointing to the spaceships. "Does it look . . . *special*?"

The bedspread does look less pilly and gross than it did before, the blue background more blue, the yellow stars more like space. I don't know if I'd go so far as to call it *special*, though. "Lemme try one more."

This time as soon as I exhale, my feet and legs get heavy and light at the same time, like the feeling right before your leg falls asleep, except it never crosses over into pins and needles. My whole body tickles from the inside, like TV static filling up every cell, rustling them against each other in a slow buzz. Suddenly I realize how much extra energy I've been using sitting up straight, propping open my eyelids, holding on and keeping it together. I flop back onto the bed, my muscles melting. "Whoa."

"All *right*!" Clint says, and turns the music up. Immediately I understand prog rock. The arrangements interlace with overwhelming complexity; I can hear every note's relationship to every other note. It's like a language, the music, or math: it seems incredible that people are capable of creating this. Behind my eyelids everything looks like Colin's space landscape T-shirt and the stickers on the back of Clint's van. Ground and gravity dissolve and I'm falling and floating, solid turned to liquid, mattress turned to air.

"Ah, the first time," Clint says to Colin, and I fall back farther.

I lie on the mattress for what feels like two hours; when I finally sit up, a third guy is on the couch. He's chubby and wears wire-rimmed glasses and a tie-dyed T-shirt with a dancing teddy bear on it. He has shortish brown hair and a face like a baby, soft where Clint is sharp. He's plucking out *Uncle John's Band* on a guitar; he looks up from the strings when I sit up. "Hey." He nods. "I'm Bennett."

"Hey."

Suddenly I'm starving, a black hole grumbling in my stomach. Clint orders us two pizzas, mushroom and pepperoni. They are the best thing I have ever eaten in my entire life. I polish off almost a whole one by myself and hardly even feel full.

Bennett hands Colin a Baggie half filled with thick

clumps of green pot. Clint checks it out. "Ah, the Kind," he says, "as the Deadheads would say." He laughs and looks at Bennett. Bennett rolls his eyes. Colin hands him money, slides the bag in his pocket.

"All right, we're gonna head out," Colin says, standing up and reaching for my hand.

"Have fun," Clint says, looking straight at me.

Clint's place is halfway to Colin's. On the way we listen to *Close to the Edge* by Yes.

"I am *so* glad you wanted to get stoned!" he says. "Are you?"

I'm a little groggy; I can't speak quite as easily as usual. But I manage to squeak out, "Totally. It was awesome." It was.

"I've been wanting to get you high *forever*. But I didn't want to bring it up, you know?"

"Kind of," I say.

"Well, you know, 'Just Say No' and all that. I wanted to make sure you wanted to do it for yourself. Wouldn't want any Peer Pressure." He makes an ooga-booga face and wiggles his fingers; I laugh.

"No, it was amazing." I want to describe it more, but I can't find the words.

"Well, it's a whole new world," he says, and turns up Yes.

. . . . .

When we get there, his place is cold, January air seeping through the cracks. I rub my arms, pick up a flannel off his floor.

"You won't need that for long," he says, pushing me back toward the bed with a smile. "I'll warm you up." He leans down on top and kisses me, then stands back up and pulls the bag out of his back pocket. He gets a pipe from the nightstand, rainbow swirly glass, packs it full and hands it over.

I'm not sure I can handle smoking more; my head's still heavy from before. But he seems eager in a way I haven't seen him, and I don't feel like I can let him down. I don't want to make his happiness go away. I take the pipe.

"You'll love it," he whispers in my ear as I light the bowl. "It makes it so amazing," and I can tell by the way he says it that he's talking about sex. I'm overwhelmed imagining those two things put together, so cut loose and open, so far from any solid ground. I don't know what would keep me from coming apart.

He breathes near my ear; it feels good but also kind of creepy. "Make sure and inhale," he says. "With the pipe you have to kind of try and swallow it."

I do, and then I cough.

"Good," he says. "That means you got some."

He takes a hit, and then another one, then hands it

back to me. After I inhale once more, he takes the bowl from my hands, sets it on the nightstand, and pulls me down onto the bed.

I'm looking for that good staticky feeling from before, the one like TV snow inside my skin, but all I feel is spinning. Colin's pressing on me from above; his mouth takes up my entire universe, and it's hard to breathe. He's so into it I can't say anything. I don't want to interrupt. I make a little sound, hoping he'll be able to tell that I feel panicky. I want him to ask if I'm okay, give me a little space to breathe, tell him I'm scared, that I need to slow down, but I think he takes it different because it makes him kiss me harder. His hands run down my hips, pressing them down into the bed. My heart is beating super fast.

He always feels more than I do—I can tell. His body shudders and he shuts his eyes, lost in some place that's a mystery to me. Sometimes I wish I was lost with him, just so I could keep him nearby. I wonder what it would feel like to be lost too. But now I am, cut loose and spinning, and I don't feel any closer to him. It's just scary, the blur of my thoughts and the weight of his breath, the closed-in feeling of underneath and underwater. It makes me feel like I'm alone.

He opens his eyes to take my shirt off, but he doesn't stop to look at me. Then he flips us over.

On top of him I'm freezing, but at least I can

breathe. The air pricks my skin; I arch backward, shivering. He makes a noise. I try it again; he makes a noise again. And suddenly I realize: I can make him feel things by how I make myself look. That's how you do it. That's the way that I can keep him close. A little chill runs up my spine, and I wonder if it's what "turned on" feels like. It's different from what he's feeling, I can tell, but maybe that's the difference between guys and girls. I don't know.

I lean over him, twist my spine and make a sound. It works again; he goes trembly underneath me and I feel a power that I've never felt before. He's like a puppet. It's so easy.

I've never been the one who could make people do things: it's always been somebody else besides me who's in charge. My dad can drive away and never write and I just have to live with it. My mom can pack us up and put us in the car; she can come home at four a.m. or never; she can get what she wants from anyone with a flick of her eyes or a lilt of her voice, and then tell me what to do and I have to do it. I guess part of that's being a kid, that you have to do what grown-ups say, but it also always felt like part of it had to do with me, like I was a branch and the world was the wind, and I just had to bend where it blew me. I didn't ever know how I could be the force that made things move.

Colin is an adult, but now he's the one on puppet

strings. Not me. I'm pulling them. For the first time in my life. He finishes and melts into the sheets. "Didn't I tell you it was amazing? Was I right?" he says.

"Totally," I say, and smile.

Seventeen

· · ·

Hold your learning in the innermost chamber of your heart, where nothing but the Divine can enter.

I've seen Avinashi a few times since that day at the Amrit; she just sits and sucks her braid and watches while I eat or get a cushion for the Program. She doesn't try to talk to me. Sanjit's gotten string-bean tall in the last couple months, his Adam's apple showing. Meer still hasn't hit puberty, and across the cafeteria I can see him get more puffed-up and hostile each day that goes by without a growth spurt.

I'm scraping the remains of breakfast into the compost bin, the world warmly blurred by this morning's wake-and-bake, when Sanjit and Meer come up to me. I put one hand in my pocket on the little bag of weed that Colin gave me, paranoid it'll fall out. My jeans are tight enough that it's not really realistic, but I want to be sure.

I've never had an interaction with someone who didn't know that I was stoned. Colin always pays the pizza guy; not me. Everything inside is so intense I can't see myself from outside; I don't remember how I'm supposed to act.

"Hi," I say to them, just standing there. I'm sure my eyes are red.

"Hey," Sanjit says. "We had a question."

Meer looks up from under his eyebrows, like a bodyguard.

"Yeah?" I scrape tofu-scramble off my plate. It seems to take forever to get the little bits from my fork to the bin. They tangle with tamari and sprouts, clump together. It's sort of fascinating.

"Where are you always going in that van?"

My head snaps up and I completely forget about the tofu bits. It's like someone changed the channel in my brain.

"What are you talking about?" I look straight ahead.

"That van. The red one. We've seen you drive around in it. And a couple months ago it dropped you off at main entrance once."

"Late," Meer says.

Oh shit oh shit oh shit. I knew I'd have to make up a story eventually, but I was expecting it to be for Devanand. I know how to talk to him, at least sort of; these kids are an unknown variable. My thoughts whir. They're staring and I'm starting to sweat, and I have to steer the ship, even if I steer it wrong.

Finally I say, "It's *seva*."

"Huh?" Sanjit says, highly skeptical.

"I know, it's weird, right?" I scramble. "But the Guru has me doing special *seva* errands for the kitchen up at Guru's quarters."

"At night?" Meer asks.

"Yeah, sometimes even at night. You'd be amazed when he gets hungry. He eats so much!" I laugh. "Sometimes he wants junk food. Cheez-Its are his favorite. Usually, he'd send a kitchen *sevite*, but my mom's important up at Guru's quarters, so—" I drop the end off the sentence, like they should know what that means. It means I'm special. And that I get to do what I want. And that they shouldn't question me.

"Wow," Meer says, impressed.

"Cool," Sanjit says.

"Yeah," I say, and turn to walk away.

That mostly sobered me up, but I still need to be alone until the wake-and-bake wears all the way off. Problem is, when I get back to the room my mom is there. And not only is she there, she's wearing my Walkman. Not only is she wearing my Walkman, she's listening to my tapes. Holy shit.

I keep Green Tea Experience wrapped up separate, but she was in my stuff, so there's no guarantee she didn't see it. I scan the bed, breath high in my throat. "Pretty in Pink," "Upstairs At Eric's," "Modern English," "Kiss Me Kiss Me Kiss Me." By some miracle, Green Tea's not there. Thank god. It's enough to make me believe in the sublime intelligence of the universe.

But then I get closer, and I see what she's got in the Walkman. It's worse. It's worse than if she found my dad's tape. She's got the mix tape that Colin made for me last week, the one with *Sweet Emotion* and *Heart of Gold* and *Kiss Off* by the Violent Femmes. Every single song that's ever been a part of our relationship is on that tape. And my mom is listening to it. My entire life could come crashing down right now.

I don't worry whether she'll be able to tell I'm stoned. I have larger concerns. "What the hell are you doing?"

She pulls off the headphones. "Well, this is a very nice collection of music, Tessa."

"Yeah. It's mine," I say.

"Did someone make this for you? It's not your handwriting on the label." Thank god I hid the case; it says *Love, Colin.*

"No."

"Well, is that your handwriting?"

"Yeah." It's obviously not, but what's she going to say?

"What, your handwriting changed?"

"Yeah."

She sighs and puts the headphones back on.

"What are you *doing?*" I can't stand that she is listening to it. "That's *mine!*"

She puts her fake-serene smiley face on, trying to prove a point. "Oh, yeah? Who bought this Walkman for you?"

"*I did!*"

"Oh." There's a pause while she figures out her strategy. "Well, I'm your mother, Tessa. And I have the right to know what you're listening to."

"Why?"

"Because I'm your *mother.* I don't need another reason."

It's such bullshit. She spends her entire life trying to get away from me so she can have her adventures and pretend she doesn't have a kid, and then she suddenly pulls this "mom" crap. She's never even here. "That's bullshit, Mom. You're never even here!"

She's stung, but then she comes up with an excuse. She always does. "Tessa, when I'm not here I'm at work. Doing *seva* and spiritual practice, just like a job. That doesn't change the fact that I'm your mother. I'm allowed to know what music you're listening to."

"Why do you even *care?*" I yell. The calmer she acts, the madder it makes me. And the madder it makes me, the calmer she acts.

Her voice stays steady. "It's important for me to check in sometimes." Like she's some kind of responsible mom.

She is so self-satisfied I can't believe it. So convinced she's totally right, even though she is completely wrong. And she is so close to my most important and most secret things. The thought of just the cells from her skin on Colin's tape makes me furious. My palms throb; I want to throw her stuff across the room. I want to run out of this place and slam the door. I want to reach down and rip my Walkman off her.

She looks at me beatifically. I glare at her, exhale hard like a bull snorting, then turn and leave her sitting on the bed. I swear two things: One, I am finding that journal of hers and seeing how *she* feels when I dig through her private stuff. And two, I am hiding everything that means anything to me from this day forward. So deep that she can never find it.

After an afternoon with Colin I feel better, even though we had to go to Burger King with Clint and Bennett in the Spacemobile, which meant an hour-and-a-half discussion of Emerson, Lake & Palmer's 1978 tour. Afterward, though, we went back to Colin's van and had sex. When we were done, Colin went to find his T-shirt in the back, and I put on the eye shadow I appropriated from my mom. In the rearview mirror I looked just like a girl in someone's music video: not just pretty. Hot.

Colin and I are in love. We haven't said it, but he keeps saying things like *I care about you* and *I like you so much* that are almost like *love*. And he signed the mix, "*Love, Colin.*" And anyway, I know it's true. My mom always said when it's love you just *know*, with every fiber of your being; it just takes you over, changes everything, and you don't have to think about it at all. I was always confused because she used to say she was completely and utterly in love with my dad, but when he visited they would scream at each other during *Sesame Street* and she would throw things at him, and now she says he's dead to us. I never really got how that could be love. She said it was mysterious.

Now I have my own love, and it is better than hers. It takes me over, every fiber of my being, and I *know*, just like she said; but Colin and I don't scream or throw things, ever. We've never even had a fight. It's sort of amazing that I'm only fifteen and I already know how to be in love better than my mom.

When Colin drops me off by Atma Lakshmi, I sway my hips walking down the path. He whistles out the window; I laugh and shake my hair, long enough to swing between my shoulder blades.

On my way into the lobby, Ninyassa grabs my arm and stops me. My heart bangs.

"Um, Tessa? Could you come over here a minute? I'd like to have a word with you."

Shit.

She takes me behind the front desk, past the flower arrangements into a little office. Pictures of the beard guy, files, wood paneling, desk.

"Sorry to take up your time. I, ah, just wondered if I could speak with you."

"Sure."

"I'd like to tell you something."

"Okay."

"Well, there have—there have been some complaints."

"O-*kay*," I say, like, *Go on*. She doesn't. "What kind of complaints?"

She makes a face like something smells. "Well, Tessa. I assume you may have heard of the Guru's recent decrees regarding relations between men and women?"

I am not giving her any more information than whatever she already has. "Um, sort of?"

"Okay. Well, the Guru has given us some . . . shall we say, *parameters*. For example, I assume you've noticed men and women sit separately at programs now."

"Yeah?"

"These parameters are meant to deepen our practice."

"Yeah?"

"And—"

"Yes?" My face is hot.

"Well, it's come to my attention that you've become, shall we say, sort of a *distraction*. Which, given the new decrees from the Guru, has made *sadhana* a little more difficult for some of our devotees."

Wait. What is she talking about? "What do you mean?"

"Well." She nods down to my sweater, which I stole from my mom. It's thin purple wool and fits me perfectly. I like the way it makes my boobs look. "For example."

"What, my sweater?"

"Well, and those jeans are quite tight."

I don't say anything.

"And the makeup."

I'm wearing blue eye shadow and frosty pink lipstick. My mom doesn't use makeup anymore, so she never notices when I steal hers. Today I wore mascara for the first time. Mascara is amazing.

"There have been complaints that it's disrupting focus for—some of the men."

"Wow." I don't know what to say.

"Yes." She just looks at me.

"So," she starts again, "it would be appreciated if you would exercise more modesty. Particularly as there is a festival beginning in a few days, and devotees will be arriving from around the country."

"Well, I don't—"

She interrupts. "The Guru would appreciate it." She looks at me with raised eyebrows and a stern mouth. I'm not going to get anywhere by arguing.

I walk through Main Building toward the Amrit, face burning. First of all, how dare Ninyassa tell me what to wear? Second of all, these stupid goddamn assholes gossiped and complained behind my back, like I did something wrong, when all I did was wear my clothes. But third: I "distracted" grown-up men who I don't even know. Hot shame mixes with a flush of power, and I feel small and dirty, proud and strong, all at exactly the same time. At the Amrit register, the pimply cashier stares at me too long; I blush. My body feels somehow too obvious, announcing itself even through the wool of my sweater and the denim of my jeans.

The next morning, the beard guy's in solitary meditation preparing for the festival, so my mom and Vrishti aren't up there cooking, which means I have to eat with them. Today we're having tofu steaks for breakfast. I don't really see how it can be steak if it's tofu, but whatever. I don't look at my mom; I don't want to talk about my goddamn mix tape that she ruined for me, or anything else. She doesn't talk to me either. Vrishti is glowing.

"Guhahita," she says meaningfully, and squeezes my mom's hand.

My mom looks up from her tofu steak.

"I—I have to tell you something."

My mom tilts her head like a curious dog. "What is it, Vrishti?"

Vrishti's breathless. She lowers her voice to almost a whisper. "Okay, you can't tell anyone I told you this." She looks at me. "You too."

"Okay."

Vrishti turns back to my mom. "I'm supposed to keep it secret. But—I have to share. But swear it. You won't tell." ·2 2 3.

Christ, they're sounding like popular girls again.

"I swear," my mom says, leaning in, eager. "What is it?"

"The Guru—has asked for a companion."

My mom suddenly gets very still.

"And they've been evaluating several candidates—"

My mom gets even stiller.

"And apparently I'm in the final round."

"Wow," my mom says carefully. "What kind of companion are they talking about?"

"Well, I mean, nothing *non-yogic*, of course." Vrishti rushes on like white water, oblivious to my mom's stick-straight spine. "It would be within the laws of celibacy. But, you know, *companionship*. Be in his presence, assist with things, you know. That kind of stuff."

"Wow," my mom says again. "And you're in the final round, huh?" There's a hint of an edge in her voice, but not mean or sharp; more like she knows something that Vrishti doesn't.

"Yes." Vrishti beams. "Isn't it amazing? I mean, I don't know what kind of karma I must have to be in this position. I just feel so *blessed*. God, it feels so good to tell someone."

"That's fantastic, Vrishti. Really, what an honor," my mom says, smooth as silk, a tiny bitter smile on her lips.

Eighteen

· · ·

The seeker must also be a warrior, fiercely fighting
the lure of subjective emotion.

Vasant Panchami is a festival that's apparently supposed to mark the beginning of spring. It's ten degrees out here, but maybe it's warmer in India. Devotees come from all over the country and everyone dresses in yellow, which is supposedly the color of the goddess Saraswati, whose birthday this supposedly is, and they all fly kites. Show me someone who flies a kite in January in upstate New York, and I will show you someone celebrating another country's holidays. The good thing is that Saraswati is the goddess of music, so the musicians play all day and everybody chants.

My mom is off somewhere doing something, as usual, so I'm going to the introductory celebrations on my own. I put on a yellow leotard and rust-colored cords and pull out my weed, sealed in a Baggie wrapped in a handkerchief and then a scarf, stuffed into a sock and then a sneaker, stashed in the back corner of my closet with all the other things that matter. My tapes, my weed, my Walkman, Green Tea Experience, Colin's flannel: all hidden, tucked away where she can never find them. Almost as hidden as the person I've become.

I blow smoke out the window screen, cold air doubling back to bite my skin, and once I'm high I head out to Shanti Kutir. I walk up and over and out through the courtyard of gods, which is a very cool environment to be in stoned. The brass statues twinkle, Gandhi leaning forward on his walking stick, Ganesh waving elephant arms, Buddha closed-eyed and serene, fresh flower garlands insisting spring against the January air. The last snatches of a rainbow sand mandala drift with the wind on the ground. For a minute I think I could be happy here, if it weren't for all the ashram people. And my mom.

As soon as I round the bend I see the mass of devotees, the crowd a single yellow organism pulsing against the white sky. Whoa. One second I'm just me, a single person, and then the next I'm part of that breathing yellow mass, bodies packed together tight enough that it doesn't even feel cold. Familiar faces mix with new ones and I give myself over, letting myself move with the crowd down the hill. At the bottom I grab a cushion, drop off my shoes, and sit in the middle of everyone, far away from the Guru's special circle in the front.

In the throng of unfamiliar faces I'm just another girl in yellow. Not Guhahita's daughter or Devanand's *sevite* or the girl who wears tight clothes. Just me, anonymous, myself. The drone starts; I close my eyes. The music is amazing stoned, finger cymbals tinkling crystalline; it's just as mathematical as Rush and Yes but more organic, less American. Plus we get to sing along, which you can't do with prog rock. The chant kicks in: the sounds start in my chest, move toward my mouth, and as they leave my lips they rise from the huge crowd like a giant cloud, drifting up into the air above us, hovering. All the ashram stuff drops away, all of everybody's individual bullshit everything, and we're just one knot of people, tied together with invisible threads of harmony and melody, chords and counterpoint, riding the chant like a river, this huge and beautiful thing made up of all of us.

I chant for hours and the stoned turns into something clearer, just as high but clean as water, streaming up through my spine to the spot between my eyes. The music speeds up and slows down, speeds up and slows down, and when it finally curls around itself and goes to sleep, I feel more awake than ever. I'm not thinking about anything, and nothing hurts. I flow outside with the crowd, hardly noticing when I get jostled or pushed forward, just trying to breathe in and out and in and out and keep the feeling going.

By the time I get to Atma Lakshmi, it's settled into a warm buzz between my eyebrows, encircling my skin. I climb up in Colin's van and kiss him on the mouth, look bright and straight into his eyes. "Hey," he says, catching a contact high, and kisses me again. "Hey."

"Hey," I say, and laugh. I lean back, leave my seat belt off. "Where we going?"

I want to have sex, but we have to go to Clint's first; Colin's out of weed. We knock and no one answers, so
we just go in. "Led Zeppelin II" is blaring; Clint and Bennett are on the couch, heads back, eyes closed, mouths open.

"This is some good shit," Clint says when he finally lifts his head and notices we're there.

I'm still bright and open from the chanting; everything seems beautiful, even Clint and Bennett. We smoke and it *is* good shit, strong without the blurry, and I sit on the floor, look for a long time at a space landscape poster of green-and-blue-rock arches rising out of water. Then I shift my gaze to the three guys on the couch—friends as long as I've been alive, they know each other inside out, what to laugh at, what to listen to, all that shared history I can hardly imagine. My body feels loose and open and connected to the rest of me.

"You guys are beautiful, you know that?"

They all lift their heads and look at me at once. It's like something from a Three Stooges movie; I crack up. Colin and Bennett turn to each other, wondering what's so funny. Clint just looks at me.

"You're beautiful too, Tessa, you know *that*?"

I smile. "Thanks, Clint."

"Sure." He smiles back.

My muscles fill with feeling and I feel like lying down, so I do, on the floor, stretch against the rough carpet, arms over my head, toes curling.

"Just *beautiful*," Clint says.

Bennett chuckles to himself and flips the record · 2 2 9 . over. *Whole Lotta Love* comes on and the guitars mix with the stretching in my muscles; it feels super good, molecules moving against each other, my leotard and the carpet and the music and the air. I wiggle around.

When I open my eyes all the guys are watching me. "I gotta get some water," Bennett says suddenly, and goes over to the yellow kitchen.

"You really are," Clint says. He turns to Colin. "She really is."

Colin gives him less than half a smile. Clint keeps his eyes on me but talks to Colin: "You are one lucky man, man." Bennett comes back with a Big Gulp and plops on the couch, watching me like a TV.

I can tell they think I'm hot. And not like the weird gross old "distracted" guys at the ashram, a cloud of embarrassed and Ninyassa hanging over it, but like Colin does, the way that's strong, that gives me power. I squirm against the floor again, testing it out. Clint and Bennett laugh.

"This is awesome, man," Clint tells Colin.

"C'mon, Tess, we better go," Colin tells me.

In the van, he is mad.

"What the fuck was that?" he says.

"What do you mean?" We're still high.

"You can't do that, Tess."

"Do what?"

"You know what."

I sort of do and sort of don't. "No I don't."

He makes a martyr noise, like he doesn't want to explain but he will because I'm making him. "You can't—roll around on the floor like that."

"Why?"

"Jesus, Tessa, are you playing dumb?"

I guess I am a little bit, but I also don't see what's so wrong. I was just feeling good and being beautiful, and they appreciated it. It's natural. "What's wrong with it?"

"You can't act like that in front of guys."

"Why? I act like that in front of *you*. A lot more than that!" I tease, expecting him to laugh. He doesn't.

"Guys—have reactions to that stuff."

"So?" I can tell he's getting frustrated, but I just don't think there's any reason to. It's not like I'm going to cheat on him with Clint and Bennett, for god's sake.

"That's okay. It's natural."

He makes a noise. "Yeah, I know it's natural. But they're my *friends*. And you're my——" He trails off.

Is he going to say *girlfriend*? "I'm your what?"

"You're my girlfriend, Tess."

He's never said that before. I flush with pride.

"I am?" I nuzzle up to him, breathe on his neck.

"Yes, Tessa, you are, okay?" He seems exasperated. Which is weird.

"Good. That's really good." I smile at him and squeeze his arm.

But he doesn't touch me back; he just says, "Okay," and fiddles with his keys. I try to catch his eyes with mine, but he won't let me.

My heart starts beating and my mind gets panicky. I don't know why, but I have to get his gaze back. He has to look at me.

I rub his knee, seductive. "I'm glad that I'm your girlfriend, Colin."

"That's great. I'm glad too. Okay?" I go higher up his thigh. But he won't stop being distant. And my mind won't stop racing.

I have to give myself a reason he won't look at me, something that's not about him being mad or not wanting me or wishing he could leave. I have to tell myself something good or I'm going to panic and everything will suffocate. *Maybe he's mad because he's jealous of them*, I tell myself. *Maybe that means that he loves me.*

And then it hits me. There is no better time than now.

"I love you, Colin."

His eyes widen; he almost looks scared. It dangles out there like a raindrop on a twig, swelling and swelling before it drops. The moment stretches out, and I get terrified. He's not going to say it back. This is horrible. It's the worst moment of my whole entire life. But then he runs his fingers through his hair, looks out the window, like his normal self.

"Look. I love you too. Whatever. Just don't act like that in front of them, okay?"

He said *I love you too*. I will do anything he asks me to. "Okay."

He's quiet the whole ride home, but I just watch the road and play it over and over in my head like it's a tape. *Look. I love you too. I love you too. I love you too.*

The cafeteria's packed like a can of tuna. Chanting pipes through tinny speakers, and the line for food is very very long. There are so many brand-new blank-canvas faces that I'm surprised to recognize one. Jayita's even thinner than before, jawbones jutting out, elbows sharp. She sees me and doubles back, beelining with her tray. There's nowhere to go: slow-moving devotees with trays of tempeh stroganoff surround me on all sides and I can't move. Skinny, she slips through the cracks in the crowd.

"Tessa," she says when she gets close. "How are you?"

"Uh, I'm fine?" I haven't talked to her in months.

"Good. That's good. Listen," she says, jumpy. "I think you're smart."

"Thanks," I say.

"Yeah. You're a smart girl. You know right from wrong."

I have no idea what to say to that. "Okay."

"So I think—I think maybe you should talk to your mother."

"What—what do you mean?"

"I think you should talk to your mother," she says again, without explaining. "He's"—she stops, then starts again—"he thinks there are no consequences. But giving up your will, it's—it's dangerous." She looks down, almost like she's talking to herself. "It's not an illusion." She shakes her head, grim. "I don't think it's an illusion."

Part of me wants more than anything to ask her

what she's talking about, but part of me really does not want to know.

After dinner my mom's still out somewhere, so I dig in her nightstand drawer. I have a sick feeling in my throat, and I want to see that journal. I sift through stray earrings and half-crumpled scraps of paper, but it's not there. I lean over the edge of the bed, check under it, beneath her pillow. No dice.

In the Burger King lot, I want to talk to Colin about everything.

"I talked to Jayita," I tell him.

"Oh yeah?" He raises his eyebrows. "Cool."

"It wasn't, actually," I say. "It was actually super creepy. She's really skinny now and kind of—I don't know, kind of intense. And she came straight up to me and told me I should talk to my mom. Twice. Isn't that weird?" I want him to tell me what it means, what I should think.

"Yeah," he says. "Weird. Well, you know those people are weird, Tess," and he turns up the volume on Cream. "Man, Clapton, man," he says, shaking his head at the guitar solo.

"Yeah, but don't you think that's kind of strange?"

I press him. "I mean, more than usual?"

"I don't know, Tess, how would I know? All those people are crazies. She was probably wearing some white robe and a red dot on her forehead, for god's sake. You can't think about it too much."

It's true: she *was* wearing a white robe and a red dot on her forehead. But she's still a person. I don't like Colin saying those people are just crazy. My mom is one of "those people."

"Yeah, I guess. She's just my mom, you know?"

"Well, sure." He pauses.

I'm about to start talking again, but he goes on. "But at some point you've gotta have your own life. I mean, look at me. I don't go around stressing out about my parents. And believe me, I could." He snorts. "But, you know. They do their thing, I do mine."

"Right." I wish I could feel that relaxed. Maybe you have to be twenty for that. "Right," I say again.

He turns the volume up more, till it's too loud to have a conversation. "Poor Tess," he says, and reaches for me, hands sliding up my shirt. "C'mere."

That night at Clint's I just want to get back to the ashram. I want to see my mom, stand on the solid ground of her eyes and cheeks and mouth. Even though I hate her. I drink Mountain Dew from a Smurfs glass. Caffeine mixes with the weed and I imagine Evening Program happening right now, all those visitors packed into Shanti Kutir, sitar and chanting and special *prasad* for Vasant Panchami, and I am antsy to be missing it.

We are listening to "Drums and Space," which is the section of a Grateful Dead show where they make strange non-melodic noises on their instruments for approximately an hour. They do it at every single show. This particular "Drums and Space" is from a show at Veterans Memorial Coliseum, I've been informed by Bennett, which was "legendary." I don't even know where Veterans Memorial Coliseum is. "Drums and Space" is making me uptight.

Clint is sitting too close to me on the couch, and I can't scooch over because Colin is right up on the other side. They both have their eyes closed. Once in a while the Dead make a particularly weird noise and Bennett says, "Oh, man!" Clint seems to be moving closer to me, and I can't tell if it's real or just the weed, but I keep feeling more and more smushed. I don't think Colin notices.

"Hey." I finally nudge him, whispering, "Hey, Colin, will you drive me home?"

He's super stoned, but he says yes. "I hate 'Drums and Space' anyway." He grins at me when we're outside, out of Bennett's earshot. I'm relieved: at the smile, the ride home, the cold and open air. It was getting hard to breathe in there. I roll down the window and let the freezing air stream in.

I get there just as Evening Program's ending. Throngs of people swarm around me, searching for their shoes. I just stand there like a rock in the middle of a stream. Sanjit weaves near me in the crowd, head bobbing on his Adam's apple neck; he's with a bunch of other kids my age, strangers. They're here for the festival. Some are pale and weird like him and Meer, but most of them are normal: ripped jeans, hippie skirts, bandannas. They're laughing. They all act like friends. A feeling rises up in my throat that I don't even know the name of, and suddenly I feel so tired, more tired than I ever have in my entire life. I want to be one of them. I want to not have to lie and not have to be alone and not have to be sexy and not have to be cool anymore. I want to laugh with other kids. I want to be a kid.

When I turn around I'm face-to-face with Avinashi; she's arm-in-arm with a black-haired girl in a Pac-Man T-shirt. The girl looks nice. Avinashi looks happy.

I have this impulse to tell them about Colin. It's right at the edge of my lips. I'd tell them and they'd giggle, "Oh my god!" and ask all about it, if I'm anxious or happy, confused or in love. They'd ask me what it feels like, what we do. If it ever scares me. If it ever feels too big. If the secret ever feels too huge to keep. I'd tell them and they'd say, *Wow*, and let me spill all of it, and we'd stay up late like at a slumber party, and my secret would be outside of me and I could breathe again.

But I know that if I actually did it that's not what would happen. If I actually did it, their faces would fall, go dark like they just swallowed something sour. They'd say, *That's wrong, you know. He's way too old. You mean you've been lying all this time?* And then they'd go tell someone, pull an ace out from the teetering, fragile house of cards I've built, and make it all smash on the floor.

I swallow everything and walk away.

Nineteen

. . .

As the ego is destroyed, great pain arises.
Beyond that pain is the true self.

My mom's going to be gone overnight, working for the festival; she'll be back before breakfast tomorrow. It's the first thing she's said to me in a week. I don't know why she announced it; usually she just waits till she thinks I'm sleeping, then leaves.

I looked for that journal two more times, combed the room before the cleaning lady came, but nothing's turned up. I still don't know where my mom goes most of the time, and we still don't talk about anything. She's changed, though; I can tell. Since that day with Vrishti she's turned inward and inward till all she is is one big secret. She's getting thinner, like Jayita, and that waterfall thing doesn't ever happen anymore—the warm flood of joy that used to fill her up sometimes is gone. Her eyes are dull, except when they dart around and wheels spin in her head. She's like a shell made out of chants and prayers and secrets. I almost even miss hearing about her spiritual journey, just to have her talk to me. But she won't talk about anything, and there's nothing I can tell her.

In the row of pay phone booths, I spin on the black plastic stool. A glass wall folds me in; I know no one can hear me.

Colin picks up. "Hello?"

"Hey there," I say, sneakers pressed against the phone booth wall.

"Hey." His voice curls into a smile. "What's up?"

"Oh, nothing," I say. "Except that my mom's out all night tonight."

There's a pause. "Really?" he says.

"Yes, really."

"Hmm."

"Yes, hmm."

"So what are you proposing?"

Colin says the best feeling known to man is waking up in someone's arms. He says there's nothing like it. It's weird to think of how he found that out, but he is twenty. I can't expect a clean slate. And the weirdness goes away when he says to me: *I wish that I could wake up in your arms.*

"You wanna wake up in my arms?"

He laughs. "Yeah. Totally. Your place or mine?"

· · · · ·

I decided my place. It feels safer somehow than sneaking out to his house overnight. No one can see me come or go, watch me pull up in the van. All we have to worry about is smuggling him into the room, and then we're golden. There's the lobby and the stairs, or there's the fire escape. The lobby and the stairs both have the risk of people, but the fire escape's back by the parking lot. If we wait till dark no one will see.

I skip dinner, stomach jumping; run up to my room to get ready. I've never spent the night with someone, and I realize all I have is pajamas and big T-shirts. Shit. ·241· You're supposed to wear a negligee. I head for my mom's dresser drawers. The top drawer is underwear; she does have some lacy stuff, but that's too gross. I dig through, looking for something else, I don't know what, when my fingers hit paper. I pull out a purple card with a laven-der mandala on the front. Inside it says, *"Guhahita Prapati: who lives in a secret place in my heart. Only surrender. Guruji."*

It makes me feel gross, even though it's just a card. I hold it at the edges like it could get my hands dirty, slip it back beneath her bras. I root through the other draw-ers, trying to think about clothes. In the last drawer, there's a nightgown. It's short and sheer and is made of silk from India. I put it on. It fits. I wear my orange underwear, plain cotton but at least bikinis, and go to put on makeup.

When he knocks on the window, I'm in bed waiting. I wish he could've just climbed in like Romeo and seen me with the covers perfectly arranged, but the window's locked. I open the latch and lift it; then there's a screen. "You have to get the screen off from the inside," he whispers, not noticing my negligee.

"How?"

"See the screws at the corners? You have to undo them."

"I don't have a screwdriver!"

"Shit."

I stand there freezing, waiting for him to come up with something.

"Okay." He thinks. "How about a tweezers?"

My mom has a tweezers in her makeup bag. I run and get it.

It works; I lift the screen out of the window, and he crawls in. After he brushes off and closes the window, he finally sees me. "Wow." He looks me up and down. "Beautiful."

I beam. He swoops me up like a 1950s bride over the threshold. It surprises me: I kick my feet and giggle, cracking up all the way to my mom's bed. He lays me down; my heart is pounding. There's only a thin wall between us and the rest of the ashram. Good thing I locked the door from inside.

It feels strange to be in my territory, closer somehow. At his house I'm separate from the rest of my life; eventually I always leave and come back to this place he's never seen before. But now he's inside it, inside the rest of my life, inside me, and there's no place to go back to, nowhere that's just mine: he's everywhere. It feels scary and a little crowded, but also brave. This is what being in love is like, I think—letting a person in the most you can, into every corner of yourself, not keeping anything reserved. "I love you," I whisper into his eyes above me, out on a limb of a tree I didn't even know existed.

Afterward we get stoned and then do it again; finally, we fall asleep. I sleep light, dreams high on the surface of my mind; and the moment dawn starts to peek through the curtains, I'm wide awake. "Hey. You have to go," I whisper loudly, rustling his shoulder.

"Mmm, wait," he says without opening his eyes. "Lie back down."

I almost forgot: waking up in his arms. I lie down on my side, stomach pressed against him. He puts both arms around me. I'm already awake, but it *is* pretty good. I'm about to drift off when I hear voices in the hall.

"Okay," I say, almost shaking him. "You *have* to go."

He rubs his eyes, bleary, smiling. "Do I *have* to?"

"Yes."

That crowded feeling from last night is worse now, running underneath my skin. My mom said *before break-fast*. Every set of footsteps in the hall sounds like hers, and I'm completely sure we are going to get caught.

"Nah," he says, shuts his eyes, rolls over toward me. "Just another minute."

I jostle him again; he doesn't move. I lie there for a second, watching the ceiling. I'm starting to get panicky. I want my room back, clean and empty, free of the thick risk of his presence. He's twenty. If he gets caught, it doesn't really matter. His parents won't get mad; nobody would give him any consequences. But I'm fif-teen; that's three years until I'm on my own. It would ruin my entire life. It almost makes me mad at him, that he doesn't think about that, that he's not looking out for me. I wait another minute. It seems like a year.

"Okay," I finally say, out loud this time. "You gotta go."

He yawns, moans, sits up. Thank god. His clothes are sprawled out on the floor, and he takes his sweet time gathering them. In the meantime I fold my mom's negligee, slip it back in her drawer, and pull a T-shirt on. He's putting on his sweater when I hear my mom's voice, chanting. Shit.

"*Colin*," I stage-whisper. "That's my mom."

He raises his eyebrows. "Where?" he whispers back.

"Down the hall. You gotta get out of here. Now."

He stuffs his feet into his sneakers, starts to tie them. "Leave it," I say. "Don't lace them up. Just go." I hear her voice again, closer. I'm sweating. He's hustling. I feel like the walls of everything are closing in on me. I push him toward the window and out onto the fire escape, his spine hard beneath my fingers. When he gets out he turns to kiss me, crouching down. "Bye," he says. "I had fun."

"Me too," I say, not sure if it's true. "Go go go." And he's gone. I grab the screen, start screwing it back in as my mom's key turns in the lock.

She cracks open the door, but the second lock catches it, the chain we never use. "Oh," she says. ·245.

"Hang on," I call. I turn the last screw. "Coming."

When I unlock the chain a gust of cold air blows through from the crosscurrent. "Brr," my mom says. "The window's open!"

"Yeah," I say, thinking fast. "I wanted some fresh air to wake me up."

"Why'd you do the chain?" she asks. "We never do the chain."

"I don't know," I say, buying time.

"Well, there must've been *some* reason."

"I was nervous sleeping here without you," is what I finally come up with.

"Really?" she says absently. Like she's going through the motions.

"Yeah."

"Well. See? Nothing happened. You were fine."

I don't say anything.

"Right?"

"Yeah. Yeah, I was fine."

I'm exhausted, but she makes me go with her to the Temple for some special prayer. She says it's a purifying practice and it's necessary for me spiritually. I don't know why she even cares. She's always gone and gone and gone, right up till I need to be alone, and then she suddenly shows up and makes me go someplace with her. She's got big black smudges of mascara underneath her eyes, left over from last night it looks like, like a junkie or a rock star. I haven't seen makeup on her in months.

At the Temple, you have to wear a skirt and cover your shoulders: by the shoe cubbies they have a bunch of huge plain black skirts with elastic waistbands, and also shawls. I put on both and look like a Quaker from the eighteenth century.

"Go on in and sit," she says. "I have to help get ready."

The Temple is a small octagonal room with a giant gleaming gold statue of the beard guy in the middle, heaped with pink orchids and roses. Everyone sits in concentric circles and has loud breathing experiences. There's no place to look that's not intense. The beard guy, the real one, is here, and he stares straight at me, eyes poking through my skin to the inside. I wish I could be in a plain white room, alone, no statues or flowers or energy, no stories or lies. I close my eyes and try to listen to the quiet, but then the finger cymbals start.

My mom comes in, waving an incense tray, singing a chant, Vrishti beside her, two other women behind. At the start of the verse, my mom messes up the words. Right away the beard guy's face clouds and he yells, "Stop!"

They stop.

He turns right to my mom, picking her out. "What is this sloppiness?" His face looks like when I saw him with Jayita.

"What is this sloppiness?" he yells louder.

One woman holds her breath; another tries to blend into the carpet.

My mom steps forward. "Guruji," she says, giving him a weird and private look, "come on now, of course we're doing the best that we know how."

He draws his neck back. "What did you say?"

Everyone else in the Temple is frozen, anticipating something, but my mom goes on like everything's okay, like she's got some special dispensation to say whatever she wants. Her hips tilt forward. Vrishti watches her, wheels turning in her head. "I said we're doing our best. I know you know that." Her tone's familiar, chiding, like a wife on TV.

And then she tilts her chin down and looks up at him from underneath her lashes, sexy, like his name is Mick or Bud or Billy. Except there's no warmth beneath the look, no soft, no animal; it's just plain power. Just manipulation. And he locks his gaze with hers, and something passes between them, and Vrishti sees the whole thing and freezes, her eyes turning to ice.

My mom takes a step toward the beard guy, hips loose, tries to pull the power into her hands. But then his eyes spark and he yanks it back.

"Are you suggesting my judgment is subjective?"

She catches herself, backtracking. "Well, no—no, of course not—"

"Do you really have so much ego?"

"No, I didn't mean—"

"Pride is the strongest demon, Guhahita. Surely you are familiar with this truth."

"Of course—"

"Then what place do you think you occupy that you may question my judgment? What great state do you believe you have attained?"

"I—"

"Let me tell you right now. You've attained nothing." He pauses, to let it sink in deep. "You disappoint me." She's a deer in headlights, stock-still and stunned. Everyone's staring. The beard guy spits on the ground and makes a noise that sounds like *peh*.

And then from inside my mom's shell all these tears come up, hot and wet and loud; I didn't know there was that much left inside. She falls to her knees in front of him. Vrishti stiffens, folds her arms tight. Everyone else backs away. My mom looks so alone up there, stripped down to nothing, so much more alone than even I have ever felt. No one comes to her rescue. She's begging his forgiveness. She didn't do anything wrong. Everyone is staring. I feel completely ill.

"Oh, Guruji, I admit I know nothing. Thank you, thank you, thank you for this lesson in surrendering my pride." Her eyes are lost and desperate, body clenched. It's humiliating.

What are we doing in a place where this happens?

I ran out of the Temple before the chant ended, beelining for the pay phones. Now I'm locked in the stuffy booth, hiding. It's the only place I can find where I know I won't see my mom or the beard guy or anyone from that room. Colin isn't answering his phone, even when I let it ring a million times. Goddamnit.

· · · · ·

I want to run. I want to run away from this place, climb out the window and into anything with wheels and drive and drive and drive. Except I can't; I don't know how to drive a car. All I can do is sit there in the passenger seat while my mom or Colin steers the wheel. And they're not here. There's no one here to take me away.

So instead I do the opposite. I close myself in our bathroom, the smallest space that I can find, and lock the door. I sit on the cold closed lid of the toilet with the shower running and sob till my ribs hurt, until the steam gets thick and hot enough to choke me. The air is clos-

ing in, making my head spin, when I hear the pounding on the door.

It's like hide-and-seek and I'm cornered—there's nothing to do but let myself get caught. Fists pound. "*Tessa!*" It's my mom.

I twist open the lock, but I keep the shower on. That teary, pleading, deer-in-headlights lady from the Temple is gone, or turned inside out, or something. Her eyes blaze. She's just as unhinged, just as scary, but now she's filled up to the edges with mad. And it looks like she's mad at *me*. She storms in and grabs me by the arm, jerks me up and off the toilet hard enough to hurt.

The first thing I think is *Colin*; my mind starts scrolling through the million possible ways that she could know. The shower's still running, enveloping us in a hot cloud. My face is slick with sweat. Her nails are digging into my arm. "Mom, wait—"

"Goddamnit!" She wrenches the water off. Steam mats her hair around her face. "*Goddamnit*, Tessa. You little liar."

I don't want to give myself away, so I play dumb. "Mom, what are you—"

"I just came from the front desk, Tessa. Do you know who called this afternoon?"

That's weird: Colin wouldn't call.

"How about a guess?"

I shake my head.

"Come on, Tessa, don't play dumb with me. You know what you did."

I really don't. "I really don't—"

She looks at me like she wants to spit.

"You're going to make me say it. Okay. Fine. When I was on my way back from the Temple"—she looks away when she says *Temple*, like she's trying to hide what happened there—"Ninyassa called me to the desk. 'You have a call,' she said." She pauses like I'm gonna know who it was. I just look at her: I don't.

"It was your *father*."

The bottom drops out from my stomach.

"That ring a bell?"

He called. I can't believe he called. So many feelings rush through my body I don't think I can hold them all, and all of them are opposites. I never knew you could be ashamed and overjoyed and terrified and embarrassed and excited and pissed off and grateful all at once. All I can think to say is one thing. It comes out quiet: "Did he call for me?"

She softens. Just a tiny bit. "No. No, Tessa. He didn't call for you."

"But he must have——"

"Well, he called because you told him you were here, if that's what you mean. He got your *letter*. Care of his *record* company." She looks at me like she knows everything, like she found out all my secrets and she is shoving them back inside me with her accusing beady eyes. "I heard you sent a few."

I don't defend myself. Right now being in trouble with my mom is so much less important than knowing every single word my dad said in that call. "Then that means he called for me——" I can hear the desperation in my voice. It sounds a little like my mother in the Temple. I don't care.

"No, Tessa, it doesn't. He didn't ask for you. He didn't want to talk to you. Okay? Your dad was drunk. He called to yell at me."

"Wait——"

"You went behind my back and did the one thing I've *ever* told you not to do! You *know* that we don't talk to him! There are reasons for that! There are——"

She's getting hysterical. I have to calm her down so

she can tell me what he said.

"Look, Mom, I'm sorry, okay?" I'm not sorry. "I'm sorry I went behind your back. I missed him. He's my *dad*." I use the tone of voice the swamis do. She slows down just a little. "What did he say?"

"He said what he always says, Tessa. That I'm an unfit, irresponsible mother. That he's sorry he ever met me; he should've skipped that stop on tour. This time, thanks to whatever you wrote to him, he said I'm in a *cult*. And he said to tell *my daughter* to quit bugging him."

I feel like it's dodgeball and I didn't get out of the way fast enough, and some kid lobbed a hard one right ·253. into my gut. I stop breathing. I don't hold my breath; I just stop breathing. Even if I knew what to say, I can't talk.

"Sorry, Tessa. Sorry, okay? That's what I've been trying to tell you."

And then she turns around and gathers up her things and says, "I have a private *darshan* now. He's giving me a special meditation, so I may be staying up at Guru's quarters for the evening."

She fixes me in her gaze. "I think you have a lot to contemplate."

TWENTY

. . .

The depths of hell and the heights of heaven
exist within a single mind.

·254. Colin is picking me up early this morning. I can't wait to get out of here; I even skipped breakfast. My hair's still wet from the shower. My mom didn't come home last night, of course, and I didn't sleep. All last night I just told myself over and over: in six hours you can talk to Colin. You can finally tell him everything. He'll help you understand.

At 8:05 a.m., the Spacemobile pulls up instead of Colin's van. Rush is playing. Clint is driving. "Hop in," he says, and the passenger door swings open. Bennett slides over on the bench seat; Colin's in the back. They're all stoned as hell.

Shit.

"Let's get out of here," I say, strapping myself in. *At least I'm leaving*, I tell myself.

"No way, man," Clint says. "We gotta see this place."

"Dude, totally," Bennett says.

"We're takin' a tour." Clint revs what's left of the engine and drives straight toward the main building.

"You guys, come on, what are you doing?" I say.

"She's worried, man!" Bennett says. "That's 'cause it's an *adventure*. Adventures are scary sometimes!"

"I'm not worried," I say, even though I'm completely terrified. Clint and Bennett and wake-and-bake plus the ashram is a recipe for disaster. I try to sound blasé. "It's just lame here. We should go."

"Dude, no way, man," Clint says. "We've been hearing about this place for like a year. It's Crazy Central. All those chicks in robes? We gotta take a look."

We are clattering down the bus route to Shanti Kutir and I am freaking out inside. "Let's just go," I say. "Get something to eat or something."

"Nuh-uh." Clint is resolute. "Colin finally agreed to give us the tour. We're not passing that one up."

I spin around toward the backseat, shoot Colin a look. He just shrugs. All I want in the entire world is to get out of here, and he's going to get me killed.

"Come on, you guys. I'm gonna get in trouble."

Clint turns to me, smirking, a glint in his eye. "Don't you worry, little lady. We'll protect you."

Somehow that isn't particularly comforting.

We drive the entire bus route, past the Amrit and Shanti Kutir, the parking lot and the dorms. Clint and Bennett laugh, talking about the devotees' outfits and women that are hot.

"So what, is everyone here married to each other like a commune or some shit?" Clint asks me.

"Yeah, are they?" Bennett asks.

"*No,*" I say, puffing up. "It's not like that." I don't like them talking about the people here. Not that I don't hate them all. But I *know* them. They don't.

"Well then, what? Does everybody do, like, mind-control experiments?"

"No." I roll my eyes. "No. I don't want to talk about it. Can we just go, please?"

"Whoa," Clint says to Bennett, who raises his eyebrows. "I think the little lady's mad."

"I'm not mad."

"C'mon, little lady. We'll find something fun to do."

I do not want to find something fun to do. I want to get out of here. People are starting to stream out of the buildings, headed toward the dining hall for breakfast. I sink down in my seat. The Spacemobile pulls up to the courtyard of gods.

"Wow," Bennett says.

"Awesome," Clint says. "Look at that fuckin' elephant!"

Colin doesn't say anything. He's stoned out of his mind, spacing to the music, useless.

"Yeah, that's Ganesh," I say. Maybe a little information

will satisfy them. "He's the remover of obstacles. You're supposed to pray to him for help with stuff in your life."

"Weird, man," Bennett says.

"Look at *that!*" Clint points at the statue of Kali Ma. Kali Ma is the destroyer goddess: she wears a necklace of skulls and a skirt made of arms and no shirt, standing on the body of Shiva with her tongue sticking out.

"Nice tits," Bennett says.

I'm not superstitious and I know that gods are symbols, but everybody says you do not want to piss off Kali Ma.

"You shouldn't say that," I tell Bennett. He looks at me like I'm crazy.

"Dude, who's that?" Clint asks, nodding toward Gandhi. "He looks fuckin' hungry."

"He's got the munchies!" Bennett giggles.

"That's *Gandhi*," I say. "Haven't you heard of Gandhi? He was like Martin Luther King but for India, in, like, the thirties?"

"He's fuckin' skinny, man," Clint says.

"Yeah, he's skinny because he went on hunger strikes."

"Nah, dude, he's skinny cause he's got the *munchies*," Bennett insists.

"He needs some Cheetos," Clint says. "And a Big Gulp."

"Dude!" Bennett says. "We gotta take Gandhi for some Cheetos!"

"Man!" Clint says, jaw dropping. "You are *right!*"

Wait. What are they talking about?

"That's what the Spacemobile is for, man. Good deeds."

"Good deeds." Clint puts the van in park but leaves it running.

"Wait, hang on," I say before he can leave the van. "What are you guys doing?"

"Feeding the hungry!"

I turn toward the backseat. "Colin!" I say. He doesn't open his eyes.

"*Colin!* They're taking Gandhi!"

He lifts his head six inches, peers at me through heavy lids. "That's cool, man."

"No, it's not cool! There are people everywhere! We're gonna get *arrested!*"

"Dude, chill out. It's cool. It'll totally be fine." And he lays his head back on the seat.

Clint and Bennett are outside the van already. If I yell I'll only draw attention. Clint's digging at the feet of Gandhi with a stick; Bennett grabs Gandhi's head and wrestles him up. Apparently I have to keep lookout, since no one else is going to. We're half hidden by a hedge, but Clint and Bennett are making grunty noises and at least two people crane their necks to try and see around the hedge.

"*Psst*," I whisper loud through the open window. "*Hey*." Bennett turns around. "People can see you."

"Okay, hurry up," he says, and starts yanking harder; Clint kicks the bottom of the statue till it finally breaks free.

"All right, one, two, *three*," he says, and they hoist Gandhi onto their shoulders, head back toward the van.

"Open open open!" Clint yells; I sit there frozen.

"The back!"

Colin's clearly not gonna get up to open the door. I just want to get us out of here. I run to the back and open the latch; Clint and Bennett heave Gandhi up and throw him in. He hits the metal of the van, making a horrible clanging noise.

"Run!" Bennett says; they slam the doors, we pile in, and Clint steps on the gas.

They're all cracking up, of course, practically falling over themselves as we speed down the bus route. Clint's eyes squeeze shut from silent-painful laugh, and once I even have to grab the wheel to keep him from swerving.

"Did you see that, Tessa? Did you—" Clint hollers.

"Just *drive*," I say through clenched teeth.

He heads straight for the main entrance, where there are about a million people. I hold my breath and shrink down in my seat. A familiar voice yells, "Hey!"

and in the rearview mirror someone chases us, but the transmission drowns it out and we speed past, hurtling toward the highway, Gandhi crashing in the back.

On the road the guys roll down the windows and yell.

"Wooh!" they howl, faces aimed into the wind. I roll my eyes and shake my head. Clint reaches across Bennett to poke my ribs. "Hey," he says. "We got away!"

"Hooray."

"Aw, c'mon. Wasn't it a *little* awesome?"

"No."

"Not even when we hurled him in the back?"

"No."

"Not even when we drove past all those ashram people chasing after us? '*Hey! Wait! Stop!*'" He imitates them running after us, making a spaz-out face. I laugh a little, in spite of myself.

"See?" he says, poking me again. "See, it's fun." He smiles at me.

Finally I decide to let him win me over. It's easier than trying to fight. "Okay." We round a bend; Gandhi clunks against the wall.

At Colin's, they unload the statue while I smoke up. If I can't talk to Colin about last night, then what I need is to forget. I need to make myself go away. I need to blot it out, blur everything till you can't make out the outlines and it all just runs together. I polish off three bowls by myself, until my head is thick enough that I can tell myself I just dreamed the temple and the guru and my mother and my dad. Until everything that's happened to me dissolves, and I'm not carrying it inside me anymore, and all that's left is what's happening just exactly now. I make a promise to myself: Today, just for today, there will be no such thing as memory. No such thing as stuff that happened in the past. No people except the ones I'm in the room with. All that will exist will be ·261. what's happening in this moment, here and now. Everything else is dust.

I let go of myself and give the morning over to the guys. We stopped at 7-Eleven on the way, and now the guys spend at least an hour building an elaborate shrine in the yard: a ring of Ding Dongs encircles Gandhi's feet, a Big Gulp perches precariously on his head, and he's festooned with Cheetos. Everyone thinks this is hilarious. I sort of like Gandhi—the person, not the statue—so I wonder if it's disrespectful. I'm stoned enough to recognize that it is kind of incredible, though.

"Good deeds!" Bennett yells, and high-fives Colin when they're done.

"Attention, all," Clint calls out in a fake town-crier voice. "Please gather round for an important announcement." Everyone just stares at him. He waves us over. "I said, *Please gather round*." Bennett finishes the Cheetos; I put down the bong and head toward the guys.

With a flourish, Clint produces a tiny Baggie from his pocket. It's folded in half and then in half again, so small you can't imagine it's even holding anything. "I have here"—another flourish—"your tickets to a new reality."

"Aw, man, you scored," Bennett says. "No shit. Really?"

"Really," Clint says with a nod.

"That is *awesome*," Colin says, slightly sobered up and more awake.

"What?" I ask. Everyone seems to know what Clint's talking about but me.

"Oh, Tessa." Colin turns to me. "You're gonna *love* this."

"Really?" What am I gonna love?

"Oh my god. Yes. Totally."

"What is it?"

"Have you ever heard of acid?"

"What, like battery acid?"

He laughs. "No. Like LSD."

I *have* heard of LSD, in junior high health class when we had two weeks about dangerous chemical drugs. Mr. Fishman said that people take it and jump off buildings, thinking they can fly; he said some people scratch their skin away, sure they're covered with bugs. He also said there are people who never come down. I pretended I was taking notes while I imagined unseen bugs crawling on my skin forever, how terrifying it would be to take a pill and never get my brain back.

"Oh. Wow. Isn't it—scary?"

Colin's eyes are wide and focused. "No. Totally not. It's *amazing*."

"Aren't there—don't you think there are bugs on you and stuff?"

Colin shakes his head. "Urban legend, man. Just like the perpetual-tripping myth. Everyone knows someone who knows some guy who dropped too much and tripped forever, but the secret is it's all the same guy. And he doesn't exist."

"Are you sure?"

"Positive."

"Because in health class—"

"Propaganda, dude," Clint interrupts. "What'd they tell you about weed in health class?"

He's right: they told us marijuana leads to heroin use, erases your memory, and turns you psychotic.

"Hm. Then what's it like?"

"Oh, *man*," Bennett says.

"Wooh," Clint says.

"Basically it's like waking up a whole new brain you didn't even know you had," Colin says, and grins.

"Wow. Like what kind of brain?"

"Like the *awesome* kind," Bennett snorts.

"Have you ever heard of that saying, We only use ten percent of our minds? It's like all of a sudden you've got access to the other ninety. And it's totally beautiful. Like you can finally *see*."

My mom said that when we first got to the ashram: *I can finally see*. I wonder if acid is like the stuff she talked about: electricity flowing through you, a liquid silence ocean. I wonder if I'll finally find out what she meant. "Is it like the universe and stuff?"

All three guys laugh. "Exactly. That's exactly it."

"It's like the universe," Clint says, as he reaches into the tiny bag with tweezers and pulls out a square of paper. "Open wide," he says, and sets it on my tongue.

For almost an hour and a half I don't feel anything. I keep telling the guys there's something wrong, but they keep telling me to chill out. "It takes at *least* an hour. Minimum," Colin says. "Sometimes longer."

At approximately eighty-six minutes I feel a weird feeling. It's kind of like too much coffee but there's a chemical part too, a clangy feeling in my nose and mouth. "Drink some orange juice," Clint says. "It'll make it come on harder."

He hands me the carton and I chug. The juice is

viscous and tangy. Somehow I can feel it in the inside of my skull. My mouth gets thick and sticky and I smack my lips.

"Ah, that acid feeling," Colin says.

Clint puts on *And You and I,* my favorite Yes song. It's long, with all these movements, delicate acoustic parts morphing into space noises and epic orchestral swells, then back to quiet. When the sci-fi crescendos start in, suddenly I can hear the sounds in space. Except it's not just hearing, because I actually experience them spatially—geometry of the notes, the gaps between them. Hearing and seeing combine into a whole other ·265· way of perceiving, and all of a sudden I realize there aren't just five senses, there are totally way more. When I close my eyes I see separate planes stretching out and out and out, notes weaving between them like electric threads. Being stoned makes music special but in a feeling way, fuzzy and lush in your body and imagination. This is actually real, crystal-clear and sharp, like it's always there and I just saw behind the curtain.

The song spirals into resolution, *And you and I climb crossing the shapes of the morning,* and I tear up at the beauty of it, note-threads looping into perfect filigreed patterns that make the shape of love, and when silence comes again I open up my eyes. They've never been so open: it's how I imagine babies feel, looking at the world for the first time, pure. My face is a clean slate.

"Welcome to acid," Colin says, and takes my hands, staring right into my mind.

Pretty soon after that, time stops meaning anything. "How long have we been tripping?" Bennett asks, and I look at the alarm clock and immediately crack up. Those little ticking hands, so meaningless, such a tiny insignificant human way of trying to measure something infinite and vast. Ridiculous. I throw the clock across the room, laughing.

"Time doesn't exist," I say, realizing it as the words spill out my mouth. "It's actually the same as space, but that's too big for our minds to comprehend, so we invent calendars and clocks and minutes and hours and run our lives by them, but all that stuff's made up! It's just *made up*. Oh my god, it's made up."

"It's *made up*!" Colin yells to the rafters, laughing.

"Made up!" That's Clint.

"Okay, so in the arbitrary system of random symbols we call time that doesn't actually exist, how long have we been tripping? I want to know how soon we're gonna peak." That's Bennett.

"Soon, I think," Clint says, giggling.

"Yeah, very soon," Colin says.

And then we're peaking.

I can't move, because everything else is. The walls

are breathing, the floor is breathing, so's the ceiling: everything around me is alive, the world continually and infinitely collapsing like double waterfalls into a single point between my eyes. And that's when I have my eyes closed. When I open them, that point is wherever I'm looking, multiplying till there's a million vortexes everywhere, white light fractured into rainbows, air fractalized and prismed, flowing eternally into itself in the infinite breath of the universe.

A little voice in my head hears me think, *Infinite breath of the universe,* and says, *That sounds like cheesy ashram talk,* but then I recognize how small that voice is, ·267. how much tinier than the reality I'm experiencing, and words like *universe* and *infinity* are coming to me like dictation, not like something I'm trying to make up, and that's the difference: Whether you really see it or you make it up. Cheesy happens when you fake stuff. If you really see it, it's just real.

Colin and Clint and Bennett and I lie down on the floor, tops of our heads touching, feet pointing outward in a circle or a cross. Colin takes my hand and I'm thankful for the tether, keeping me from sliding off into infinite space. I feel his pulse in his palm and our veins interweave, life joined to life. Everything's alive. *Everything's alive.* I move my free hand in front of my face and it turns into fifty hands, my arm to fifty arms, and suddenly I understand the courtyard of gods. That's why

Ganesh and Kali Ma and Saraswati have a million arms. It's a picture of *this*.

And then suddenly everything's a picture. The kitchen, the poster, the bed, all of them are paintings of themselves, like Van Gogh or something in a museum. I realize: the painting is the outer manifestation of the thing, how the world sees it, what it wants you to think it is. But underneath that, each thing has an essence. I look at Colin, and Bennett, and Clint: it's the same thing with them. Their faces and bodies and clothes, presentation, personalities—all of that's a painting, and beneath that is their life force, which is what they really are. And I get it: that's what the swamis mean by *ego*. The painting part's the ego, and the essence part's the soul.

That's such a cool thing that I want to say it out loud, but my mouth won't make words. Thoughts are coming so much faster than my teeth and tongue can turn them into language. Nobody else is talking either. I think I have to just stay quiet.

Those words echo in my head, *Stay quiet*; thoughts fall away and I'm just breathing. My ribs turn vast and transparent; when I close my eyes there are those planes again, stretching out in infinite directions till they disappear or turn to everything, and I realize everything and nothing are the same, it's all a liquid silence ocean, stretching on forever, and then I remember that I've heard that phrase before.

This is what my mom meant. This is why her eyes blazed and she tried and tried to tell me. I know it. A wave of love and relief floods over me. I wish I could go back to that walk in the woods when I made the dumb televangelist joke; I wish I could take it back, tell her I understand. The thing is, now, I'm not sure she'd even care. She's so far away. Even though I know that *near* and *far* are just illusions, that they're really the same thing, I still can't find her.

I'm starting to get overwhelmed thinking about my mom, far away with the beard guy. I flash on last night in the bathroom, the steam, her fingernails digging into my arm. I get a whiff of claustrophobic anxious black oil creeping in the edges of my rainbow mind, and I know I have to stop it, now. I have to pick my mind up off that subject and put it down in a wholly different place. Now. Before it's too late.

I open my eyes, point them toward the white ceiling, try to slow things down enough to stand up. There are fractals moving on the stucco, but things are breathing less; the infinite collapsing has stopped being quite so infinite. I get up.

"I'm going for a walk." I'd forgotten I could speak.

Outside is amazing. Nature is perfect. It's freezing and the wind bites past my clothes, through my skin, between my cells; I'm cold down to my bones, but it's not uncomfortable. I'm part of the air. If you don't resist it, cold is just another way of being, as natural as a warm bath. Branches tangle, interlace in the woods around me like nerves or lace, black against the bright white sky. Snowflakes sprinkle out from whiteness—crystalline, miraculous. Everything is so clear it's like I've got extra-strong glasses. My world was blurry and I didn't even know it.

Behind me is Gandhi; I go to see him. He has Cheeto powder on his face, Dr Pepper running down his head. It was funny before, but now I see it isn't right.

He needs to be cleaned. I try wiping him off with my sleeve, but there's too much junk on him. I understand why they call it junk food—it really is. It doesn't have life force like nature does, or sprouts. Suddenly sprouts sound really good. My sleeve is soaked with Dr Pepper and I'm smearing it on his face. That won't do. I pull my shirt over my head; a rush of goose bumps shoots up my spine. *Don't resist*, I tell myself, and breathe deep, nothing but my bra between me and the winter wind. Snowflakes melt onto my skin. *You're part of it; it's all the same thing. There's nothing outside of you to fight against.*

I use my shirt to clean Gandhi, every inch of him, and think, *This is what devotion is.* I'm in an ancient temple or a ceremony, communing with the spirit of the statue, making sure he's clean and pure. I run the corner of my sleeve around the rim of his glasses, creases of his nose. Snow makes a thin film on his head and shoulders. When he's finally clean, he smiles at me. I smile back.

We're standing there, staring at each other, when the guys spill out. I feel their energy, loud and tumbly and male, even before the screen door slams.

"Hel-loo," Colin calls out.

"I'm here with Gandhi," I say, still reverent from the cleaning. They come over.

"What do you think?" I show them my handiwork. They nod, solemn. It's an improvement.

"That really is a beautiful statue," Bennett says, looking at Gandhi.

"Yes, indeed it is," Clint says, looking at me.

Colin comes up behind me, wraps his arms around my naked torso. I wasn't fighting the cold, but the warm feels amazing. I lean back into him, soak up the heat of his chest with my back. He grabs my hips, turns me around and kisses me.

It's insane kissing on acid: weirdly more and less than sober or stoned. We fall into each other's mouths, energy circling between us in an endless figure eight, like an infinity sign, and again I understand: that symbol's not just a drawing, it's a picture of something real, a picture of *this*. At the same time, the actual kissing part feels weirdly hollow, almost silly—just muscles, tongues swimming around each other. Bodies are just bodies. We give them all this importance, but they're really so rudimentary, empty vessels. He opens my mouth deeper and I don't feel the sex of it, just the energy.

Meanwhile Bennett has found a tree trunk to stare at. "Man, look at this *bark*," he says. "It's like *moving*. I should totally take this home and put it on my wall like art."

Colin stops kissing me for a second, laughing. "In eight hours it isn't gonna look like that anymore, man. You can't take it with you." Then he comes back to my mouth.

"Aw, dude, you're *right*," Bennett says. "Wow. Perception is wild, huh?"

"Wild, man," Clint says. My eyes are closed but I can hear he's near me.

Electricity runs through me, strong, and I realize that I'm shuddering. My whole body's shivering hard; it's funny, I don't really feel cold. I stop kissing and look down at myself. Colin does too. "Wow," he says. "Why didn't you tell me you were cold?"

"I didn't feel it," I say, and look into his spinning eyes.

"C'mon," he says. "Let's go inside and get you a shirt."

His flannel feels like the essence of hot cocoa. The bed is the essence of bed. He puts on water to boil, and part of my brain says, *Hot stove = fire*, but then I start watching the walls and forget. When the teakettle whistles, he remembers to turn it off, which is good because I wouldn't have. He brings me a Garfield mug full of mint tea. It says, "Give Me Coffee and No One Gets Hurt." Garfield is out of control. I stare at his face for a minute and then it's too much; I have to stop. I cover him up with my hands.

"You good?" Colin asks me.

"Mmm," I say. I am.

"Cool, then I'm gonna go outside and run around a little." He smiles into my eyes. I smile back. That was nice, how he took care of me, brought me in and put a flannel on me. That's what people are supposed to do with each other. That's what love is, I realize: just looking out for the people around you, thinking about what they might need, and giving it to them. So simple. He's my ally.

"Thanks," I say.

I lie back on the bed and close my eyes for what seems like hours. Grids of vibrating electric light stretch out in all directions, farther than my mind can even see; I track them back and back and back till suddenly they disappear and everything turns to space, like in *Star Wars* or cartoons, but vast, and real. Twinkling in the emptiness are a million tiny jewels, and when I stay with them, I see they're all connected by delicate threads, gossamer thin, and the net that they make is the universe.

In the distance I hear the door open and swing shut, far off, all the way across space. Then a voice snaps me back into the room.

"Hey, Tessa," Clint says.

I rub my eyes, disoriented, not sure which reality I'm in or if it's both at once. Transcending dualities is confusing. It's dark outside.

He sits backward in a kitchen chair. "Trippin' out, huh?" His weasel eyes are blazing.

I smile. "Yeah."

"Didn't know all that stuff existed, did you."

"No. Well, sort of. But not like this." It's hard to talk. "You know."

"Yeah, I do. You want something to eat?"

Eat. Whoa. My body is not sure how it feels about that. "I don't know."

"Yeah, I know what you mean. But try this." He brings an orange from the kitchen, digs his thumbs into the peel. It sprays, pungent. "Smells good, huh?"

"Yeah."

"Wait'll you taste it."

He finishes peeling, splits it in half. It's incredible just to see. It's like the mandalas at the ashram, perfect patterned circles, except this one's made by nature. I swear, nature is amazing. He pulls a segment off.

"Open wide," he says, just like when he put the acid on my tongue. The thought, *Why does he keep feeding me?* flashes through my mind, but then it flits away. I open my mouth; he slides the orange in. It's amazing. So intense I can feel it in my whole head, and also in my blood. Suddenly I understand food. This was made by nature to sustain me, who is also part of nature. I feel the interconnectedness of everything as I chew.

"Wow," I say into his eyes.

"Toldja," he says.

He feeds me another piece. Then he hands the orange over to me. "You don't want any?" I ask.

"Course I do." He grins. "Now it's your turn."

He means feed him. I guess it's only fair. I peel off a piece and hold it out, stopping a few inches from his mouth. He darts forward and bites it from my fingers like an animal.

"Mmm," he says, chewing, staring at me. I squirm a little. He swallows.

"Another," he says.

This time his lips brush my fingers as he takes it from me. A shiver goes through my skin. I've never touched another guy besides Colin, unless you count Randy Wishnick. It surprises me how much touching Clint is the same as touching Colin. Except then he looks at me with those beady weasel eyes and it's not.

"Why'd you put that flannel on?" he says.

What does he mean? "I was shivering."

"Too bad," he says.

Too bad I was shivering, or too bad I put the flannel on? "I guess." Suddenly I wish I could close my eyes and go back to glimmering jewels in space. My heart starts to thud. I'm not hungry anymore.

The door creaks open, interrupting Clint's stare, and Bennett walks in, pulling off his sweater. He's got a tie-dye T-shirt underneath, and the swirls of color undulate across his pudgy belly. I stare.

"What, the tie-dye?"

"Yeah," I tell him. "Totally," because suddenly I understand tie-dye. Acid makes you suddenly understand a lot of things you've seen a million times before.

"Where's Colin?" I ask Bennett.

"He went down by the creek," he says. "Grabbed a flashlight, went exploring."

I wish he would've taken me. "Oh."

"He always does that when he trips. Vision quest. He'll be back eventually," Bennett says. "He knows the woods around here super well."

"Okay."

"Tessa and I were just having an orange," Clint tells Bennett, raising his eyebrows.

"Yeah?" Bennett says.

"Yeah," Clint says. "She was feeding me." I blush. "Maybe if you ask nice she'll feed you too."

I want to say, *No way,* but I don't want to seem paranoid. *What's wrong with sharing an orange?* Clint would say, and I wouldn't have an answer.

Bennett turns to me. "Tessa, would you please feed me some orange?"

My stomach burns. "Okay."

I peel a piece off, put it in his mouth. They both just watch me.

They're not doing anything wrong. They're being nice, and smiling, sharing food. But the acid gives me X-ray vision, tunneling through the layers, and there is something underneath that's unfamiliar, thick and sticky and a little frightening. I'm starting to get that feeling that I had before, black oil creeping in the corners of my mind. I start to remember last night again. I feel like I don't have any parents. I feel like I'm still too young to not have parents. I want Colin to come back.

"It's hot," Clint says, and turns to Bennett. "Don't you think it's hot?"

"Totally," Bennett says. I don't think it's hot.

Clint stands up and takes his shirt off. He's skinny: you can see the outline of each muscle, his chest concave, stomach a perfect six-pack. His body is bright white, moles and freckles standing out in stark relief. He strides over to the sink to get a glass of water, easy in his skin. He gulps it down and puts "Led Zeppelin III" on the stereo. *Immigrant Song.* He turns it way, way loud.

Robert Plant's voice screams out echoey: *Aaaah-ah!* It sounds like Halloween.

Valhalla, I am coming. Bennett smokes from the bong. I can't imagine being stoned right now.

Clint says, "Aren't you hot, Tessa?"

"Not really," I tell him.

"Yeah, but sometimes acid messes up your sense of temperature," he says. "Remember before when you didn't realize you were cold?"

It's true; I didn't. "Yeah."

"I think it's the same thing now. It's super hot in here. You should be careful not to overheat."

"Really?" I can't tell if he's messing with me or not. Everything's a collage of contradictions; I can't tell what's real, if everything or nothing is, or somewhere in between. My gut says he's messing with me. But what's "my gut"? Maybe it's just fear. Maybe I need to overcome it. Maybe that's my challenge from the universe.

"Totally," he says. "You shouldn't be wearing all that heavy flannel."

I have to be brave in order to know the truth. I start unbuttoning.

"You're gonna be way safer," Clint tells me.

I let the shirt fall to the floor. Cool air feels good against my skin. I'm just in my bra and jeans. Bennett is staring at me over the edge of the bong.

Clint cracks a grin. "See, isn't that so much better?"

I wish there was a word for *yes* and *no* at once.

Clint sits down by me on the bed. Led Zeppelin wails. It's pitch-black out the windows. He reaches out his hand, puts it on my leg, and suddenly it's like a vortex opens up, one I could just spin into, no bottom, no floor, no one to catch me or pull me back; just endless empty space. I peek over the edge, teetering.

Then the door cracks open again.

It's Colin. My heart leaps in my chest: thank god. My body fills with love and I understand the phrase *sweet relief.* "Colin!" I stand up, pulling away from the black hole of Clint. "You're back!" I go to throw my arms around his neck, kiss him like before, minds melding in infinity signs, but he hangs back.

"What's up?" I ask him, eyes wide open.

He looks down at my bra and stomach, then across the room to Clint.

"Nothing," he says, but he doesn't mean it.

He eyes the orange peels on the floor, then walks to the refrigerator and opens it, staring at the empty inside. I follow him.

"Are you mad at me?" I can read him better than I can read Clint and Bennett.

"Nope," he says, staring at the mustard.

Reality is shaped like nerves or branches, and he's gone down a fork where I can't follow him. I remember this morning, how all I wanted was to talk to him. How

I stayed up all night waiting for it, imagining how I would finally tell him everything and he would hold it, hold me, keep me from spilling. He was so nearby. Now he's down a whole road I don't recognize. I want to reach through the crowded air between us, past the skin of thoughts that wraps his mind. I want to pull him back. "Hey," I say, and run my fingers down his cheek.

"Hey." He turns to me and wraps me in his arms, slides a hand onto my hip and grabs, but it's rough, not pure like energy and babies' eyes. Then he kisses me, too hard to feel the figure eight between us. I squirm. It doesn't make me stop spilling. Clint and Bennett are watching from the couch. Out the corner of my eyes I spot the alarm clock on the floor from where I threw it a long time ago. It's four in the morning. I can't imagine ever sleeping.

"Let's go for a walk," I say.

"Tess, I just got back from a walk. A really long one," he says. "Besides, don't you want to be in here with everyone?" He eyes my chest again, then looks to Clint, his shirt off too. "It kind of seems like it."

I shake my head.

"Kind of seems like you want to hang out with Clint."

"Not really," I say.

"Really? Hmm," he says. He sounds hard, and far away. It scares me: I can't find him, even though he's standing right here. "Well, I still don't feel like going out again. You can if you want."

It's pitch-black; I'd get lost out there in the woods by myself. I need to find something to hang on to.

"No, it's okay. Let's listen to some music."

Colin puts on the Doors. "Break on Through." I've heard them before and I know all about Jim Morrison, but they are different on acid. Especially closed up in a little cabin, especially in the middle of the night. *Tried to run, tried to hide, break on through to the other side.* The Doors were made for taking acid. I start dancing. I'm the only one but I don't care, I shut my eyes and shake every- ·281. thing as hard as I can, trying to get it all out, cross over, push through. I tell myself: *Just spill. Disintegrate. Give up your attachment to holding things together.* I remind myself: *Your challenge from the universe is to overcome your fear.*

I dance till my muscles are wobbly and I'm covered with sweat. Now I'm glad I'm only in my bra. I flop down on the bed; the room spins around me, tilty, orbiting, like Saturn's rings. The world of my mom and my dad and the ashram and even Colin dissolves and my universe becomes the circus world of the Doors, carnivals and lizards, snakes and deep dark corners. Clint sits next to me, leaning in and singing along: *You know that it would be untrue; you know that I would be a liar. . . .* He holds out the bong and I take it, inhale deep.

The next song comes on and Clint keeps singing

right to me: *The men don't know, but the little girls understand.* I just watch his lips move, till I can't see them anymore because they're pressing into mine.

I go with it for a second, just a second, before my brain says, *Stop.* Then I realize what's happening. The last thing I want to do is kiss Clint. His breath is hot and he looks like a rodent or a fox and he is scary like Jim Morrison. And he is my boyfriend's best friend, and what the hell is he doing kissing me? My mind swirls. Shit. I have to get away. I pull back, press my hand against his chest. "Stop."

"What's the matter, little lady? You scared?" He leans in again.

"No. Yes. I don't know. Just stop it."

He doesn't stop. He's crowding me with his breath, and I look over his shoulder, search for Colin with my eyes. I know he'll get me out of this, say something that's just the right mixture of funny and firm, pick me up and hold me, make it so I can breathe again. I plead with my eyes: *Come get me.*

But he doesn't. He takes a swig of water from his glass and looks me straight in the eye like he's accusing me of something. And he leaves me there.

Clint leans back in and I say, "Stop," again, and he says, "C'mon, Tess, break on through." I put my elbows in front of my chest, try to make a space between us, but he pushes them away, pins my arms on the bed. My

mind is a zoom lens; the room is spinning out and everything is way too intense, his hands and face and the con-
fusion; *this is the end, my only friend* and Colin by the
refrigerator, not moving, just leaving me there, Bennett
saying, "All *right*," and Clint's hard body on top of me all
bones and angles. I'm trying to push through my fear,
push past it, go where the universe takes me, but the
harder I push the harder it pushes back, and the push
grows and the fear grows and the push grows and the
fear grows until there's an epic battle inside and on top
of me, every fight that's ever existed replicating its
essence in my body and my mind, threatening to ·283.
explode my skin from the inside.

"Jesus Christ," Colin says and slams his water down.
"I'm going for a walk."

I decide I will kiss Clint. I can't fight it, so I'll do it as an
experiment. To see what an unfamiliar human being
feels like. Or something. The universe wants me to be
brave, so I'll let myself kiss him. But that's it.

It goes on for what seems like forever, and the
whole time I feel like I'm on the edge of a razor. It could
cut me anytime and I would bleed and bleed and nothing here would stop it. I could bleed till I'm empty, till
there's nothing left but the painting of me. "C'mon,
gimme a little love," Clint says, and I know he wants me

to act how I do with Colin, the squirming and the sounds, and I can't. I can't do it. It's fake. All that power I think I have with Colin, it's all fake. He still leaves the room and Clint's on top of me, and no matter what noises I make it won't change that, and I'm starting to wonder what is on the other side of my fear, and if I'll ever get there.

Bennett comes over and sits on the bed. He just watches us. Clint looks up at him and grins. "Awesome, huh?"

"Awesome," Bennett says.

I ram Clint in the ribs with my elbow and run outside.

I can't find Colin. I run and run, breathless, freezing in my bra, wind washing my lungs like water. My heart pounds hard, harder than it ever has, till I start wondering what a heart attack feels like. I could die. I could die out here and nobody would stop it; I could die at any second, anytime. Fear bears down on me like a tidal wave and I'm running to outrace it, find some hiding place where it can't reach. Everything turns primal; *this is the most basic thing*, I think; terror runs through my veins and I'm alone. Totally, completely, essentially alone.

Branches scrape my shoulders, leaving welts; my skin looks too alive, grotesque in the predawn light. I run through the woods. *"Colin!"* I yell on the edge of my breath. "Colin!"

Finally I find him, down at the creek, on the other side from me. His jeans are rolled up, his shoes off. He's staring at the water; it floods between us like a boundary on a map. We're two separate countries, him and me, and I don't know what war we had to get that way.

"Colin!" I call across the creek. He looks up. His face is angry.

"What do you want?" he yells back over the rush of the water.

I want you, I think. But I'm too scared to say it. And in some way, for some reason, it partly isn't true.

I roll up my jeans, lose my shoes, and wade in.

I was cold before, but this is a whole new level. The water's glass through my skin; the current's hard enough to knock me over and I feel like I'm a pioneer crossing some huge and ancient river, my entire survival hinging on getting to the other side.

"What're you *doing?*" Colin shouts, and I can't answer, too focused on the mossy rocks beneath me, struggling not to slip. Halfway through my ankle catches in two sharp-edged stones, wrenches hard and I fall, twisted backward with the current, soaked. A hot arrow of pain shoots up my leg.

"Tessa!" Colin yells.

I brace myself, slip my foot out, hoist back up; but

when I try to walk, the arrow fires harder and I fall again. I start hyperventilating.

"Just wait there." Colin wades into the creek.

I sit, water flooding around me, and try to slow my breathing, hold still in the rush of it. Finally he gets to me, puts his arm around my waist, slings my arm over his shoulder, and lifts. I lean on him; I have to.

Finally we get over to the other side, collapse on brown leaves and soft dirt. The sun is rising. I'm still breathing hard. My ankle throbs.

"What the hell were you doing, Tess?"

I can't tell what he means: when I was crossing the river, or with Clint in his cabin? My head is crashing with so many things. I'm relieved I made it here, and terrified; furious at Colin for leaving me with Clint, but thanking god he waded in and got me. My entire body's shaking. "I was trying to get to you."

He looks at me for a long time from far away. His face is like the day after we first kissed, when he told me that it couldn't happen anymore—except harder, and older, and full of too many things for me to count or know. Suddenly I can feel my own face and I know it looks the same. That border's still between us, even though I made it across the creek. I feel old, and scared, and young, and angry.

"Take me home," I say, and then I'm sobbing. "Take me home."

Twenty-one

. . .

The question: How do you get there from here?
The answer: You go around and then you come back.

We hike up, my arm on his shoulders, till we get to a ·287.
bend in the creek that's narrow enough to cross. I wait
by the van while he goes and gets me clothes, and I
change outside when he comes back. I don't want to see
Clint and Bennett.

My ankle's dulled to a low throb, but I can feel
there's something very wrong. I brace myself against
Colin's bus to change, wince hard when I lean on my bad
foot. Colin's cords slip off my hips, but I roll the waistband, tuck his flannel in the back to hold them up. His
clothes are big enough for me to drown in and I'm glad;
hidden in the folds, my body finally feels safe.

"What time is it?" I ask him.

"Five thirty," he says. "It's been fifteen hours. You
should be down by now."

"I'm not," I say. The world is still too clear, my

thoughts too big; everything's still flooding in too fast.

His eyes dart at me. "Really?"

"Yeah, I'm still tripping. Is that weird?"

He pauses. "No," he says, not looking at me. "No, it's not weird."

I don't believe him. But I don't want to ask him any more.

In the bus, I check out my ankle. It's purple and huge, like a rotten fruit. The fragility of my body overwhelms me; a wave of nausea passes through. I flinch and look away. Out the window everything is spinning. It's a kaleidoscope: there's no solid place to look, the world spilling in an endless tilting circle. My head is spinning too. Space has turned to time, expansiveness to speed, and things are moving way too fast. My tether snapped; he let me go and I slid off to someplace not safe. There is nobody to catch me. Not Colin, not my mother, not my father. There's no one left; just me. I'm too exposed. Clint and Bennett, even Colin: they all crowd me out and make me naked, roll me over, bare my belly, then act like I did something wrong. I don't know what I did, what I'm doing, how to roll back over and protect myself, and Colin isn't talking.

Just go home, I tell myself. *Just sneak into your bed and close your eyes and crawl between the sheets.* Alone and quiet I can piece myself together; the world will slow to steady and I'll find solid ground again. I tell myself later

Colin and I will talk and he'll hold me, arms around me like a blanket, warm and soft, and it'll be like the beginning, when I fell into him beneath his favorite tree and it was safe. I'm not sure it's true, but I tell myself, *Believe it.* Because otherwise I'm going to panic and dissolve.

We zip past Atma Lakshmi, toward the front. "What are you doing?" I ask him.

"Well, you can't *walk*," he says, like it's my fault. "How're you gonna get there unless I take you all the way?"

"I don't know," I say, ashamed to need his help.

The nearer we get, the faster my heart thuds. This is too close, the main entrance in broad daylight, right at the end of morning meditation. *Just breathe*, I tell myself. *Breathe and make yourself invisible. If you're small enough they won't see you.*

When we pull around the corner I see that that's impossible. There's a crowd out front: a big one. I can feel them buzz from here. My heart goes high up in my throat; adrenaline floods my veins.

Then I see through the people—there are cop cars. Two of them. My blood goes still and the tense floods out of me, but I don't relax. I'm like an animal—hunting or hunted—every nerve on alert, yet stiller than I've ever been.

Someone yells, "Hey!" and points, and it's too late to turn around. I look at Colin. He looks at me. Time stretches out.

"Shit," he says, and puts the bus in park.

They swarm up, Ninyassa and Vrishti and a bunch of people I half recognize. Not my mom, though. My mom's not there. The cops go around to Colin's side. They're in uniform and everything, two of them. They open his door hard; one of them grabs him by the shirt. "Come with us," they say, and I see fear flicker through Colin's eyes.

"Wait," I tell them. "What did he do?" I've never talked to a cop before, haven't even seen one except on TV or pulling someone over on the highway. But I know Colin can't argue with them, so I have to stop them from taking him away.

The fat cop peers at me. "I think you know what he did, young lady." He says it like a warning.

"No, I don't—" even though I kind of do.

He cuts me off. "Robbery, trespassing, corrupting a minor, statutory—"

Colin looks at the steering wheel. "Fuck," he says quietly. Then he turns to me, slow. "Tessa, let me go."

Tears are streaming down my face and I'm still tripping. "No," I scream at the police, like it could stop them. "You can't. You can't do that."

"Oh, yes we can," the tall cop says. "And you better watch it, kiddo, because we're gonna be talking with you next about that statue."

I grab Colin's arm and hang on hard enough to hurt

him. My nails dig into his skin. I can't let him go. Something is ripping in two parts inside my ribs, like velcro but made of flesh and blood, and it hurts more than anything I've ever felt. *Let him go.* I can't. I can't I can't I can't. "I love you, Tess," he says to me, and his arm yanks past my grip, and they pull him out of the bus and toward their car.

This is like a horror movie, the worst thing I can imagine actually becoming real before my eyes. The only way it could be worse is if they took me away too.

And then the door on my side opens and Ninyassa and Vrishti grab my arms.

"What the hell do you think you're *doing?*" Vrishti yells at me in front of everybody. I stumble, trying to stay off my bad foot. Vrishti's pretty face isn't pretty anymore, curdled with anger, bright pink against the orange of her hair. "I saw you. I saw you steal that statue. I know everything." Everyone is staring. Ninyassa stands there with her arms crossed.

My head is spinning. Everyone's faces are distorted, like a fun-house mirror or a freak show; pain throbs up my leg. People buzz and ogle me like a car wreck.

Vrishti goes on. "I know *everything.*" She gives me a gross, knowing look. "I talked to Devanand." My eyes go wide. "Yes, I did, and I know what you were doing with that—*man*. And let me tell you, if you think the Guru's going to stay with someone whose daughter acts like *that*, you've got another thing coming." All of a sudden she's off on some hysterical tangent about the Guru and his "companion," ranting and raving. She's so mad it's like she's crazy. "He has standards, you know. And you can bet when he finds out about all this he'll be done with both of you. He wants companionship that's ethical and pure. Not a family of whores. And betrayers," she says through tears. "And liars. That's what you are. Liars." She's crying hard now; her voice is acid, full of hate. She called me a whore. She's talking about my mother. I want to shrink into the sidewalk.

"Where's my mom?" I squeak out.

"Probably up at Guru's quarters whoring around like her daughter. Runs in the family, you know," Vrishti yells, freaking out, and then Ninyassa's arm's around my back.

"You're coming with me," she says, stern, and leads me through the entrance.

She marches me through the lobby, limping, everyone staring, and then around behind the desk. "Where are we going?" I ask her, and she doesn't answer.

My mind whirs, trying to make up a story to slip out of this and save myself. I don't know what people know and what they don't, who told what to whom; some things I can't explain away. Devanand knows we were kissing. Meer and Sanjit caught me leaving in the van. Vrishti saw us steal the statue, and everybody knows that I was gone all night. I try to put something together that includes it all, but my thoughts sprawl in a million different directions, refuse to weave together into a single thread. And underneath, that black oil creeps in at the corners when I think about the Guru and my mom.

Ninyassa takes me to the tiny room behind the front desk, fluorescent lights and a table and a hard plastic chair. All my stuff is on the table; my weed and pipe unwrapped from their sock and scarf and handkerchief and laid out there, spread out with all the other things that matter. My Walkman, the mix that Colin made me, all my tapes. Green Tea Experience is there. And next to them is my mom's journal.

Ninyassa sits me in the plastic chair. My butt bones ache. My ankle is in agony. "Where's my mom?" I ask again.

"I don't know," Ninyassa says. "The police are on their way to talk to you," and leaves me there.

I stare at the wood-paneled walls for I don't know how long. The grain swims. I'm still tripping. It's supposed to last twelve hours; it's been almost sixteen now. I let those guys tell me it was just an urban legend: you couldn't drop too much and not come back. But what if they were wrong? What if that guy who tripped forever *does* exist—and he turns out to be me? I start to mourn my mind. I loved my mind. I loved how it listened to music and thought about things, how it could be quiet and rest. I miss the mundane of breakfast and brushing my teeth, sneakers and small things and engine parts. Now I'll never get it back.

I think about taking my weed from the table, slipping it in my pocket or the trash so the cops can't see. But they'll see. They know. Ninyassa knows. There's no getting out of this. I'm going to go to jail, on acid. I cannot believe this is my life.

My mom's journal is sitting there staring at me. I know I shouldn't pick it up. The cops could come in, or Ninyassa, catch me reading, fingers in the pages like a cookie jar. But I'm already tripping forever, and I'm already going to get arrested. My life is over anyway.

Fuck it. What more can they do to me? I pick it up.

The pages are rice paper, her handwriting like calligraphy or lace. I thumb through it, looking. It's the inside of my mother's mind. The place I've spent the last six months trying to find.

It starts with things I've heard about: the liquid silence ocean, electricity and light. How glad she is to have finally found her people. That this is what she's been looking for, all this time, since she was just nineteen. That she's finally free. Then it says *I can tell Tessa doesn't like it here.* It says *I don't know how to make it better. I don't know how to make her understand.* Then it says *I'm so goddamn pissed at her. All I want to do is open up my heart, and she keeps rejecting everything. I want to make her happy, but not at the expense of my own fulfillment, and it makes me so mad that she keeps making me have to choose. How can I even be a good mom if I'm not happy?* And then, later, it says *I think the Guru wants for me to be his love. This is more intense than anything I've ever known. I'm scared of it. I'm worried that it's wrong. But I can't give up this opportunity; I know that it's the courageous thing to do.*

She's been having sex with him for months.

I feel dirty reading it, wrong and gross. It's way too much information, so much more than hearing about all her dates and lumberyard guys back in Ohio. But I can't stop. This is what she's been keeping from me; this is why she's gone. She talks about giving up her power, surrendering and how it scares her, how she has to force herself past the fear, give up, give in, demolish her ego till the person that she thought she was is gone. That she has to be ruthless in destroying her desires and fears. That even though their relationship is perfect in the eyes of God, that no earthly soul can ever ever know. And she says that he's her soul mate. That this is what she's been really looking for for fifteen years; she's traveled and traveled only to land at his feet. And that now that she's finally found him, she can never leave.

My heart cracks. *She can never leave.*

She's gone, spiraled into some place I don't ever want to be, a universe that terrifies me, full of orders and obedience, power and surrender, destruction of who you are and what you want and everyone you love. I think about what happened in the temple, how her self just all drained out of her, and I want it back. I want her back. She's never coming back.

The doorknob clicks; I wipe my eyes and brace myself for cops.

But then it opens and it's her.

Her eyes turn into saucers and she runs to me. Life floods back through her like a dying plant in a rainstorm. "Tessa!" she yells, and lifts me from the chair. She squeezes so hard I can't breathe, and all her bones poke into me. She's so so thin, but she hangs on to me as strong as iron. She buries her face in my hair, breathes in deep. "Oh, Tessa," she says. "I was so scared you were gone."

"I wasn't gone," I say, even though I sort of was. And then I can't say any more because I'm crying, hard, and so is she, shoulders wet with both our tears. I can't tell what's her and what's me, and it scares me, but it also feels safe, safer than anything I've felt in too long. "I wasn't gone," I say again, thanking god she noticed I was missing.

We stay like that a long time, till there's a knock on the door and Ninyassa comes in. My mom pulls away from me like taffy. She doesn't even hold on to my hand. I guess I shouldn't be surprised.

"Well," Ninyassa says, looking at the two of us. "Well, well." And suddenly I feel like my mom's in trouble too.

"So we'll have to talk," Ninyassa says.   ·297·

"I just have to tell you——" my mom starts in.

Ninyassa cuts her off. "I have to say a few things first."

I look at my mom sideways. She's staring at the floor.

"There have been some serious transgressions here," Ninyassa says, eyes ping-ponging between us. "To the point of the criminal. On multiple fronts."

The room's so quiet you can hear fluorescents buzz.

"There are rules, you know. These transgressions have to be addressed," Ninyassa goes on. She turns to me. "Tessa," she says.

I face my mom, try one more time. *Please have my back. Don't make me talk to her alone.* But she keeps her hands in her lap and her eyes on the wall.

"Tessa," Ninyassa goes on, "it's come to my attention you've been carrying on an illicit—*relationship* with a young man who is not only not a part of our community, but who is an adult, thereby making that relationship not only immoral, but illegal. You've been dishonest with Devanand for several months, abandoning your *seva* and your responsibilities to the community, and you've abetted trespassing by encouraging this young man to sneak into your room at night." My mother shoots a look at me. "This is not to even begin the discussion of the robbery of the statue, or your use of drugs on ashram premises. As I'm sure you know, these actions of yours carry serious consequences." My cheeks burn. I want to say, *Quit rubbing it in*, but that would be a bad idea. My mouth stays shut. Ninyassa turns to my mom.

"Now, I believe you share responsibility for this, Guhahita," she says. "As you know, we have a firm policy that ashram guests are responsible for the actions of their children. On both the literal and metaphorical levels. And I believe Tessa's actions would not have gone unaddressed for so long were you not engaging in unethical, dishonest behavior of your own."

"Ninyassa, I just have to say—"

"I'm not finished." Ninyassa stares her down. "Despite all that, this ashram exists as a place of service to the Guru. We follow his infinite wisdom here, even when it seems mysterious to our own more limited minds. And he has been consulted, and he has come to the conclusion that under no circumstances are you to be disciplined, Guhahita, for your personal breach of ethics, unless you choose to compound that breach of ethics by discussing it publicly." She pauses. "Do you understand what I'm saying?"

"Look, Ninyassa, I'm not sure—"

"Do you understand what I'm saying." It's a statement, not a question.

"I—think so," my mom says, trying to read her eyes.

"Not only are you asked to stay, but you may maintain your"—pause—*"position,* with the understanding that you will exercise immaculate discretion, advising your fellow devotees that to believe in rumors of illicit activities on the part of our beloved Guru is to strengthen the illusions of the mind."

My mom looks like she swallowed something rotten. Ninyassa turns to me.

"Now, Tessa. About the robbery, and other crimes."

Jesus Christ. Does she have to keep saying *crimes?*

"Assuming your mother abides by the agreement I've just mentioned, and you as well, the Guru will refrain from pressing charges. However, you'll have to tell us where the statue is."

I'm confused. "What does that m—"

"That means you won't have to deal with the police."

Oh. Wow. No jail. And all I have to do is tell her

where it is? A ten-ton weight lifts off my shoulders. "It's at Dee's Cottages," I blurt out. "In the yard." Secretly I hope that Clint and Bennett are still there, and that the cops will find them too.

"Good," Ninyassa says, clipped. "The police are currently holding the—*young man*. Since we're agreed on all the other issues, the ashram won't be pressing charges against him for the robbery. You can discuss among yourselves whether you will choose to press charges in the areas of corrupting a minor and statutory rape. That choice is, of course, ultimately up to you, Guhahita, as you are the parent here, and thus, the legal guardian." Ninyassa stares her down for a second, like she doesn't think my mom deserves to be my legal guardian. At this point, I kind of agree.

My mom doesn't say anything. Ninyassa points at her, like giving an order. "But if you do decide on pressing charges, remember: *ultimate discretion*."

And then she turns and leaves.

My mom looks at the ground. Not at me. Even after all of this, she still won't look at me. She seems so miserable, like the night before we came here when she sobbed into her Lemon Zinger tea and said how men would always let you down. Except now she looks way worse.

I don't know why she feels so bad; she just got everything she wants. We got out of trouble. She gets to stay here with her precious fucking soul mate, be obedient and keep it all a secret, and everything will be just exactly how it was for her, and I'll be stuck here all alone with everybody watching me and judging me and knowing everything I've done.

I'm glad I don't have to go to jail, but I'm not sure if this is that much different.

I don't have anything to lose. She's already gone. It doesn't matter if she's mad at me. I take a breath.

"Mom, you remember when we were on the way here, how you promised you would stay with me? Well, you didn't. You didn't stay with me. And you never do. ·301. You're always leaving every place we ever are."

"Tessa, come on, that's not fair," she says. "We've just been looking for where we finally fit in. And now we've found it." She tries to make her voice soothing, like those guys in the cafeteria with Jayita, trying to calm her down. "We can stay here, Tessa. I'm not going anywhere."

What's left of the acid makes it so everything is clear, so I can see the things she's doing even when she doesn't say them. She's just trying to get me to say okay and go along with what she wants. She's trying to comfort me without actually giving anything up herself.

"*We* haven't found anything, Mom. *You* found it. You never asked me if I wanted to come here. You never ask me if I want to go anywhere. You just do what you want and drag me along, and I'm just invisible, so fuck it, I don't matter." The force of it surprises me. "Do you know you haven't asked me what I want since I was, like, six years old? You only talk to me about yourself, and you only do it when there's no one else to talk to, and I don't care if you want to spend the night with Rick or Dan or the fucking weirdo beard guy, I'm your *kid*, and you're not supposed to leave me alone. And I don't care that you never got to go on the road and be a hippie. It's not my fault. I wasn't even born yet. So quit fucking making me feel guilty about it."

She looks like she's been hit by a truck. I don't care that I'm crying; it feels good to make her finally shut up about herself.

"And you know what, Mom? I know you hate my dad for leaving you, and I know he doesn't want me bugging him, and maybe I *do* think he's an asshole, but he's my *dad*. You don't get to decide how I'm supposed to feel about him. You don't get to make me think the things you think. Okay? So fuck you. Just *fuck you*."

Suddenly the words stop: that's all there is. And it's just silence. She isn't saying anything. And it's like the ground dissolves beneath my feet, like there's this open space that's bigger than anything I've ever felt or seen, the world broken apart like an earthquake, and I don't know what will fall into it before it closes up again. It could be everything.

Her eyes fill up with something I don't recognize, and I can see her think. Hard, like she's working an equation in her head. After a long, long time she nods to herself. She found the answer.

I brace myself for a proclamation, an announcement, a new statement about her journey. For the earth to close back up and seal itself like nothing happened. I brace myself to say, *Okay*, even if it's not at all, because I know there's never any other option.

She turns to me.

"What do you want to do, Tess?"

The wind goes out of me.

She's never asked me that question before.

She says it again. "What do you want to do?"

"You mean—what? You mean about pressing charges?"

"Well, yeah, that, but I mean . . . do you want to stay here?"

I can't believe it. "We don't have to?"

Her eyes fill up with tears. She shakes her head. It's hard for her to say.

"No, Tess. We don't have to."

If I trust this, and then it goes away, it will be me that drops into that chasm, falling and falling till everything breaks apart. "Where—where would we go?"

"I don't know, Tess. I don't know." There's a long pause.

Then her voice goes soft. "Maybe you could tell me what you want."

It's weird: this is what I've wanted more than almost anything forever, what I've been asking for from some god I don't even know if I believe in. And now that it's here, I'm terrified. More afraid than coming here, or being left, or sneaking off with Colin; more afraid than getting caught or facing cops or staring down the Guru. More afraid than being alone. But then it pops back into my mind: *Your challenge is to overcome your fear*, and suddenly I can tell the difference between when you're supposed to listen to your fear and when you're not. This time I know for once that pushing past it is what I really am supposed to do.

"Okay," I say. "Let's go."

She wants to go right up to our room and pack, but I tell her I don't want to. And she says, "Okay, Tess, you do what you want," and I can tell she actually means it.

I take some paper and an envelope from the room we're in, and I go to my table by the window at the Amrit, and I start another letter. The last one.

Dear Colin.

It's weird to write to somebody besides my dad.

I just wanted you to know that I'm not mad at you. And I'm not going to get you in any trouble. And that my mom and I are going, because I finally told her what I want, and she finally listened. Thank you for showing me how not to be afraid. I love you too.

I fold the letter into thirds and seal the envelope up. I drop it in the mailbox on the way back to our room. And for the first time it's okay if I don't get an answer back.

We drive straight into the sunrise. It burns our eyes, bright orange, but we don't turn around. Cardboard boxes fill the car to overflowing and I help her see out the rear window, change lanes, keep moving forward. Neil Young is on the stereo; I picked the tape. *Old man, take a look at my life, I'm a lot like you; I need someone to love me the whole day through.* We don't know where we're going yet, but it doesn't matter. We'll decide. Rearview Buddhas clink in open-window air and I hold my mom's hand on the gearshift, our hair whipping in our faces as we speed down empty open highway, two gypsies finally about to land.

Jessica Blank, an actor and writer, has appeared in several films, including *The Namesake, On the Road with Judas,* and *Undermind*; and several TV shows. She is coauthor (with her husband, Erik Jensen) of the award-winning play *The Exonerated*, based on interviews they conducted with more than forty exonerated death row inmates across America; and *Living Justice*, a book about the making of the *The Exonerated*. She is also the author of the critically acclaimed novel *Almost Home*. Jessica lives in Brooklyn, New York, with her husband and their dogs, Zooey and Yoda.